THE REMAKING OF PROFESSOR BOBBINS

CEDRIC SALDANHA

ALKIRA PUBLISHING

Also by Cedric Saldanha
Quest for Freedom

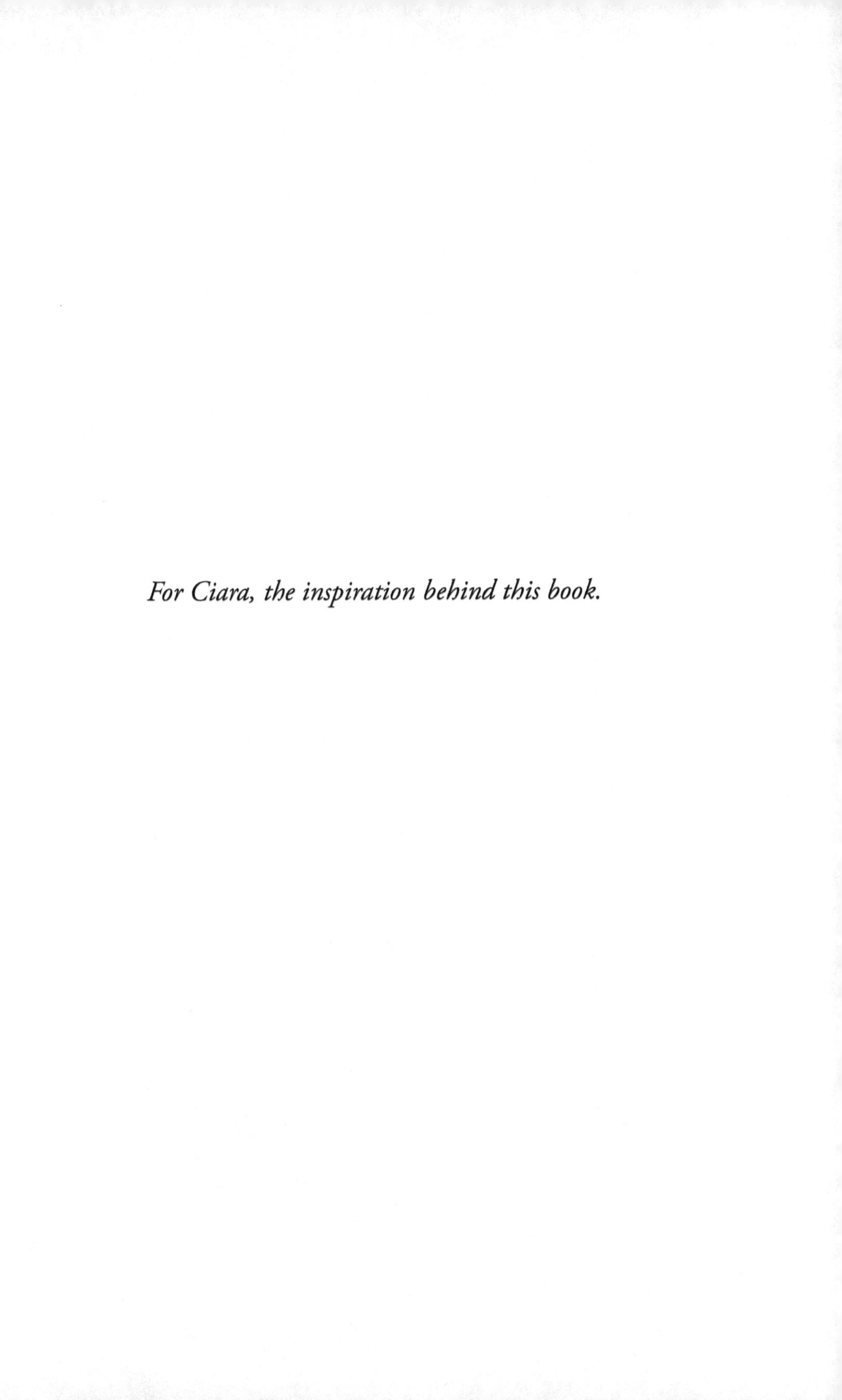

For Ciara, the inspiration behind this book.

ONE

The phone rang in the far distance. Faint but tenacious.

Alex ignored it. The sound persisted, resolute in its haunting. Reluctantly, he dragged open a bleary eye. The room spun, his head exploded, and the light hurt. He shut the eye in protest.

The ringing continued, dogged, like an irritating itch. He tried again, opening the other eye.

Christ! Not even in his bed. *Where am I?*

A vibration reached him. Something felt wrong. His pyjamas never had pockets. Further, he always switched his phone off before bed. Why would anyone in his right mind want to be disturbed by a call in the middle of the night?

The ringing and vibration continued.

Reluctantly, he decided to attend to it. His right hand reached out, searching, eyes still closed. Surprise, surprise. The phone nestled in his jacket pocket. What on earth had happened? Why was the jacket still on? Had he fallen asleep wearing it?

He pulled the phone out, put it to his ear, and tried to focus.

'Alex, you okay?'

Who the hell was calling him? The voice sounded familiar, but he couldn't place it. The room still spun. His head pounded, and his mouth tasted sour.

Why wouldn't they leave him alone? And why so bloody early? This was the weekend, right?

'Alex? Are you there? Can you hear me? It's Thomas.'

Alex Bobbins finally came awake, startled to find himself on the sofa in the living room rather than in his bed.

'Alex?'

'Yes, yes. I'm here, and all buggered up. Who is this again? Where am I? Some idiot has banged me on the head.'

'This is Thomas, Alex. You okay? No one whacked you on the head. You simply have a giant hangover.'

It came back in a rush. The farewell party at the university the night before. The laudatory speeches. The fulsome praise. The camaraderie he would so dearly miss. The company of bright, young, inquiring minds, a source of motivation for the years spent in research and teaching. All of it was now part of the past.

'Alex? Are you there? You okay?'

'Yes, Thomas. Yes. And thank you.'

Professor Alex Bobbins struggled to sit up. His nose wrinkled at the sight of his crumpled suit, his overweight body slumped on the living room sofa, his shoes still on.

'You must have helped me get home, Thomas. Jesus. I've probably made a fool of myself. I don't even remember how I got home.'

'No worries, Alex. It turned into a great party. We gave you the send-off we wanted to, and you delivered, as always.'

Now he remembered. After leaving his farewell party at the university, he had weaved his way unsteadily to the tram stop, helped along by Thomas, one of his assistant professors.

It had been an eventful evening. Speeches, hugs, toasts, and gradually getting high on alcohol and the warmth of his staff and students. A farewell to remember.

This marks the send-off you receive, he reflected, *after over forty years of dedicated research, teaching, and collaborative academic ventures.*

He would miss the university—its brick-lined walls, its gracious gardens, and its soft, luscious lawns. No more sounds of youthful laughter, lively discussions, and raucous debates.

Most of all, the daily polemics, the stimulation of theoretical contests and contentions that he loved to engage in with his peers and his students, now belonged to the past.

The field of economics had always fascinated him—the dynamism of its constantly evolving theories, paradigms, and real-world applications. He endeavoured to instil in his students a sense of curiosity and the tools to understand the intricate dance of supply and demand, the complexities of market structures, and the profound impact of economic policies on societies.

He knew that one day, it would all come to an end. That day had come. It was nice, though, to have departed his work at the uni embraced by the warmth of fellow travellers.

Then reality hit home. He was now jobless. No more waking up to days of purpose, lectures to be planned, colleagues to be consulted, conferences to be organised. He sighed as he contemplated his depressing future. It didn't look encouraging, he reflected, as he licked his dry lips and scratched his stubby chin. His shoulders slumped. He stared into the nothingness of the future.

'Will you be okay, Alex?'

Alex smiled as he visualised the eager face of his replacement at the university, his long brown hair falling over his bespectacled countenance, a look that might be mistaken for old-fashioned seriousness if not for the frequent, slightly awkward smile and boyish flush that seemed ever-present on his cheeks. Thomas Beckham had been his loyal, dedicated assistant for over ten years. Alex had now handed the baton over to him, admittedly with a degree of nostalgia and regret. But he would not have been happy if his position as head of the department had gone to anyone else. Fortunately, the authorities saw it his way. He was leaving the department in safe hands with Thomas as its new head.

'Would you like me to come over and take you out for breakfast, Alex?'

'Thomas, thank you again. But no,' he replied in a slightly gruff voice. 'You've been kind enough. You better get on with your life and leave this old, retired, and pensioned-off professor to his devices.'

'Come on, Alex. You may be retired, but you're not old. It's time now for some well-deserved leisure and perhaps some attention to your health.'

Alex looked down at his protruding breadbasket. It was true. The doctors had told him he was playing with fire by not taking his health seriously. He had high cholesterol and even higher blood pressure. A terrible diet didn't help, including consuming too much wine. But then, was life worth living without a glass of full-bodied, cherry-toned Shiraz before his meaty dinner, and perhaps a second to help the food go down? Sometimes a third to keep him company during the quiet after-dinner hours of the evening.

He smiled cynically. 'Leave it, Thomas. You're a good lad.

Now, get on with your day. Love to Beatrice and the kids. And thank you again for helping me home last night.'

He rang off before Thomas launched into one of his haranguing lectures on all the exercise routines he should consider.

Alex grimaced as he moved his feet to the ground. Gremlins were playing havoc inside his head. Every muscle seemed to scream in protest. The sunlight from the large bay windows blinded him. He scowled as he noted the pungent smell of alcohol still encompassing him. He was a disgusting mess, he decided, and slouched back on the couch, unable to find either the motivation or the energy to get up and clean himself.

He looked around, eyes still bleary. A sunny morning. Too sunny for his liking. The living room sat squat, sparse, silent. Nothing but the three-piece sofa set, a centre table, and the TV, and in a corner, facing the windows, an armchair next to his desk and computer. The attached dining-kitchen room was also relatively bare. Hardly used. Till yesterday, the university had been his real home after Mabel had passed away. He spent twelve to fourteen hours a day there and enjoyed every one of them. There was nothing at home for him to do. Besides, everything here just kept reminding him of Mabel, his sweet petite blonde-haired wife of thirty years. Dearest Mabel, to whom he owed so much and whom he so dearly missed. Her cheery, always-smiling face, her down-to-earth practicality. Her rare gift for lightening up the room, her warm, bright laughter that never failed to wrap around him like a favourite old sweater.

He remembered when Mabel and he purchased the house some thirty years ago. It was small and cosy. Its attraction was the huge bay windows, which overlooked a lovely sprawling back garden with a couple of gorgeous leafy oaks. It was a house of light, north-east facing, allowing it to capture maximum sunshine whenever the Melbourne weather favoured them. Mabel and he had enjoyed their time here with their only daughter, Kay.

Alex smiled, and his heart warmed as he recalled those good old days. The house had been a joyous place. Mabel filled it with her love, her caring, and her industriousness. Little Kay, their only child, brought in squeals, laughter, and merriment. As Kay grew older, mother and daughter bonded ever more strongly. He, however, grew increasingly obsessed with his career at the university.

Kay then left home when she married, and almost on cue, Mabel fell ill. Soon, she was no more. And now the house stood empty and silent.

~

Seven years earlier

Alex sat by Mabel's bed, caressing her fragile, bony hand. He'd taken leave from the university to spend Mabel's last few days by her bedside.

He blinked away his tears. They never seemed to stop these days. He couldn't believe how quickly the cancer had reduced this warrior of a woman, his lovely, vivacious Mabel, to this brittle, pitiful body. Her once-vibrant eyes, usually sparkling with mischief, were now dimmed with pain and fatigue. Each shallow breath seemed like a monumental effort, the rise and fall of her chest a constant reminder of her fading life force. Despite her physical decline, a flicker of her familiar smile played on her lips.

Their eyes met. 'Alex,' whispered Mabel.

'Yes, dear?'

'Promise me one thing. Will you?'

'Yes, of course, dear. Anything.' He leaned in closer to her.

'Please stay close to Kay.'

Alex sighed and looked away. This was a painful subject for both. 'Mabel, dear, you know well that's not up to me. Kay's decided my obsession with work has been responsible for the deterioration of your health. I ought to have read the signs earlier and got you into therapy quicker. I don't think she'll ever forgive me.'

'Alex, we both know that's not true. I'm a nurse, and I ought to have read the signs early on. But that's all water under the bridge. We are where we are. But I don't want to leave wondering if the two people I love the most will continue to live lives apart.'

He saw the pain in her eyes. It hurt him even more. But he was helpless. Kay had made up her mind. And once she did, little would move her. But this wasn't the time to argue.

'I promise, dear, I'll keep trying. That's all I can do. Please rest easy. You don't want one more burden on your mind.' He squeezed her frail hand reassuringly.

'Alex, I'm also going to talk to Kay about this. I'll tell her it's my dying wish that you both come together again. I wish I was there to see our grandchild. Kay tells me it'll be a girl. It's bad enough the child won't have a grandmother. I definitely want her to enjoy a grandpa.' She smiled bravely.

Alex smiled with her, but a deep sadness enveloped him. They both knew Kay was not in a good place. Six months into her wedding and pregnant, she was now estranged from her husband. Then Mabel's illness overtook them, suddenly, like a meteor crashing into their lives.

'Perhaps it's the strain of her circumstances, Alex. She'll come around. She needs you now, more than ever.'

Alex nodded, reluctant to argue. Possibly, she was right. But Alex also knew Kay's accusations had a degree of truth. He had indeed allowed work to consume him. He'd been determined to become the head of the economics department. He'd allowed his ambition to blind him to his family responsibilities. And poor Mabel had carried the burden.

~

Current day

Alex surveyed the silent house. *It'll now become home again.*

After Mabel had departed seven years ago, consequent to her short but severe illness, he'd hardly spent any time in this house. There seemed to be little purpose to life besides work. And work he did, often seven days a week and late into the evenings. He'd lost himself in his career. Kay and he had made attempts to rekindle their relationship, but they were half-hearted … on both sides.

Mabel wouldn't be happy, he mused, almost out loud, as he scratched at his cheek again.

But he'd tried, perhaps less hard than Mabel would've liked.

He'd also neglected his diet. He never did any exercise, not even the walks that Mabel and he had done every evening and enjoyed so much. The house had become a place to sleep his nights. The university had become home.

Now, with his career over, the silent house seemed desolate and lonely. He had known this was coming, the feeling of abandonment once the stimulation and pressure of work disappeared, along with its purpose.

He was going to miss Mabel's company even more deeply. If she were here now, she'd have goaded him to get up and clean himself before she helped him make his breakfast.

Dearest Mabel. Why did you have to go so early? Life was so good while you were here. His shoulders sagged as he stared down at his hands. He wiped his teary eyes and sighed deeply.

Mabel had been the down-to-earth nurse who'd consistently shoot down his esoteric economic theories. The no-nonsense companion who'd make sure he ate a healthy diet, accompanied her to church each Sunday—non-believer though he was—and who took on without complaint more than her fair share of managing the house and Kay.

Now that Mabel and his career had disappeared over the horizon, he wondered what was left. Did going on with life make sense anymore?

With an effort, he pulled himself up out of the sofa and staggered to the bathroom. He didn't recognise the person in the mirror. His face was puffed. His hair was tousled, a greying untrimmed bush. His bloodshot eyes screamed that his best was past, with nothing to look forward to.

With a sigh, he got to the clean-up task, and a half-hour later, he emerged feeling cleaner and a little more sane and sensible. He went straight to the kitchen, where he gulped down three glasses of water. *Perhaps some fresh air would help.* He decided to walk to the shopping strip and get a decent coffee rather than the swill he'd normally make himself.

He stepped out gingerly, still a bit unsteady on his feet, and wincing slightly at the enthusiastic sunlight.

'Morning, Alex. Where you off to?'

It was Ella Webster, his inquisitive neighbour. *Predictable,* he thought, as he examined her critically, taking in her wiry frame, garden gloves, and sun hat. *The woman spends most of her day pottering in her garden. God alone knows what she does there.* He sniffed. *The garden certainly doesn't show much for her effort.*

And her arrogance! As if I'm answerable to her!

Ella Webster had become insufferable of late, monitoring his comings and goings. Made him inclined to consider moving. Though it would be too much of an effort to pull up roots from this neighbourhood after thirty-odd years.

He forced out a civil greeting. 'Morning, Ella. Coffee.'

He usually answered her in monosyllables or as cryptically as possible.

'Rather late in the morning for a breakfast coffee, right?'

He snorted and marched on, ignoring her. But he knew she didn't miss his unstable gait. She rarely missed anything.

The walk to the local shopping street wasn't long. His path ran past houses of varying architecture, each with fronted gardens, a few with barking dogs.

The area presented a curious and eclectic mix of house designs, which he usually enjoyed examining and critiquing on his walk to the shopping strip. Some showcased Victorian architecture adorned with cast-iron lacework and ornamental brick facades. Others displayed Edwardian and Californian bungalow styles featuring red-brick exteriors, stained-glass windows, and open verandas. All generally in good taste and stately. The newest constructions, though, were not to his liking. Built by newcomers to the neighbourhood, they projected a sense of pretension with their dubious designs. His economist's mind also typically speculated on the financial circumstances of each house owner based on appearances.

But today, he was in no mood for his usual appraisals. His head still hurt. His body ached. His eyes struggled with the bright sunshine.

At the local shopping centre, he made a beeline to a quiet little café. He favoured its coffee over the three other larger and busier cafes on the strip, which he also frequented. Now, he needed quiet.

He settled at his preferred table by the street-facing glass window. As he savoured his coffee, a sense of normality gradually descended. The water had helped. The coffee cleared his head, though a vague nausea continued to linger. Breakfast held no appeal this morning. Hopefully, by the afternoon, he'd feel like himself again.

Nursing his second cup, he mused over the humble coffee bean and its remarkable journey into the lives of hundreds of millions. A recent article came to mind—coffee ranked as the second most-traded commodity worldwide, just behind crude oil, with a value exceeding one hundred billion dollars. More than twenty-five million people played a role in its production, distribution, and sale as the bean travelled from plantation to coffee cup, crossing international borders and geographical barriers. Countless intermediaries shaped its path, from small-scale farmers to exporters, importers, roasters, and retailers. A complex web of volatile factors— weather conditions, politics, currency fluctuations, and speculative trading—all influenced his morning ritual. He marvelled at the interconnectedness of the world. The cup before him linked him intimately to farmers thousands of miles away in South America.

His reflection in the wall mirror caught his eye as he watched the traffic through the expansive floor-to-ceiling windows. The sight unsettled him. A sagging face, tired eyes tinged with sadness, and a body utterly out of shape stared back. Little remained to look forward to. Retirement had crept up on him unannounced. He'd never planned for it, never considered what he'd do once it arrived. But it had come, and he now faced it unprepared and adrift.

Yes, the million-dollar question was: *How will I spend my time?*

Outside of the university, his circle of friends barely existed. Not that it mattered—they were all caught up in their own professional and personal lives. Thomas had suggested he start writing papers for publication. The university would even support his efforts, maybe publish some of his work. But the thought of sitting alone at his computer at home, churning out papers destined to be read by only a handful of academics, felt suffocating.

For him, the real joy of academia came from the daily interactions—meeting colleagues over coffee and lunch, debating the issues of the day. He thrived on supervising PhD students, guiding them through ground-breaking research, and chairing workshops and seminars that tackled the complex challenges facing Australia and the world.

He needed intellectual stimulation. Without it, a void yawned before him.

Take the current issue of supply chain disruptions, for example, and their massive implications for the sustainability of globalisation …

His phone rang, snapping him out of his thoughts. A twinge of annoyance surfaced. Probably Thomas again. He just wanted to be left alone with his thoughts and his coffee.

The screen displayed Kay's name.

He hesitated before answering. 'Hi, Kay. How you doing?'

'Hi, Dad. How did the retirement party go? Did you enjoy it?'

They kept in touch, though they rarely met. It felt like they were fulfilling an obligation, honouring Mabel's wish for them to stay connected. But the distance remained. He wondered what prompted this call.

'The party? Ah, well, yes and no.'

'Yes and no? How does that even work? You either enjoyed it or you didn't. Which is it?'

He sighed. 'Can we not argue today, Kay? I'm not in the mood. What's up?'

'I was just wondering … Are you free for lunch today?'

Lunch? With Kay? The idea took him aback. She normally avoided him, keeping their conversations as brief as possible. Their relationship had always been strained.

Then a flash of guilt swept over him. The last seven years hadn't been easy for Kay. Sarah's birth had come the same year Mabel died. Kay had separated from her husband before Sarah was born, and the divorce followed soon after. Navigating life as a single mother and a professional must have been overwhelming. He'd offered her a place at his and Mabel's home, but she refused, insisting on her independence.

That refusal had felt like a line drawn in the sand. Swamped by his own work commitments, he failed to provide any help with looking after the child. Though he'd offered to help pay for Sarah's childcare. His offer was refused with disdain. Thereafter, their awkward relationship became even more distant.

So what was this lunch about? It then struck him that perhaps she'd found someone and wanted to remarry. That would be great. He hoped she wanted to meet to share the good news with him.

'Sure, Kay. Is everything okay?'

'I'll explain when we meet. How about Betsy's near your place?'

They agreed on the time.

His legs protested when he pushed himself up from his chair. He'd take a stroll, clear his head, then head to Betsy's for lunch with Kay. No point going all the way home.

TWO

It had taken days for Kay to arrive at the decision. She'd spent hours debating options in her mind and then discussing it further with June and Han, her best friends. They'd have liked to help, but she knew how difficult it would be for both. She finally arrived at what she thought was the optimal solution, though she disliked it.

Kay entered Betsy's café, lips pressed, forehead creased, hoping her chosen option would work. She brushed down her black bob and straightened the jacket of her neat moss-green skirt and jacket ensemble. She spied Alex in a corner, sipping a glass of water and looking out the window.

Alex rose when he caught sight of her. They exchanged strained smiles and a cold hug before seating themselves. *A stranger wouldn't say we are father and daughter*, she reflected.

He looked drawn and tired. Kay wondered why. This was his first day of retirement, and she thought he'd be excited about the prospect of a more relaxed life. He'd always worked long hours for as long as she could remember.

They ordered lunch: a salad for Kay and a meat pie and chips for Alex. She raised her eyebrows as she heard his order, but he ignored her. She couldn't understand why he continued to disregard his health and diet. He was obviously overweight, probably didn't have regular medical check-ups, and certainly didn't look healthy.

'How was the farewell party, Dad?' she asked. 'You didn't quite answer me when I called you earlier.'

He shrugged, eyes dropping to the table. 'Was okay, Kay. Got caught up in the celebration and had a little too much to drink, but Thomas helped me home. Anyway, that was the last I'll probably see of the university and classrooms. It was a goodbye. And goodbyes aren't always joyous occasions. I'm now jobless.'

'You sound regretful. Aren't you happy you'll now have all the leisure time in the world? I'd love to be in your place.'

'Kay, the retired are the discards of society.' His shoulders drooped as gloom appeared to settle over his face. 'They want us out. Yes, out and away. Either because we've passed our use-by date, or because we cost too much. But certainly, because we need to make way for the next gen.' He laughed bitterly as he ran a hand through his straggly greying hair.

'Come on, Dad. You've had a great career. You rose to head of the department. You're still a respected economist. There's heaps more you can contribute in your area of expertise.'

'I don't think you realise how closed academia and research circles can be, Kay. Once you've formally exited their ranks, you've lost your platinum card and access to all the privileges that go with it. There are no more invitations to speak at conferences. Powerful people aren't interested in your opinion anymore. Professional publications are not so welcoming of your research. You're viewed as a has-been—an

old tome that is best left to gather dust on a forgotten shelf.'
Alex's shoulders slumped even further.

'Self-pity doesn't do you justice, Dad,' she said.

'It's not self-pity, Kay. It's realism.'

Their lunch arrived. She eyed his rather generous pie and chips, but didn't say anything. 'To my knowledge, the university has no compulsory retirement policy. So why did you retire if you feel so strongly about losing your position?'

He sighed. 'Lots of reasons.' He picked up a chip and savoured it. 'First, I found that, as I've aged, I have less and less patience and capacity to deal with the inevitable politics and the onerous administration that goes with a head-of-department position. Every year, it becomes worse. My age is also telling on me physically. I find I tire more easily these days.'

'It's not your age, Dad. It's your diet and lack of exercise.'

He ignored her comment and continued munching his chips. 'A time also comes when the hints that you should be moving on become too hurtful or obvious to avoid anymore. Besides, I owed it to Thomas, who's been a selfless, committed assistant head for the last ten years.'

'Doesn't the university have work available for ex-professors?'

'The university offers ex-professors the title of emeritus, with the possibility of research and consulting projects. Despite the officious-sounding title, it's essentially an empty, hollow, soul-destroying position. I've seen how they treat emeriti. You're always looking for opportunities, not begging, but virtually pleading for them. No thanks. I'll not lower myself to that.' His nostrils flared as he railed against how retired academics were treated. He looked at her defiantly, challenging her to counter his view.

Kay shook her head, unconvinced. 'I still think you should leave the door open.'

'Never mind me. Now, how is Sarah? Is she doing well? Where is she now? I've not seen her in a while. How old is she?' He cut his pie in half.

Kay frowned, feeling irritation rising within. *He doesn't even remember Sarah's age!* She'd always felt that he'd been a bad-enough father, but now he'd turned out to be a worse grandfather. He'd never had time for Sarah. *Sure,* she argued with herself, *he was willing to help pay for her childcare, but all he was interested in was his work and career.*

'She's at a friend's house today,' she said curtly. 'She's seven now and has a mind of her own. She's a very determined and opinionated little girl.'

'Just like her mother, I suppose?' ventured Alex.

Kay smiled and took the jibe in stride. 'I want to talk about Sarah, in fact,' she said.

'Oh?'

'You look surprised. Were you expecting me to discuss something else?'

'Well, I thought perhaps you wanted to share news of a possible new relationship. You've been single for almost seven years. Sarah could do with a dad.'

Kay stopped eating and looked at him, wide-eyed in astonishment. She screwed up her face. 'Are you suggesting that's reason enough to hitch up with some idiot man?'

'Not all men are idiots, as you term them, Kay. In fact, I notice that, unlike my generation, young men these days are much more sensitive to the needs of their partners.'

'Pity they only move in your circles, Dad. I've yet to come across a man who does not think primarily of himself and his career first.'

'Perhaps it's time to lower your expectations a bit,' he said.

'They're already rock bottom, and males still can't live up to them.' Her remarks seemed to increase his guardedness, so Kay settled back into her seat, cleared her throat, and looked directly at him. Perhaps it was time to drag him out of his glasshouse.

'Look, Dad, I've come across many men in my life, and I've decided I have no time for any. The Peter Pan types are simply out to have a good time—lots of fun, but zero interest in any serious relationship. The egotistical narcissist like my ex, Dan, is self-centred, boastful, arrogant, and manipulative, with an insatiable need for validation. Don't tell me you've not noticed. I've no idea how on earth I ever found the bastard attractive. I'm well rid of him.'

Her dad seemed taken aback by her venom; he even stopped eating his pie—which made her smirk. But Kay still nursed her hurt; it was always there. She couldn't forget how her ex had treated her.

'Kay, I know—'

'I've not finished, Dad. Then you have the emotionally unavailable stoic, like some from your academic circles.' She hoped the dig would find its mark. 'They project the image of the intellectual, the know-all, and impress you with their knowledge. But when it comes to emotions, they are either dried-out cabbages or would rather not waste their emotive energies.'

Alex moved in his seat uncomfortably. He seemed increasingly uneasy with her rant, but she wasn't finished. She had an inkling it was triggered by her own latent anger against him.

'Finally, there is the perpetually unfulfilled wanderer. The one-night-stand men.' She paused and crossed her arms.

'Somewhat like the Peter Pan types, but even blunter about their base intentions. I've tried them all, Dad, believe me. I'm convinced they exist on a different plane to me, trapped in perpetual adolescence or in self-absorption and emotional detachment. They are quick to promise the world, but when the rubber meets the road, they vanish into the ether, leaving me holding an empty bag of promises.'

He sighed and started to comment, but she interrupted. 'I've been told by some of my girlfriends that I'm too independent, too strong-willed, too demanding. That may be, but I'm happy with myself. I know my worth, and I'm not ready to settle for anyone who treats me otherwise.' She then grinned at him and shrugged. 'Sorry for that barrage. I needed to get it off my chest.'

He nodded and smiled back. 'I suppose I asked for it,' he remarked ruefully, though he didn't seem convinced by her exposition. 'Okay. Never mind the relationship topic. Tell me what you want to talk to me about. I'm intrigued because you and I rarely have a decent chat.'

She smiled, silently acknowledging the fact, and sipped her coffee. 'I've accepted an assignment from the Department of Foreign Affairs, commonly known as DFAT, to provide health policy advice to the government of Papua New Guinea for three months. It's part of the Australian aid program.'

Alex nodded approvingly. She'd expected he would. He'd been instrumental in persuading her to graduate in economics. She'd grudgingly followed his advice, but only after encouragement from her mother. The choice had proven brilliant. She fell in love with economics and excelled at her grades. She then chose to do a master's in health policy, pleasing her mum with her interest in the medical sector.

'That's great news, Kay. But it's going to be quite a challenge.

The state of the economy in PNG is not encouraging, nor is the quality of governance. Its fiscal situation usually does not allow it to adequately finance—'

'Dad! I'm not here to listen to a lecture on PNG's economy. I've briefed myself on PNG in detail before taking this assignment. I want to discuss Sarah.'

Her dad's expression grew puzzled. He was probably wondering what the connection between PNG and Sarah was.

'As you know, Dad, the law-and-order situation in PNG is dicey currently. DFAT has informed me that it's preferable I leave Sarah here, back in Melbourne.'

Alex appeared aghast. His eyebrows shot up. His forehead creased into a frown. 'But she's only seven. You can't just send her to boarding school for three months.'

'Exactly. Which is where you come in.'

Light finally seemed to dawn on him, followed by a look of dismay, his eyes widening in disbelief. She wasn't surprised that it took him so long to decipher what she was leading up to. It showed how buried he was in his own journey. She saw resistance building on his face as he blinked and digested the news.

'I want to leave Sarah with you, Dad. Please,' she said, despite his obvious reluctance. It wasn't easy to ask for a favour from him. She hated being dependent on him, but she'd examined every other option. Only this one ticked all the boxes.

Alex sat back, speechless. His body had frozen; his mouth fell open, and he took in a shaky breath. He seemed to be in shock, and she could understand it. He'd just heard her tirade about the inadequacies of men. He would have rightly assumed this included him. Now she wanted to entrust her seven-year-old daughter to him? A sixty-five-year-old man who had never before taken any interest in assuming family responsibilities. In her view, it was about time he did.

'You're retired now, Dad. You have all the time in the world. This'll be an opportunity for Sarah and you to bond. I've spoken to Sarah, and she's excited.' Kate saw doubt and opposition building, but she wouldn't let him get away with it.

'Look, Kay'—hesitation filled his voice—'I don't think you've thought this through.'

'I most certainly have.' She firmed her chin, indicating he had little hope of changing her mind. 'This arrangement is the best option. I definitely can't send her to boarding school. She wants to continue with her current school. All her friends are there and live in our neighbourhood: yours and mine. I have considered asking June and Han, my best friends, who also live in the neighbourhood, to look after her. But it would be too much of an imposition. They both work long hours, and each has helpers for their own kids. And I certainly can't entrust her to any other guardian. Also, she already knows you and is excited about the opportunity of looking after you now that you're retired.'

'What? Looking after me?'

Kay bit her lip, trying not to laugh at the consternation on his face.

'I don't need any looking after, Kay, as you well know. And by a seven-year-old? You must be joking,' he replied indignantly.

'Sorry. I had to sell the idea to Sarah, and she's quite taken with it.'

He still appeared unconvinced. This was going to be difficult. She'd hoped, with his retirement, he'd see this as an opportunity to bond with his grandchild. But obviously, he saw this differently.

'I leave in a week,' she persisted valiantly. 'This was a sudden vacancy in the position of health adviser, and DFAT felt I suited the position perfectly. It's simply too good an opportunity for me to miss. Besides, the compensation is very attractive.'

She paused. 'I thought you'd be enthusiastic. You know how you keep saying applied economics is the real challenge, especially in a developing country. Not the esoteric stuff they keep arguing about in the journals and newspapers. I couldn't have asked for a more attractive challenge than the PNG assignment.'

'I agree. Completely. But the idea that I can look after a seven-year-old girl for three months in my home is completely bonkers.'

Kay stiffened her back. 'Dad. Can you, for once, accept some family responsibility?'

He looked like he'd been punched in the chest. But it was the truth. He'd never really accepted responsibility for family matters. It had always been her dependable mother. This time, there was no escaping. She wasn't taking no for an answer.

He kept shaking his head, seemingly getting used to the idea that he would now become the guardian of a little kid.

'I've spoken to June and Han, who live in the neighbourhood. Their kids are friends with Sarah and attend the same school as her. They've reassured me that they will reach out to you and help in any way you need. Okay?'

Alex sat silent, looking somewhat stunned by the responsibility being offloaded onto him. He'd put down his cutlery and was blinking furiously. She took his silence for acquiescence. In any case, he wasn't getting out of this responsibility. Her mum would have been a hundred per cent behind the decision.

'Look, Dad. Sarah is on her school holidays for the next month or so. I'll bring her to your place on Wednesday, and we'll begin the process of gradually moving her in. I leave on Saturday. Believe me, Dad, you'll enjoy her company. She's an intelligent little one, though sometimes a bit of a challenge.'

She left him befuddled, probably wondering how he'd cope with this unwelcome challenge. *Good for him,* she thought. *About time he thought of someone other than himself.* It would work out. June and Han would help. And she'd brought up Sarah to be as self-sufficient as possible.

The only issue was whether they'd get on. Sarah could be bossy. She had a mind of her own, and Kay was aware that her dad wasn't the most caring of people. But it was only for three months. The first month, though, would be challenging. After that, Sarah would be in school for most of the day.

She left smiling. Alex Bobbins had finally been cornered into being the hands-on grandfather he probably never thought he'd ever be.

THREE

Wednesday morning arrived, and the doorbell rang impatiently. Imperiously. *A sign of things to come*, Alex grumbled to himself.

He sighed and rose from his armchair. He'd enjoyed three days of peace and quiet, catching up on his reading, reacquainting himself with the ambience of the house, and doing domestic chores that he had long ignored. He thought he was adjusting rather well, despite his qualms about retirement. But the routine he'd set up was about to end. A new, unfamiliar challenge awaited. This would be more difficult.

He'd returned from his meeting with Kay last Saturday with growing misgivings. The more he thought about it, the more daunting the task seemed. It was a significant responsibility to look after a child. More so Kay's child. She was a demanding person. She'd have all sorts of expectations and stipulations about how he went about this responsibility. Would he be able to live up to them?

Kay had said they'd come that morning to initiate the move. He lay his newspaper aside and gingerly ambled to the door as he scratched his hairy chin, wondering what awaited him on the other side of the door. The doorbell continued ringing.

He opened it and looked down. Looking up was a bright little girl, sparkling eyes and turned-up nose, jumping up and down with a grin that lit up the neighbourhood, while her auburn-coloured pigtails danced wildly from side to side. With a teddy bear in hand and her little backpack slung over her tiny shoulders, she seemed a bubble of energy.

He couldn't help but smile. How he envied that energy, that enthusiasm for life.

'Grandpa, I'm here,' she announced to everyone in earshot.

Ella Webster, in her garden, waved at him and grinned. He assumed Kay had briefed her.

'I guessed, Sarah. I see that you can now reach up to the doorbell.'

'I'm here to look after you, Grandpa. Mum says you need help. You know I can make breakfast for you, help you make up your bed, and teach you new games. Aren't you excited?'

She was cute and precocious, he decided. Very much like the little Kay he remembered.

Behind her stood Kay, also beaming and loaded with colourful boxes of Lego sets, dolls, books, and an iPad. 'Thought I'd begin today with some of her toys,' she said.

Alex noted the determiner 'some' with raised eyebrows. He groaned inwardly, but put on his best face and welcomed them in.

Sarah skipped into the house and headed straight to the three-seater sofa. She clambered up on it and jumped up and down, testing its springs while surveying the room with disapproval.

'There's nothing here to play with, Grandpa. Only books and papers,' she declared. 'You must be bored. I've brought some of my toys, and my teddy bear, and my iPad. So don't worry. We'll have lots to play with.'

He followed them into the living room. Kay dumped the toys she was carrying on the centre table. With hands on hips, businesslike as usual, she said, 'Okay, Sarah. Let's go to my room to see how we can fix it for you.'

With that, they left a confused Alex wondering what had descended on him and what the future held. He was suddenly at a loss for what to do. Kay obviously knew the house where she'd been brought up and had decided she'd introduce Sarah to it all.

Then the implications of Sarah's actual living there descended on him in full measure. He'd have to cook for her. Jeez. That was going to be a challenge. His repertoire ranged from frying eggs to making sandwiches with processed meat. Perhaps shoving readymade pies and sausages into the oven. He only ever ate at home on weekends. During the week, he was at the university till late and either ate at the café or ordered take-away from there. How was he going to manage this? There was nothing in the fridge just now that Kay would approve of, he was sure.

The toys lying on the centre table distracted him from his worries. He walked up to examine them. *There must be well over a thousand dollars' worth of stuff there.* The toy industry had grown by leaps and bounds since he was a kid. It'd become truly global, with China at its core with its gargantuan production capacities. He often quoted the industry's advances in his seminars on neoliberalism. Free trade and deregulation had allowed the likes of Lego to become a household name.

The brilliant Danish innovation had introduced bricks with polished modularity and compatibility that allowed them to be connected in innumerable ways. He was now going to encounter the famous Lego like he'd never done before. In person, playing it with a child.

He noted the kid-friendly Amazon tablet lying on the table. Its games had taken the toy world by storm. Next to it sat the iPad, probably the most expensive toy on the table, and adding daily to the bottom line of Apple. Barbies had their pride of place as well, the Mattel product that was now universally loved.

He reflected on his own toys when he was a kid. The only ones he ever got were for his birthday and for Christmas. Just two toys each year. It was left to his ingenuity to create playthings from items that were freely available. He loved stones of beautiful shapes and different sizes. He picked them up on the way home from school each day for his collection. He and his friends used tree branches for the sticks-and-stones game they played or for cricket wickets, and discarded wood planks made acceptable cricket bats.

The world is different today, he reflected. They lived in a consumption economy. And evidence for it lay on his centre table.

He heard Sarah complaining about something upstairs and wondered what she was unhappy about. The sound of human voices echoing through the house was unusual. No one ever visited, not that he'd wanted anyone to. He was hardly ever at home except to sleep.

~

Sarah wasn't impressed with her mum's room, now to be hers.

It was plain as plain could be. No pictures on the wall. A desk and chair, with nothing on them. The bedspread was dull white. Though there was a nice window overlooking a really big garden. She ran to it to check out the view and liked what she saw, especially the two big trees, which had lots of leaves. *Maybe I can make a cubby house there?* A bird flew from the tree to the windowsill, hoping for some food. She kissed it through the windowpane.

'What do you think?' her mum asked.

'It's okay.' Sarah shrugged, trying to be helpful. She knew her mum was worried about how she'd settle into her grandpa's house. 'The window and the trees are nice,' she added. 'But the room isn't. Nowhere near as nice as mine at home.' She scrunched her face. 'Everything is so plain and boring.'

'Look, love. We'll decorate the room tomorrow, okay? Get wall stickers and posters from Kmart. Butterflies, birds, maybe your favourite animals. We'll buy them this evening, and tomorrow we'll transform this room.'

That sounded better. 'Can we make it just butterflies, birds, and fairies, please? And can I bring my own doona? I hate this cover.'

'Sure. Now, come on. Let's join Grandpa downstairs, and you can show him your toys.'

Sarah walked downstairs to the living room and stared at the old man in the armchair. He looked really old and tired and fat. His cheeks hung down his face, and he was definitely unhappy. Why? What made him so unhappy? She felt a little sad for him. And then doubts crept in. How was she going to live with him? For three months?

Maybe she'd be able to make him cheerful again? But how was she going to keep him entertained? Would he be interested in playing noughts and crosses, or word games, or perhaps Pokémon? She sighed. *I'll just have to teach him*. She wasn't sure what her mum meant when she said he needed to be looked after. But she'd do it. For her mum.

When she heard her mum was going away for three months, she'd burst out crying. How could her mum do that to her? How would she do without her mum? Why not take her along? What did her mum mean by saying the place she was going to was dangerous? Then why did she want to go there? She didn't understand.

Anyway, she was here now … and she'd look after her grandpa. She'd promised her mum. Yes, he did seem to need looking after. First, she'd make him shave. Yes. Definitely. The hair on his cheeks and chin looked very untidy. He almost looked like Mr Grimble Grumbles in the *Puddle Lane* books. Then he needed to smile. Perhaps he would be happier if he got to know her dolls. She'd better start on that already.

'Grandpa, can I call you Alex?'

He looked surprised. Why? Alex was shorter, much better than Grandpa if she was going to be friends with him.

'Sure, Sarah. If you want to.'

'Okay, Alex. I want you to meet each of my dolls. You'll like them. Mum does. All my friends do. They'll be living with us, and you must get their names right. You can't be mixing them up. They'd be very upset if you called them by the wrong name.'

He nodded, but it didn't look like he really wanted to. Sarah thought her mum looked amused, and she wondered why. But she carried on. Each doll had a story she had to tell him. They were her children, after all, each with likes and dislikes, and it was important that Alex understood them all. She began with the introductions.

She didn't like that her mum kept talking at the same

time, giving Alex instructions about what meals he should prepare, what clothes she should wear, and how often they should be washed. That was the thing about her mum. She wanted to be the boss all the time. Sarah hoped Alex would be easier to manage. She thought he would be. While he looked old and grumpy, he had kind eyes.

~

That's the thing about Kay, Alex thought. *She always speaks at a hundred miles per hour. Before you'd digested the first instruction, three more arrived.* Mother and daughter both competed for Alex's ear, and in the end, he gave up listening and trying to absorb, hoping he hadn't missed something crucial.

They finally said goodbye to an exhausted Alex, promising to return the next day with groceries and to do up Sarah's new room.

As they left, Kay waved to Mrs Webster in her garden, resplendent in her working gear—sunglasses, orange hat, green gloves, long-sleeved gardening apron and clippers in hand.

Ella Webster waved back and then came to the fence and removed her glasses. She smiled down at Sarah. 'How's grumpy old Grandpa?' she asked with a grin. She then realised Alex was at the front door. 'No offence, Alex. Just having some fun,' she announced with a wink.

Alex was not amused.

'How are you keeping, Mrs Webster?' Kay asked.

'I'm good, thanks, Kay. Lovely seeing you after such a long time. You rarely visit these days, though you live so close by. And this is Sarah, I assume, your little daughter. She's a picture of you.'

'She's going to live here for the next three months,' Kay explained.

'Really?' Mrs Webster exclaimed, eyebrows arching.

'Yes. I'm off on a three-month assignment overseas. And Sarah is pleased as punch to stay here and help her grandpa.'

'Are you sure Alex is up to looking after a little girl? No offence, Alex. I'm just concerned about Sarah. If there's any way I can help? I—'

'Get on with your gardening, Ella.' Alex glared at her. 'Of course I can look after her.'

'Perhaps you can give Dad a hand in checking on her from time to time?' Kay suggested.

'No thanks, Kay. Ella has enough to do with her garden.'

'Don't be rude, Dad. Mrs Webster's only trying to help. Thanks, Mrs Webster. Sarah, say bye to her. You'll be her neighbour now.'

They both walked off, Sarah waving, while Alex stomped in and banged the door shut.

~

Alex returned to his armchair with mixed emotions. Without having to go to the university, he didn't know what he'd do with his time besides read. He had piles of books he wanted to get through. Perhaps write a little, maybe for publication. *But for how long can one sit in a lonely house and read?*

He usually spent his weekends doing basic chores in the house and garden and replenishing the minimal groceries that he needed for the week. Then he'd go to the cafés in the shopping area, where he'd have lunch and observe, with his economist's eye, the goings-on of the local economy.

His work and colleagues in the university had encompassed

his world. Now, there was a huge gap to fill. Could a seven-year-old actually do that?

The phone rang.

'Alex. How you going?'

Alex smiled. *Dear Thomas, always the concerned one.* He was the closest to Alex and considered him his mentor, the one who'd guided and shepherded him through his academic career and to whom he owed his current position. Now, roles were switched. It seemed like Thomas was the one who had to care for him.

'Nice to hear from you, Thomas. What's it now, two to three days, that you've been the head of the department? How does it feel?'

'Will take some getting used to, Alex. You have big shoes to fill. Everyone here still talks about what Alex would do if he was here in this situation or that.'

'Sorry, lad. I promise to keep away. But if I can help in any way, you should feel free to call me.'

'The reason I'm calling is to check how you're adjusting.'

'Good of you, Thomas. But all's going well. I'll soon have a house partner.'

'Great. Who, may I ask?'

'My seven-year-old grandchild, Sarah.'

Silence on the line. Alex smiled to himself, imagining the surprise at the other end.

'You mean she's coming to live with you? I don't recollect her visiting often. What happened to her mother? I'm hoping she's okay.'

Alex briefed Thomas. Then, 'You have little kids, don't you? Any advice? If I recollect, you've been a much more hands-on dad than I've ever been.'

'Not sure what to say, Alex. One thing's certain: she'll

keep you on your toes. And maybe that's good for your figure.'

'What's wrong with my figure?' Alex frowned, irritated that the conversation these days always moved to his health.

'No offence, Alex. But for your own health, losing some weight will help.'

'You're sounding like my daughter. But look, why don't you, Beatrice, and the kids come over sometime? I understand the kids are on holidays for a while now. The children can meet each other.'

'Great idea. Perhaps sometime in the next couple of weeks.'

FOUR

On Saturday morning, Alex and Sarah stood at the departures gate at the airport, saying goodbye to Kay.

'Look, dear,' Kay said, holding Sarah's face between her hands and looking into her eyes. 'I'll FaceTime you every day. Okay? And promise me you'll look after your grandpa?'

'Okay, Mum. I'll try.' Sarah blinked away tears and put on a brave face while Kay went through all her instructions again.

It'd been a hectic week of comings and goings from Alex's house while Kay ensured her daughter would be safely and comfortably ensconced for the next three months.

She'd examined the pantry and the freezer with her eagle eye. 'What's this, Dad?' she'd complained loudly, lips pursed, face tight. 'Sausages, meat pies, frozen chips, pizzas, readymade lasagne? And NO greens! Are you trying to kill yourself?'

Alex rubbed the back of his neck, feeling like the little boy caught out. 'Come on, Kay. That's all good food.'

'Is this what you call *good*? When was the last time you checked your cholesterol?'

'Are you here to cross-examine and berate my eating habits or to brief me on how to look after Sarah?'

'That's exactly the point, Dad. You must promise me that you'll feed Sarah only healthy foods. I will stock up, not to worry. But at some point, you'll need to restock. And I need you to promise you'll buy her only healthy stuff.'

'Yes, yes. I heard you loud and clear. Let's get clear on all the healthy food you want me to give her.'

'No processed food, as far as possible. Steamed veggies every day. I'll show you how to do them. Pasta is fine, though be careful what sauces you use. I'll get you some appropriate ones. And no snacks between meals, please. I'm preparing a separate menu for her lunch boxes once school begins.'

Alex sighed and looked down at poor little Sarah. He felt sad at all the goodies she was missing out on. Sarah looked up, giving him a knowing look.

The pantry was duly replenished with milk, three kinds of cereal, whole grain bread, butter, fruit, pasta, and sauces.

'What about some cakes and chocolates for Sarah?' Alex asked, trying to be constructive. 'Occasionally,' he added lamely.

Kay glared at him. 'Dad! How many times have I told you, no sugar! And if you have any sweet things in the pantry, we need to get rid of them.'

He gave her a repentant look, but he'd carefully hidden his treasured box of chocolates and cookies, knowing Kay would object.

The house had been completely transformed. The living room had toys and books stacked in one corner, with a little table and chair for Sarah. They sat in the corner opposite Alex's desk and computer. The centre table had become the workshop base for Sarah's Lego creations. Sarah's things were easily accommodated, since he lived with minimal possessions. Once Mabel passed away, he'd systematically rid the house of furniture and curios. He didn't need the extras.

Sarah seemed happy with her room, finally. It had indeed been transformed from the bare, sterile place it had been the last seven years since Kay had moved out. Alex now stared, open-mouthed, at the makeover Kay had managed. The room was a riot of colour. Birds and butterflies of varied colours swarmed the walls. A cheerful array of pillows and stuffed animals adorned the bed. Bright patterns and cartoons spread across the doona on the bed. Vibrant curtains that matched the overall colour scheme hung from the windows. It was extraordinary! Kay had achieved a complete makeover in just a couple of days.

'Do you like it, Alex?' Sarah asked, beaming with pride.

'Absolutely love it. It's beautiful.'

'Mum will do your bedroom as well, Alex, so you don't need to feel left out,' Sarah generously offered. Kay smiled in the background.

'No, thank you, Sarah,' Alex assured her hastily. 'I'm quite happy with mine.'

Then it was off to Sarah's school. With the school holidays on, no teachers were available. But the principal and deputy principal were there. Kay introduced Alex to them, explaining her intended travel. The school was close to Alex's house. When Kay married, the newly wedded couple had moved into a house in the same neighbourhood, since Kay had been keen to keep in close touch with her mum.

Alex realised he now had a new series of tasks to wake up to each day, particularly once Sarah was back at school—preparing Sarah's lunch box, ensuring she was dressed on time, and ferrying her to school and back again in the afternoon.

Back home, Kay had sat him down at the dining table and pulled out a pile of Excel sheets she'd prepared. *Meticulous,* he noted, *as usual.*

One list outlined Sarah's daily schedule, including weekends. A second was for Sarah's meal menus. A third for her close friends and their parents, with addresses and phone numbers, since Sarah would often be at their houses. Yet another provided details on her school and the relevant contact numbers.

Kay had given Alex's email address to the school, and she told him to expect messages virtually every alternate day on issues the parents and guardians were supposed to be on top of, including homework requirements, outdoor expeditions, sports activities, and the like. The list went on. It was unbelievable, the extent to which a little kid consumed the life of a caring adult.

Alex didn't think, no, he was certain that his parents hadn't devoted that much time and attention to his needs when he was growing up. Certainly, not as far as he recollected.

And so, here they were; the day of Kay's departure had finally arrived. She gave them both her final hugs. Tears streamed down Sarah's face. Alex held her small body close to him, consoling her. Every now and then, a tremor shuddered through her, and he held her closer. Kay turned quickly before she, too, broke down. With a final flying kiss, she hurried through the security gates and was out of sight.

Wanting to console the little girl and hoping to distract her, Alex said, 'Look, dear. How about an ice cream?'

Sarah hiccupped through her sobs. Finally, she wiped her tears and gave him a weak smile. 'Okay, Grandpa, I mean, Alex. But don't tell Mummy.'

Alex grinned. 'This will be our secret. Okay?'

The ice cream calmed Sarah down. She began asking about aeroplanes and flights and whether Mum would be safe. They licked their ice creams as they made their way to the carpark to leave for Sarah's new home and Alex's new life.

~

Back home, Alex realised he needed to keep Sarah distracted for the day so she wouldn't miss her mum too much.

'I saw you've brought your scooter along, Sarah. Would you like to take it out with me for a walk?' Getting out for some fresh air would help them both.

Sarah brightened at the suggestion.

'But not too fast, okay?' he cautioned. 'I need to be able to keep up with you, and I can't run.'

Soon, they were off down the street. Sarah immediately swung into action, enjoying the freedom of wheels, her hair flying in the wind, her right leg pummelling her scooter forward at breakneck speed. Alex followed her, huffing and puffing along, and pleading for her to slow down.

She whipped around the street corner, and to Alex's horror, crashed head-on into a tall, thin man coming from the opposite direction. Both tumbled to the ground, the scooter skidding off in another direction.

Alex watched helplessly from far behind with alarm and deep dismay as he struggled breathlessly to catch up.

'Look where you're going, you bloody urchin!' the man shouted, picking himself up. Face flushed with anger and left eye twitching, he stared down at Sarah.

Sarah also picked herself up, tears streaming down her face. 'I'm sorry, Mr Hancock. I didn't see you coming.' Sobbing, she ran to the arms of the approaching Alex.

'That's not the way to ride scooters on the road, you bloody idiot! Next time I see you going so fast, I'll take your scooter away.' Hancock's face glowed red with anger.

Alex caught up with the two and wrapped his arms protectively around Sarah. Sarah heaved with sobs, her face covered in tears.

Alex bent over her, checking for injuries. 'Are you okay, dear?' he asked, deeply concerned. *This is a disaster*, he thought. *And on my first day as her guardian.* He dabbed her tears with his handkerchief.

'You the bugger looking after this little runt?' Hancock's left eye twitched uncontrollably, and his hands shook.

Alex's jaw tightened, but he kept his tone measured. 'Yes. I saw the collision. I'm sorry it happened. But there's no need to be aggressive and call people names, please. It was an accident.'

The snarl grew on Hancock's face, and his left eye twitched even faster. 'She has no business being on a scooter if she can't ride carefully. She bloody well knocked me down. You're the fat old professor from down the road, right? What the hell are you doing hanging around with little girls now?'

Alex recognised Adam Hancock. He lived with his wife, Sharon, in her parents' house a few houses down the street. Alex and Mabel had been friends with the old couple, the Andersons. Both couples had moved into the neighbourhood at about the same time, thirty years ago. The elderly Andersons had both passed away, and Sharon, their daughter, had inherited the house. Sharon married Adam about the time Kay married. While Sharon was a familiar and friendly neighbour, Adam made no effort to be sociable at all. Alex had seen him around occasionally.

'She's my grandchild,' Alex explained, taken aback by

Hancock's aggressiveness. 'I insist you avoid abusive language in her presence, please.'

'Oh, fuck off, old man. If you're supposed to look after her, you're certainly not up to the job.'

'Look, she's just a kid, okay? I'll make sure she's more careful. But please control your language and temper.'

'Don't you give me no fucking advice, old man. Just look after your kid better.' Hancock then abruptly turned and walked away, leaving Alex fuming and feeling inadequate. Hancock had been right. His responsibility was to look after Sarah, and he'd fallen short.

Alex turned to Sarah, who was his primary concern now. He put a protective arm around her and drew her to him. She was still sobbing.

'I hate that Mr Hancock,' she declared between sobs.

'You know Mr Hancock?' asked Alex, curious.

'Yes, and I don't like him, Alex. He treats Cassie badly.'

'Who's Cassie?'

'His kid. She's my friend at school. He sometimes comes to pick her up when Mrs Hancock's at work. He never allows Cassie to play with us, not even for a little bit in the school playground before going home. And he always has that funny face and blinking eye. I hate him. He's not a nice man.'

Alex had to agree. Adam Hancock was a mystery to the neighbourhood, rarely seen, but when anyone did meet him, he was always scowling. The slim young man had a drawn face and shifty eyes—one of which always twitched—and a lethargic gait. No one knew what work he did.

'Are you and Cassie good friends?'

'Yes. She, Alice, and Anya are my best friends. Can I have them over for a play date, Alex?'

Alex smiled. 'Of course. If their mums agree. I'm not sure

what her dad will say, though. We'll check it out in the next few days. For now, let's enjoy our walk—but slower on that scooter, okay?'

Sarah gave a small nod, her face brightening again. 'Okay, Alex. I'll go slow this time.'

~

The following day, Alex and Sarah sat at their desks in opposite corners of the room. Outside, the brilliant sun shone brightly and sent shining arcs through the large bay windows. Alex had opened the windows, and the fresh air and garden scents filled the house. The birds sang and the trees swayed, inviting them to step outside. But Alex was content in his corner, reading his newspapers online. He looked across and saw Sarah buried in her iPad.

Mercifully, Sarah had indeed turned out to be rather more easily managed than he'd expected. A bit bossy from time to time, though, reminding him to brush his teeth after dinner the night before, restricting his evening desert to just one serving, and checking if he'd made his bed in the morning.

At breakfast that morning, she'd insisted on making him pancakes. Apparently, it was her commitment to her mum.

'Look, Alex, you need to really shake the mixture well. Try it, and do it like I did.'

He patiently followed her instructions. When it came to frying them in the pan, he was worried about her handling the hot plate. But she was quite competent about it. Kay had trained her well.

He ate the pancakes, pretending to relish them, though he'd have preferred his bacon and eggs.

Sarah looked up from her iPad. 'This is R-E-A-L-L-Y

boring, Alex.'

He glanced at her. 'I think it's wonderful, dear. Of course I'd rather have the peaceful day to myself.' He bit his tongue, but too late to take back the comment.

'So you'd like to be alone and without me? That's not very kind, you know? I don't think my mum would be happy to hear that.'

He felt ashamed of his pettiness. 'Let's put it like this, Sarah. I'm rather old to be good company for a seven-year-old. And you're rather young to spend your days with an old man like me. Unfortunately, dear, we're together for the next three months. So we'll just have to adjust.'

'I've an idea. What if you and I do one exciting thing together each day? Just one. Will you do that for me? Please.'

Alex saw an opportunity. He was at a loss about how to occupy a seven-year-old for what now appeared to be an eternity—almost four weeks till school reopened.

'Okay. Done. One day, you decide what we do, and the next, I will. Agreed?'

'Yes, let's agree. Pinkie promise?' She held out her little finger.

This was something novel. *What does the pinkie, anatomically, have to do with a promise?* Maybe he'd learn in time.

'Okay, pinkie promise.' He held out his little finger like she did hers. She hooked it with hers. *Cute,* he thought.

'My turn first,' she said before he had a chance.

He waited with bated breath.

'You're going to put on shorts and go to the park to play tag. I love tag, and you'll enjoy it too.'

'What? Not me; not on your life. And certainly not in shorts,' he protested.

'But you just pinkie promised. A pinkie promise CAN'T be broken, don't you know?'

~

And so it was that retired Professor Alex Bobbins was seen lumbering around the park, chasing his granddaughter in a pair of shorts that clung precariously to his generously rounded waist and rump. His legs, pale and knobbly from years of underuse, moved with all the agility of a steam engine struggling uphill.

He huffed and puffed, each breath a wheeze, as he reached out to tag the sprightly seven-year-old who danced just out of reach, her laughter ringing out like the sound of tiny bells. She delighted in his discomfort, his clumsy attempts to catch her, and the ease with which she slipped his grasp each time. The poor man had no chance, and his face soon turned the shade of an overripe tomato.

Old Agatha Wallin and her companion Joan Chester were out for their morning constitutional, strolling at a leisurely pace as they always did. When they caught sight of Alex, they halted mid-step, their jaws hanging open in astonishment.

'Good heavens, is that Professor Bobbins?' Agatha's eyes grew wide with disbelief. 'The same man who barely grunts when we wish him good morning?'

Joan squinted. 'The very one. Wouldn't have believed it if I hadn't seen it with my own eyes.'

They stood there, transfixed by the sight of the famously grumpy professor—a man known for his monosyllabic greetings and his steadfast avoidance of small talk—chasing a child through the park with all the grace of a waddling duck.

'What's gotten into him?' Agatha demanded, folding

her arms. 'Has he finally lost his marbles, running after little girls? Disgraceful, though not unexpected, given how he's shut himself away since poor Mabel passed on.'

Joan shook her head. 'No scandal here. Kay's gone off somewhere, and the little one's staying with him for a while.'

'Honestly,' Agatha huffed, her lips pursed, 'rather irresponsible of Kay to leave that sweet child with such a crusty old recluse.'

Joan shrugged. 'Well, at least he's trying to entertain her. You've got to give him some credit.'

Agatha's eyes narrowed as she watched Alex stumble, his arms flailing as he narrowly avoided toppling over. 'Entertain her? He's more likely to give himself a heart attack. Look at him—wheezing like an old bellows. He'll never catch her at that pace.'

She cupped her hands around her mouth. 'Alex! You need to shape up, mate! You're about as fit as a Christmas pudding!'

Alex came to an abrupt halt and bent over, his chest heaving, hands on his knees. His face was a furious crimson, his hair plastered to his forehead with sweat. He glared at the two women, his cheeks puffed out like a blowfish, every laboured breath a wheeze.

'Thank you, Agatha,' he managed between gasps. 'I'll be sure to consult your … expert opinion … if I ever want to … win at the Olympics.'

Joan burst into laughter, and even Agatha's stern expression softened. Alex straightened slowly, his legs trembling from the exertion. He looked at his granddaughter, who was still bouncing with energy, her eyes sparkling with joy.

He let out a sigh, half exasperation, half affection. He might not be the fittest grandfather in the park, but seeing her smile made every aching muscle worthwhile.

'Come on, Alex!' Sarah's voice rang out across the field, her hands on her hips, eyes bright with challenge. 'You're not even trying!'

Alex straightened, wiping sweat from his brow, panting like a fish out of water. 'Okay, okay, dear. Here I come,' he called, forcing as much enthusiasm into his voice as he could muster.

He staggered forward, legs heavy as sandbags, wondering just how much longer he could keep this up. The vast football field spread out before him, its border of leafy trees swaying gently in the breeze. Under different circumstances, Alex would have appreciated the tranquillity of the setting. It was, he mused between gasps, a perfect spot for a leisurely stroll— certainly not for chasing a seven-year-old with the energy of a tornado. He made a mental note to visit this park more often … but for walking, not sprinting.

'Alex! You're hopeless at this game! Can't you at least try?' Sarah's frustration was evident, her little arms on her hips, foot tapping impatiently.

Alex opened his mouth to defend himself, but before he formed the words, Sarah took off like a rocket, her ponytail flying behind her as she raced across the field towards another child her age.

A wave of relief washed over him, cooling his flushed face. Gratefully, he slowed to a walk, watching as the two girls met and immediately fell into animated chatter, Sarah's hands gesturing towards him, likely recounting his feeble attempts at tag.

When he finally caught up, Sarah introduced him. 'Alex, this is Alice, my best friend from school.'

Alex struggled to catch his breath. 'Hi, Alice. I'm so glad to see you.' And he truly was. Alice was his salvation.

Alice, as tall as Sarah, with curly hair framing a round, dimpled face, looked at him curiously. 'Are you a professor?'

Alex raised his eyebrows, surprised. 'How did you know that?'

'Oh, Sarah's always bragging about her grandpa being an important professor at the university. But … I didn't think you'd be so fat.'

Alex flinched, his cheeks flushing a deeper red. *Why do kids have to be so brutally honest?* he wondered, his back unconsciously straightening. Yet beneath his embarrassment, he felt a flicker of warmth. He hadn't realised Sarah was proud of him. For a granddaughter he barely knew until recently, that was something.

The girls quickly lost interest in him and took off, their laughter floating on the breeze as they chased each other across the grass. Grateful for the reprieve, Alex hobbled over to a nearby bench, his legs trembling as he sank down. His breath came in wheezing gasps, his heart thumping like a drum. But as he watched the girls play, their energy endless and laughter infectious, he found himself smiling.

'Are you with Sarah?'

The voice startled him out of his reverie. He looked up to see a petite middle-aged woman standing before him. Slim and athletic, with bright eyes and a welcoming smile, she radiated vitality. Alex suddenly became painfully aware of his own appearance—sweat-drenched, his too-tight shorts clinging awkwardly to his round belly. *I must look like a circus clown,* he thought grimly.

'Yes,' he admitted sheepishly. 'I'm her grandpa. She's staying with me temporarily.'

'I thought so,' the woman said, her smile widening. 'Alice mentioned it. I'm Laura, Alice's grandaunt. I help out my niece, June, who—like your daughter, Kay—is a single mother. Looks like we'll be seeing more of each other now that Sarah's staying with you.'

'Well, nice to meet you, Laura,' Alex replied, surprised by how genuinely pleased he was. 'Kay's spoken of June, and Sarah of Alice. Small world.'

'Mind if I sit?' Laura asked, nodding at the space beside him. 'We might as well get acquainted while the girls wear each other out.'

'Of course, of course.' Alex shuffled to one side to make room. He usually avoided idle chit-chat, preferring solitude and the company of his books. Yet, for reasons he couldn't quite explain, he found himself looking forward to a conversation with this vibrant woman.

'So, Laura,' he ventured, trying to sound casual, 'what do you do when you're not looking after Alice?'

'I'm an economics adviser to the Australian Labor Party,' she replied matter-of-factly.

Alex nearly choked. His eyes widened, and his head snapped around to look at her properly. 'An economist? You?' He'd simply assumed she was a housewife who liked helping out with her grandniece. His own bias surprised him.

Laura's eyes twinkled. 'Surprised? And yes, I know about you too. A professor of economics, no less. Neoliberal, from what I've heard. A Milton Friedman devotee.' She raised an eyebrow. 'I hope you're giving your students a balanced view of economics?'

Alex found himself both amused and impressed by her audacity. 'I do my best to be objective, though I can't deny my sympathies lie with the free market. I suppose, being an adviser to the Labour Party, you lean towards the left?'

'I do,' Laura admitted, her tone unapologetic. 'I favour Marxian economics, but I have little patience for rigid ideologies. Facts are facts. Unfortunately, too many politicians are obsessed with dogma.'

Alex chuckled. 'We agree on that, at least. Which facts are you referring to?'

'Well, for one,' Laura began, her eyes flashing, 'everyone keeps blaming low productivity on workers. But no one mentions the oligopolies dominating entire sectors, the price gouging, or the—'

'Hold on, hold on—'

'Alex!' Sarah's voice cut through their debate, her small hands yanking at his arm. 'Come on! I want to show Alice how fast you can run!'

'What?'

Laura burst into laughter, her eyes dancing with mischief. 'Go on, Alex. Show them your speed.'

Sarah dragged him off, his protests drowned out by her giggles. And so Professor Alex Bobbins found himself running again, this time two little girls chasing him with infectious glee, their laughter echoing across the field.

Later, as they walked back to his house, Sarah skipped ahead, her energy seemingly limitless. Alex followed slowly, his legs aching, but his heart feeling strangely light. He watched her bouncing ponytail, her carefree leaps, her joy. Little kids, he realised, didn't walk—they danced through life.

Ella Webster, pottering around in her garden, greeted them when they reached their gate. 'Hello, Sarah,' she called out, her eyes twinkling. 'How are you managing with grumpy old Alex?'

'We played tag today!' Sarah announced proudly. 'Alice

and I chased him all around the park!'

Ella's eyes widened, and she glanced at Alex's ill-fitting shorts. Her mouth twitched, and she let out a bark of laughter. 'Good Lord, Alex! You're not losing your mind, are you? Dressed like that and running around like a madman?'

To his own surprise, Alex grinned. 'You should try it, Ella. It's quite invigorating. Good for the spirit … and the constitution.'

Ella shook her head, still chuckling. 'Well, I never!' Her face softened. 'I've baked some cookies for you both. I thought Sarah could do with a treat. And you … well, you've certainly earned one.'

She handed Sarah a plate piled high with cookies wrapped neatly in a cloth. Alex accepted them with gratitude, suddenly realising that perhaps Ella wasn't such a bad neighbour after all.

As they walked inside, Sarah already munching on a cookie, Alex felt an unfamiliar warmth spreading through him. He looked down at his granddaughter, so full of life, and smiled. Maybe, just maybe, this wouldn't be such a bad adventure after all.

FIVE

Evening settled in, and Alex and Sarah prepared dinner together. After the day's unexpected burst of activity, Alex was famished. Chasing a seven-year-old around the park had been more exhausting than he'd anticipated.

Kay's instructions were clear: pasta and veggies. But after all that running, Alex craved something heartier.

'Listen, Sarah,' he began, glancing at the packet of pasta. 'Your mum said pasta and veggies, but just for today, how about we have some pies and sausages instead? I'm starving. We can save the pasta for tomorrow. Deal?'

Before Sarah answered, he pulled the pies and sausages from the freezer and popped them into the oven.

With dinner warming, Alex sank onto the sofa and stretched out. His legs throbbed, and his muscles already whispered of tomorrow's aches. Still, he had to admit—it felt good. The fresh air, the laughter, the sheer joy of playing had made him feel alive, almost young again. Yet he knew his body would soon remind him of his age.

Sarah dragged her little chair over and sat beside him, arms crossed and a serious look on her face. It was a perfect imitation of her mother's disapproving glare. 'Alex, you're terrible at running.'

Alex chuckled. 'Well, dear, I don't usually need to run. I'm not as young as you. When you get older, your muscles get tired faster.'

'That's not what Mum says,' Sarah countered.

'Oh? And what does she say?'

'She says everyone needs exercise to stay fit, young and old. If you exercise, you enjoy life more and live longer.'

Alex grunted noncommittally. He wasn't keen on this line of discussion. 'How about we watch some TV while we eat?' he suggested, rising to check on dinner.

'Mum says no TV during dinner,' Sarah stated matter-of-factly.

'Oh? Then what do you do instead?'

'We sit at the table and talk. But ...' She hesitated, a conspiratorial gleam in her eye. 'If you don't tell Mum, I'd love to watch TV with you.'

Alex grinned. 'I won't tell if you won't.' He dished up the pies and sausages. 'Let's eat on the sofa tonight. I haven't had a chance to read the newspapers. We'll watch the news.'

He reached for the remote, but Sarah was faster. 'Ewwh! No news!' she said. 'They always show boring stuff like people crashing cars or fighting. Let's watch *Bluey*!'

'What's *Bluey*?' Alex asked, surrendering the remote.

She switched to ABC Kids. 'It's the best show ever! You'll love it.'

Alex settled in, ready to endure whatever mindless cartoon was currently captivating seven-year-olds, but as the episode began, he found himself intrigued. It was about a family of dogs—two little ones and their parents.

'So which one's Bluey? The dad?'

Sarah looked at him, her eyes wide with disbelief. 'Alex! Haven't you been listening? Bluey's not a boy! She's a girl! And the dad's name is Bandit. The other little dog is Bingo, Bluey's sister. And their mum is Chilli.'

'Unusual names,' Alex mused.

'I like Bandit. He's a great dad. I wish all dads were like him.' Her voice softened, and she looked down at her plate. 'You know I don't have a dad, right?'

The statement hung in the air, heavy and unexpected. Alex had always wondered how Sarah felt about not having a father around. He knew Kay had severed all contact with her ex, but he'd never been sure how much Sarah understood.

'Yeah … yeah, I know,' he said softly. He wanted to say something comforting, but words failed him.

'Some of my school friends don't have dads either, like Alice. And some have two … one real and one extra. I think it would be nice if all of us had dads, don't you think?'

Alex's heart ached. 'Yes, I do, sweetheart.' He'd observed, with some distress, how divorce rates these days had risen exponentially. Every second colleague at the university appeared to have divorced. He often wondered at the causes of this rise in divorce rates.

He'd once examined the economics of the issue, the financial impacts on families, the effect on birth rates, and the implications of these for the economy. He realised the trend seemed almost inevitable as women's patience with their male partners wore thin. Women had finally found their voice and decided if male partners couldn't contribute equitably to the household, they might as well go separate ways. He'd been fortunate that Mabel was old school and patient with him.

He had sympathy for the cause of women. But he wondered where this trend was taking society.

'Watch, Alex!' Sarah's voice pulled him back to the present. 'Bluey and Bingo are going to trick their dad!'

'You've seen this before?'

'Yeah, but I don't care. It's still funny. I love Bluey. Don't you?'

Alex looked at the screen. He hadn't been impressed at first. The animation was simple, the characters differentiated only by size and colour. Yet, the story was relatable, the humour genuine. It reminded him of *The Simpsons*—intelligent and insightful, using humour to reveal life's complexities.

'It's not bad,' he admitted.

'See? I knew you'd like it.' Sarah leaned against him, snuggling closer. Her small head fit perfectly under his arm, and Alex felt a warmth he hadn't known he needed. It was a reminder that family wasn't just about biology.

They watched a few more episodes, Sarah giggling uncontrollably at Bluey's antics, Alex chuckling along. Eventually, he decided it was time to call it a night.

'All right, Sarah. Time to brush your teeth and get to bed. We've both had a big day. But first, help me clear up.'

Sarah sprang up, more energetic than ever. 'What are we doing tomorrow?'

Alex feigned deep thought. 'Ah, tomorrow … It's my turn to choose, right?'

'Yep. But you also promised Alice could come over if her mum said yes. Right?'

Alex considered the idea. If Alice came over, the girls would keep each other busy, and he might have a chance to relax. 'Okay, I'll check with Alice's mum tomorrow.'

Sarah beamed. 'Great! And maybe Laura will come too!'

Alex's heart gave an unexpected leap. The thought of continuing his conversation with Laura was surprisingly appealing. 'We'll see,' he said, trying to sound casual.

As they washed the dishes together, Alex watched Sarah humming happily to herself. Her laughter, her boundless energy—it was contagious. He realised that she wasn't the only one adjusting to this new arrangement.

In some unexpected way, she was bringing him back to life.

~

A persistent shaking jolted Alex awake. His eyes fluttered open, his mind struggling to catch up with the world around him. Sarah stood at his bedside, her hands planted firmly on her hips, a determined look on her face.

'Come on, Alex, it's late! We need to make breakfast and call Alice's mum.' Urgency tinged her voice.

Alex groaned and sat up, his head in his hands, wishing he could go back to sleep. *This is worse than a hangover,* he thought. *This exercise business does not agree with me.* Every muscle protested, each movement reminding him of his attempts to keep up with the girls at the park the day before. His body felt like it had been trampled on by a pack of horses.

Head heavy and limbs leaden, he rubbed his face, willing himself to wake up fully. *Whoever said exercise was good for you was clearly a sadist.*

'Alex, hurry up! I'm hungry, and Alice will be waiting for you to call her mum!' Sarah's voice cut through his foggy thoughts.

'All right, all right, I'm up,' he grumbled, trying to muster a smile.

Downstairs, the kitchen came alive with the sounds and smells of breakfast. Flour dusted the counter like powdered snow, and the sweet aroma of pancakes filled the air. Sarah stood on tiptoes, vigorously stirring the batter. She hummed to herself, her ponytail swaying with each enthusiastic motion.

Alex watched her, marvelling at how much energy she had so early in the morning. He poured batter onto the sizzling skillet, the mixture spreading into imperfect circles that bubbled and hissed.

Sarah's eyes sparkled as she watched the pancakes rise. She barely waited for them to cool before gobbling them down, syrup dripping down her chin. 'Hurry, Alex! You need to call Alice's mum!'

Alex wiped his hands and shuffled over to his desk, where Kay's meticulously organised Excel sheets awaited. He scanned the columns, feeling like a detective on the trail of a missing clue. *There it was—June! Alice's mum.* He found her number and took a deep breath before dialling.

The phone rang twice before a warm voice answered, 'Hello?'

'Hi, June? This is Alex, Sarah's grandpa.'

'Ah, Alex! Nice to hear from you. How's it going looking after Sarah? I'd promised Kay I'd check in, see if you needed any help. Sorry I haven't called sooner—work's been crazy.'

'All good here, June. Thanks for asking. The girls met in the park yesterday, and they're keen on meeting again today. Would it be all right if Alice came over?'

'Absolutely! Alice would love that. My aunt, Laura, told me about yesterday. She's quite impressed with you, Alex— said you were running around with the girls like a pro.'

Alex felt his cheeks flush. 'Oh, I'm not sure about that. But I did promise Sarah I'd try.'

'Well, you did a great job. I wish more grandparents were as adventurous as you!'

Alex felt a flicker of pride. He still had it in him, even if his muscles vehemently disagreed.

'I can't come over today, though—I'm working from home—and Laura's out. But I'd be grateful if Alice can spend the day with you. I'll drop her off in about an hour. Is that okay?'

The doorbell chimed just after they'd cleared the breakfast table. Sarah bolted towards the door. 'I'll get it!' she shouted, her voice trailing as she skidded down the hallway.

Alex wondered who it was. Couldn't be June and Alice yet. Then he heard a squeal of delight. 'Cassie! You're here! Alice is coming too. This is going to be so much fun!'

Two girls burst into the room, laughter bubbling. Alex blinked, his brain scrambling to catch up. *Cassie? Who's Cassie?*

Then he saw Sharon Hancock standing at the door, looking hopeful yet hesitant. Recognition dawned—Cassie was her daughter. Alex remembered seeing Sharon's worried face around the neighbourhood, her shoulders always slightly hunched, as if carrying an invisible weight.

'Hi, Professor,' Sharon began, her voice tentative. 'Cassie saw you with Sarah and Alice at the park yesterday. She's on holiday too and begged to play with them. I was going to take her to the school care centre today, but … well, would you mind if she stayed here instead and played with Sarah? I'm at work this morning.'

Alex opened his mouth to respond, but Cassie was already sprawled on the floor with Sarah, their heads bent over an iPad, excitedly discussing some new game.

He sighed, the corners of his mouth twitching into a resigned smile. 'Of course. Can I have your phone number, just in case?'

Sharon's face lit up with relief. 'Thank you, Professor—thank you so much.' And just like that, she was off, hurrying to work.

Not long after, Alice arrived with her mum, June, who carried a plate of freshly baked cookies and Alice's lunch box. Alice's eyes widened with joy when she saw Cassie. In no time, the trio were huddled together, whispering conspiratorially and erupting into bursts of giggles.

June hesitated at the door. 'Are you sure you'll be okay with them, Alex? I'm close by if you need help. Working from home.'

Alex waved off her concern. 'They'll entertain themselves. I'll just supervise and maybe get some reading done.'

June smiled, clearly impressed. 'You're a gem, Alex. If you need anything, just call.'

But the quiet time he'd envisioned was short-lived. The house was soon filled with shrieks of laughter, the thud of running feet, and the constant opening and closing of the refrigerator.

'Alex, where's the butter?'

'Can we have some of those cookies?'

'Are there any soft drinks?'

'Can you make hot chocolate?'

'We're hungry—what's for lunch?'

Questions flew at him like arrows, each one methodically piercing his plan of a peaceful morning. The kitchen became a battleground of requests. Ham for one, no butter for another, brown bread for Sarah, white bread for Alice. Each child had their own preferences, and Alex struggled to keep up.

By mid-afternoon, Alex felt as though he'd run a marathon. He slumped into his armchair, newspaper in hand, but the words blurred together. He hadn't read more than a few paragraphs when June arrived to pick up Alice.

'Can I come again tomorrow, Mum? It's so boring at home by myself.' Alice's eyes sparkled with hope.

'Please, June?' Sarah chimed in. 'Alex loves having us here!' She turned to Alex, her eyes wide with expectation, a grin stretched across her face.

Alex opened his mouth, hesitated, then saw the unspoken plea on their faces. He managed a weak smile. 'Of course. You're all welcome tomorrow.'

His answer was met with squeals of joy and a group hug that nearly toppled him over. As the girls ran off, their laughter echoing down the hall, Alex looked on with a rueful smile.

An hour later, Sharon Hancock arrived to pick up Cassie.

Alex invited her in while he looked for Cassie, who was probably upstairs in Sarah's room.

'Can I have a word with you, Professor, before you call Cassie?' she looked nervous, almost hassled.

'Yes, Sharon. What is it? And you can call me Alex.'

'I … I … I don't know how to put it, Professor.'

'It's okay, Sharon, just tell me what's on your mind.' Alex tried to sound reassuring. He was genuinely concerned. She appeared anxious and worried as she fingered her necklace and searched for words.

'Professor, I feel ashamed to ask this, but can I leave Cassie here during the day while Sarah is on holidays? You see, I work as a cashier in the supermarket. Our family survives on my income. Keeping Cassie in school care while I'm at work takes almost half the money I earn for the day. I'd be so, so, grateful if you can help me here?'

Alex was taken aback. For a moment, he was at a loss for how to respond. 'May I ask what your husband is doing while you're at work, Sharon?'

She looked at the floor, reluctant to answer, continuing to finger her necklace. He waited, truly wanting to know about the mysterious Adam, who didn't work and wasn't able to look after his own kid. Yesterday's confrontation was still fresh in his mind.

'Professor, he's an alcoholic.' Sharon sighed and couldn't look him in the eyes. It seemed a huge effort for her to make this admission.

He saw her struggle, and he felt for her. 'Come in. Here, sit with me at the dining table. I want to hear more about this, if you don't mind. Cassie is upstairs playing with Sarah.'

Over the next fifteen minutes, Alex got an idea of all the pain and suffering this woman was going through. Not only was her husband an alcoholic, he was also a gambler and an abuser.

'So why don't you just leave him and take Cassie with you?'

She shook her head. 'Professor, the house is mine. It was left to me by my parents. It will be Cassie's inheritance. I can't just leave it to my husband. I know he wants to sell it for the money, which he will then gamble away. Besides, where will I stay? My job gives us just enough money for essentials. I have no money to rent.'

Alex saw despair in her eyes. He wanted to help, but at a loss as to how, he simply sat in empathy with her as she wiped her tears.

The children rushing down the stairs broke the spell.

'Hi, Mum. Can I come tomorrow as well? Alice is coming. Her mum has allowed her. Is it okay, Professor?'

Alex was touched that she thought to ask his permission. He smiled down at her. 'Yes, sure, Cassie. You're most welcome every day till the school opens.'

'Yay,' both girls screamed and high-fived.

He enjoyed their liveliness. Sharon Hancock teared up again and gave him a grateful look.

They were soon gone, saying goodbyes at the door.

'Hi, Mrs Webster,' Sarah called from the door when she spied Ella Webster in her garden.

'Hi, Sarah. Has your grandpa been good today?' she asked with a mischievous smile.

'He's great, Mrs Webster. My friends will be coming every day now to play with me. You too can come if you wish, though I don't think you'll like our games.'

'That's lovely of you to invite me, Sarah. Though I don't think your grandpa would like me to come.'

Alex, standing behind Sarah at the door, felt embarrassed. 'Ella, you're most welcome anytime. I know I'm a bit grumpy sometimes, but do come. By the way, we enjoyed your cookies. The kids particularly loved them.'

That night, after putting Sarah to bed, Alex lay down, exhausted but surprisingly pleased with himself. He'd been of some help today and had somehow come out with glowing reviews. Then he thought of Sharon Hancock and her situation. Of how single mothers seemed to be multiplying and how they appeared, somehow, to be holding society together despite all odds.

SIX

Alex sat at the dining table, coffee mug in hand, running his hand through his bushy hair, surveying his charges. It was lunchtime, Friday. Six little figures seated around the table, loudly slurping their drinks, chomping at their burgers, giggling and chatting, and so engrossed in their conversations that his presence seemed an afterthought.

The little girls were of varying skin colours, physiques, clothes, and personalities. *Each,* he reflected, *is different, unique, and interesting. Each is a discovery.* He almost scratched his head at the situation he found himself in. He hadn't interacted with children for years. Decades, possibly. Kay's childhood days were a distant memory.

He wondered what Mabel would make of him, seated at the head of the table, looking after six seven-year-olds. Nothing in his life and career to date had prepared him for this. She'd be shaking her head, unbelieving.

It was the end of the week, one in which he had gone from being in charge of one kid to six! He had no idea how it'd happened. It all seemed rather spontaneous, organic, even natural. The calls kept coming after the initial group of Sarah, Alice and Cassie had been formed.

Han, also a close friend of Kay, called on Tuesday to ask if all was well and if she could help in any way. When she heard that Alice and Cassie were now in a playgroup with Sarah at Alex's house, she asked if she could drop her child, Anya, as well. Alex graciously agreed. She arrived, bringing Anya's lunch as well as food for the other kids. A couple of other of Kay's friends also called in, asking if Alex could let their girls join the playgroup.

By the end of the week, the group of six had assumed complete control of the Bobbins' household.

The mums were considerate and helpful, bringing along lunch boxes for their kids and the occasional plate of cookies for all to share. So feeding the kids wasn't too demanding. Though he still needed to supplement their lunch boxes. The kids' appetites belied their size. He wondered where all the food disappeared.

Every second evening found Sarah and him making a trip to the supermarket to shop. It was fun to have Sarah show him where in the supermarket he could find what they needed. He'd never bought so much before. His needs had always been minimal. Particularly since the university had been his primary home. Now, he found the shopping cart and pantry back home filling up by leaps and bounds.

The girls were a cacophonous, vocal bunch, constantly chuckling, arguing, quarrelling, and devising games to keep themselves entertained. The idea of getting playmates for Sarah had been brilliant. It relieved him of trying to find ways to entertain a seven-year-old. He came to enjoy their constant chatter. He didn't mind the regular interruptions as they asked for something to eat or help with setting up one of their games. It was fun sitting with the girls on the floor, trying to understand their latest art project as they showed it off. He gradually learned to push the background chatter aside while he snatched a few moments now and then to catch up on his reading.

But all hopes of focused analysis and writing on economics had gone out of the window. Thomas had called him a couple of days ago, asking if he was ready to guide a young PhD researcher in the department on the economic implications of duopolies and oligopolies in some sectors of Australia. It was grant-funded and sounded like an attractive project to work on. He'd wanted to tackle this issue for some time. But he realised there was no way he could do so at this time.

'Regrettably, not for the next three weeks, Thomas. Maybe after Sarah goes back to school.'

'So she's keeping you busy, Alex?'

'More than busy, I'm afraid, Thomas. I have her friends here as well. Every day. They're more than a handful.'

'Fabulous way to spend your retirement, Alex.'

Alex wasn't sure Thomas was having him on. They agreed to talk again in three weeks.

What did develop as a challenge for Alex was acting as referee to the inevitable disagreements and quarrels which broke out, from time to time, among the girls.

One afternoon, Alice approached him, teary-eyed. 'Alex,' she sobbed, 'Cassie's taken my koala. And she's not giving it back to me.'

'Why not?' asked Alex, showing his concern. Alice seemed really upset.

'I want you to tell her to give it back, Alex.'

'Okay, dear. Let's go and talk with Cassie.'

Cassie saw them approaching. She hugged the koala even tighter, putting on a defiant face. *The koala does look very cute and cuddly,* mused Alex.

'Cassie, did you take Alice's koala without her permission?'

Cassie looked at him, defensive. 'Yesterday, she took my teddy bear. And she didn't ask my permission, did she, Sarah? So why can't I take her koala today?' Cassie looked at Sarah for confirmation.

Sarah looked cautious, not wanting to get involved.

'Cassie, I do think you should give the koala back.' Alex suggested. 'It's not good to take someone else's things without asking permission. Now, please give it back,' he requested firmly.

Cassie burst into tears. 'I want my mum,' she moaned as she threw the koala on the floor in frustration.

Alice now burst into tears. 'She threw my darling koala on the floor. I'll hit her,' she screamed as she rushed to rescue her beloved koala.

'Hold it, Alice. Let's talk about this, please.'

'I hate you, Alex, I hate you,' Cassie now decided. 'You're a bad man.'

'No, he's not.' Sarah rushed to Alex's defence. 'He's the best man there is.'

'I'm leaving and will never come to your house again. I'm going to find my mum.' Cassie rushed to the door.

Alex panicked. There was no way he'd let a kid in his charge simply leave the house. He charged after Cassie. 'Hold it, Cassie. Let's all talk about it, okay?' In the background, Alice was crying in distress that her darling koala had been thrown to the ground.

'No, I hate Sarah, and Alice, and you. Most of all, you, Alex,' Cassie insisted as she reached the front door.

This was definitely more challenging than assessing the economic implications of duopolies and monopolies, Alex decided.

Then he got a brilliant idea.

'Anybody for ice cream?' he called out loudly.

There was a sudden silence. Just for a moment. Then in unison, a shout went up, 'Yeah!'

He turned to the refrigerator, the girls running after him, all else forgotten. Over ice creams, the koala conflict became history.

Nothing like incentives to solve a problem, Alex reflected. *Good old economics. One can always depend on it.*

However, it was most difficult dealing with Sarah's complaints about one or the other girl. He was, after all, her grandpa, and she expected full loyalty from him when she approached him to sort out her wrangles. He struggled to be fair. Inevitably, the dispute ended with a little girl sobbing and crying in a corner.

Ice cream, he realised, couldn't always be the solution. He gradually learned more constructive strategies. A useful approach, he realised, was to simply sit next to the little one who was upset and reassure her that he understood her problem. Slowly, the comforting, non-critical presence of the adult seemed to calm the little girl. He would then appeal to Sarah to help her get back into whatever game they were playing.

But a fine line had always to be treaded. Refined diplomacy was often called for.

At the end of the week, Alex took stock. The group of six had by now gelled. Though they'd been friends from school, while of a similar age, they were all different and interesting with varying temperaments—some shy, some boisterous, some timid, others animated and demanding.

He noticed the uncanny similarities between daughters and mothers. The mothers, Sharon and June, were slim and of modest statures, as were Cassie and Alice, their daughters. The plump and ever-bubbling Olivia's mum, Mei, was a lady of Chinese descent. She was, like Olivia, well-rounded, always smiling and beaming, with a good word for everyone.

He recalled the day, earlier in the week, when she rang his doorbell.

'Hello, Mister Professor. Olivia is friend of Sarah. You no mind Olivia joining girls to play?' she asked tentatively when he'd opened the door. 'She worrying me too much to come and play.'

He looked down at cute little Olivia, who looked up at him, uncertainty in her eyes. He smiled reassuringly. 'Come on in, Olivia. I'll call Sarah.'

As Sarah, Alice, and Cassie hugged Olivia and welcomed her in, Alex chatted with Olivia's mum.

'May I know your name?'

'Mei.'

'May I ask what it means in Chinese?'

She smiled shyly. 'Means beautiful. But I no beautiful. Too fat.' She pointed to her size, then giggled.

Alex laughed. She was a fun person. 'Me also fat, Mei. So no problem.'

She insisted on giving him a grateful hug when leaving. 'You very kind man, Professor. I come afternoon to pick up Olivia.' She departed after leaving her phone number with him.

But it was Hanneli and her kid, Anya, who blew his mind. The mother's physique and the presence she projected struck him as special. She was tall, slender, and dark with long, flowing hair and toned muscles, in an outfit and with a demeanour that shouted, *fitness instructor!* He tried to place her ethnicity and decided she was either from South Africa or India. She had a warm smile and sparkling eyes and always spoke with gestures.

Alex felt uncomfortable, though, when they met for the first time, as she gave his figure the eye over. Inevitably, later that first week, and as he got to know her better, she invited him to join one of her fitness classes in the evening and to bring along Sarah, who would keep Anya company.

Anya, like her mum, was similarly athletic, constantly doing cartwheels, bridges and backbends. He often caught her coaching her friends in the challenging moves.

He admired the new generation and how differing ethnicities seemed to be simply taken for granted. The kids didn't appear to give race or colour a second thought. *Australia is all the better for it,* he reflected. The sooner the human race left behind its biases against ethnicity, the better.

The kids played havoc with his house. He thanked his lucky stars they weren't boys. He couldn't imagine how he and his house would have coped. He gradually taught them, with the help of their mothers, to clean up as much as they could before they departed every afternoon. But it was a back-breaking job to get the house in order once they had all departed. He found himself wondering if, indeed, he should take up Hanneli's offer and join one of her fitness classes.

'Come on, Alex, we still have to clean up my room,' Sarah urged one evening, when Alex sat on the couch, taking time off huffing and puffing with the exertion of cleaning up. His back ached, his knees felt wobbly, and he sometimes felt dizzy as he stood up from the ground. That evil little mole at the back of his mind kept berating him for how unfit he was.

At the end of the day, he often found himself wondering how Mabel would have enjoyed the company of the little ones. They certainly added colour, activity, and mess to the house. She would have been pleased.

~

The weekend arrived. At breakfast that Saturday morning, Sarah demanded they do something different for the day. Her friends wouldn't be coming, except perhaps Cassie.

Alex gathered himself for the onslaught of suggestions, and then his phone rang. It was Kay on FaceTime. He put the call on speaker.

'Hi, Dad. How are you doing, and how is Sarah?'

Despite her commitment to call Sarah every day, Kay had only called once—the day after she arrived in Port Moresby. She'd flown to the PNG highlands the next day, to check out health services in the provinces. Phone connections from there were sporadic and weak at best. She was now back in Port Moresby.

'All good here, Kay. Sarah's begging to come on. I'm passing the phone to her. Will talk after she's finished.'

'Hi, Mum. I just made Alex pancakes for breakfast,' Sarah announced.

'Well done, Sarah. I'm impressed. But don't feed him too many. He needs to lose weight.'

Sarah giggled.

Alex scrunched his face. Why did his weight always come up?

'Tell me, love, how are you enjoying staying with Grandpa?'

Sarah launched into explaining how she had a play group of her school friends at Alex's house, and it kept on growing.

There were now six of them, all girls. They played with their scooters down the hallway. They each brought their dolls and played house. Also computer games and hopscotch in the backyard. Alex had made a swing on one of the trees. 'It's so much fun, Mum,' Sarah declared, grinning at Alex.

Alex sat back, pleased to hear Sarah give him a thumbs-up for her first week with him. Truthfully, he'd not expected it to go so smoothly. He still grappled with issues like constant interruptions by the girls, their endless eating and drinking needs, and the mess left behind each afternoon after they departed. But most of all, the tiredness got him down. He'd never done so much bending, picking up stuff from the floor, or general cleaning. Each afternoon, the house looked like a cyclone had just passed through.

Thomas would probably say all the exercise was good for him. But that didn't help the fact that his limbs and his back ached when he lay down to sleep each night. What had improved, though, was his sleep. The exercise and the absence of alcohol probably put him into a deep slumber each night. There had never been a spare moment to enjoy a drink since Sarah had come to live with him. He didn't miss it much. And that was good.

It dawned on him then that he'd hardly ever thought about the university and his work there since Sarah had come. He didn't miss it like he thought he would. There was just so much to do, to plan for, and to prepare for the next day.

'Here, Alex, Mum wants to speak to you.'

Alex took the phone.

'Dad, you've done a wonderful job for me and Sarah. She seems to be doing fabulously. You're a miracle. I really didn't expect you to cope so well.'

He felt pleased despite the implied criticism of

his capabilities.

Sarah looked up from her iPad, where she'd parked herself, and smiled. He winked at her conspiratorially. She tried to wink back, but managed only to blink. He promised himself he'd teach her that skill in due course.

Kay wanted to know whether all her instructions regarding Sarah were being followed. Whether he'd been consulting her checklists. Whether Sarah had been eating her veggies. And on it went. He was short on responses, irritated by her scrutiny. On the other hand, he was more interested in the latest about PNG, the economy, the health sector; but she didn't seem keen on sharing much with him.

It turned out to be a scattershot conversation, going nowhere, both speaking on different planes. His cryptic answers seemed to be irritating her, and her reluctance to entertain questions about the PNG economy annoyed him. She finally had to call off, having to leave for work.

Sarah looked up from her iPad game, which she'd played during his conversation with Kay. 'You both fight a lot, don't you?' She'd obviously been listening intently.

Sarah always surprised him with her keen observations.

'What do you mean?'

'You're always both snapping at each other. Always. Does this happen when children become adults?'

Her perceptiveness took him aback.

'Sarah, your mum is very dear to me. After all, she is my daughter. But when children grow up, they get ideas about life different from those of their parents. And then disagreements occur.'

'I'll never allow that to happen to me, Alex. I'll always be nice to my mum.'

'Good, Sarah, good. But now, we must plan what we're

doing today, right?'

'Only Cassie is coming today, Alex. It'll be boring for us inside the house all day. Can we go to some park?'

'As long as I don't have to play tag with you guys.' He wasn't going to be caught in shorts again, running around with little girls.

She seemed to have suddenly landed on an idea. 'I know what we'll do. Let's go to the Flip Out Park. Yes, Alex. Please, pleeease.'

'What in the heavens is the Flip Out Park? And where is it?'

'It's a jumping-around park, with slides and trampolines and foam pits where you can wrestle and play games. It's a lot of fun.'

'Hmm. I'm not sure that sounds good, Sarah. What if you injure yourself?'

'Mum takes me there heaps. It's safe. And lots and lots of kids come. Only Cassie'll be here today because her mum goes to work. The others are at home with their parents. So pleeease, pleeease, can we go? I'll be so much fun.'

'Okay. As long as you don't expect me to join in your flipping-out games. Now, do you know where it is?'

'It's in Box Hill. You'll find it on Google maps. Have a look. Yeaaaa, it'll be fun.'

~

At 10:00 am, after getting the green light from Sharon when she dropped off Cassie, Alex set off for Box Hill with the two girls in tow. The kids were in the back seats, chattering away, their excitement filling the car. Alex found himself looking forward to the outing, curious about this Flip Out Park that had them so thrilled. It was a break from the usual routine, something new to experience.

When they arrived at the sprawling parking lot next to the mall, Alex was struck by the crowds of parents and kids streaming towards the entrance, laughter and excited squeals echoing off the concrete. The Flip Out Park was housed inside the mall, but its scale took him by surprise. Inside was a vast expanse bursting with colour—trampolines of every size, twisting slides, climbing ropes, and massive pits filled with foam balloons. It was a sensory overload of neon hues and flashing LED lights, all set to the beat of thumping music.

He barely had time to purchase the tickets before Sarah and Cassie vanished into the chaos, diving headfirst into a foam pit and disappearing beneath a sea of balloons, their laughter piercing through the noise. For a moment, Alex panicked, his eyes darting frantically to find them again. Then their heads popped up, grinning and waving. He exhaled, his shoulders relaxing as he realised they were fine.

The park was alive with movement and sound. Kids were everywhere—bouncing on trampolines, racing through obstacle courses, and hurling themselves into foam pits with wild abandon. The noise was deafening, a constant roar that seemed to vibrate through the air. But it was a joyful noise, filled with laughter and shouts of exhilaration.

Fascinated, Alex took in the world of colour and energy, built entirely for the young and restless. The walls soared high in vivid neon pinks, blues, and greens, illuminated by pulsating LED lights that danced to the rhythm of the kids' movement. Even the floor was a patchwork of bright pastels, adding to the dreamlike atmosphere. It was a masterpiece of design, a playground that catered to every whim of childhood imagination.

He watched as children flung themselves into foam pits, their faces a mixture of fear and exhilaration. Others navigated obstacle courses with surprising agility, while a row of trampolines hosted a series of gravity-defying flips and somersaults. It was mayhem—glorious, joyous mayhem.

The adults stood along the sidelines, some watching with a mix of nostalgia and admiration, others snapping photos and cheering on their kids. A few adventurous parents joined in, bouncing alongside their children with varying degrees of grace. Alex grinned as he caught a few pics on his phone, capturing Sarah and Cassie's boundless joy as they bounced on the trampolines, their hair flying wildly.

Before long, they were calling to him, their voices pleading. 'Come on, Alex! It's safe! You'll love it!' Sarah shouted, pointing to other adults who were joining in the fun.

He hesitated, feeling a wave of self-consciousness. But their enthusiasm was irresistible. With a resigned sigh, he climbed onto the trampoline, feeling its soft, springy surface underfoot. Sarah and Cassie immediately took his hands, and they began bouncing together. At first, he moved cautiously, testing his balance. But the girls' laughter was infectious, and he jumped higher, his body jiggling and wobbling comically.

He lost control for a split second, his bounce going too high. Gravity took over, and he crashed spectacularly, face-down on the canvas, his backside pointed skyward. The girls erupted in hysterical laughter, their faces red as they clutched their stomachs.

Alex was trying to regain his dignity, struggling to get onto his knees, when a familiar voice called out, 'Sterling job, Alex. Well done.'

He looked up to see Thomas from the university, his face alight with amusement. Mortified, Alex accepted his outstretched hand and stumbled out of the trampoline, brushing himself off.

As if his embarrassment wasn't complete, Thomas' wife, Beatrice, appeared beside him, smiling warmly. 'Professor, that was absolutely wonderful,' she said, her eyes twinkling.

They moved to a nearby café while the girls continued playing. Alex's face still burned with embarrassment, but Beatrice's warm demeanour eased his discomfort. Over coffee, they talked about Kay, her work challenges, and how Sarah had completely upended Alex's life.

He was just starting to relax when Sarah and Cassie reappeared, tugging at his arm. 'Come on, Alex! We want to try the exercise balloons!'

With a sigh, he excused himself, giving Thomas and Beatrice a quick wave before joining the girls at the balloon area. They chose the smaller, safer-looking balloons, and Alex carefully lowered himself onto one, determined not to make a spectacle of himself again. From the corner of his eye, he saw Thomas and Beatrice watching, laughing as they gave him a thumbs-up.

For the first time in years, he felt truly carefree, caught up in the girls' joy and excitement. Watching them, he remembered his own childhood, spending hours playing football without a worry in the world. Somewhere along the way, he'd forgotten how to have fun. But today, bouncing among foam balloons and laughing with his granddaughter, he was learning all over again.

SEVEN

Monday unfolded with familiar rhythm. One by one, the girls arrived, trailing behind their mothers, chattering brightly. They deposited their lunch boxes and treats neatly on the dining table, a routine Alex had firmly established. The mothers exchanged brief farewells, mentioning the time they'd return for pick-ups, then departed, leaving behind a swirl of perfume and lingering maternal energy.

Sarah had consolidated her leadership position among the girls. Decisions about games and activities were often made without Alex's input, which he observed with quiet amusement. She was so much like her mother—confident, decisive, charismatic. The resemblance was uncanny, both in spirit and in the way she held herself, shoulders squared, chin slightly raised, commanding attention effortlessly.

By eleven, the house had settled into its customary mid-morning hush. The girls were absorbed in their games—voices blending softly with the birdsong drifting in through open windows. This was Alex's golden hour, his reprieve before their hunger inevitably broke the spell, sending him into the kitchen to rustle up extra food and drinks for lunch.

The doorbell shattered the peace. It rang, sharp and unexpected. Alex frowned, glancing at the clock. Too late for another mother dropping off a child. He sighed, easing out of his armchair, his knees protesting as he moved towards the door.

Two police officers stood on the porch. The woman, tall and severe looking, appeared to be in her late forties, her posture rigid, eyes keen and unblinking. The younger man beside her looked barely out of his teens, his uniform still crisp, his expression trying too hard to appear seasoned.

'I'm Senior Sergeant Larkin. This is Officer Nelson,' the woman announced, her voice clipped and businesslike. 'May we come in?'

Alex's brows knitted. He hesitated, a ripple of unease passing through him. 'May I ask what this is about, Sergeant?'

'Are you Professor Alex Bobbins?'

'I am,' he replied, his voice firm, though his mind raced. 'Is there a problem?'

'It would be better if we discussed this inside. It may take a while.'

Alex's stomach tightened. What could possibly require a police visit? 'Of course. Come in.'

As they crossed the threshold, he noticed how their eyes flicked over everything—the children playing in the living room, the cheerful chaos of toys strewn about, the faint aroma of cookies lingering from yesterday's baking. They were assessing, cataloguing, calculating.

He gently shepherded the girls into the dining room, out of earshot. Sarah, however, lingered, her face a knot of worry, but Alex gave her a reassuring pat. 'It's fine, darling. Just grown-up stuff. Go on now.' She nodded, though her eyes stayed on the uniforms a moment longer before she joined the others. He noticed, though, that she edged back slowly to be in hearing range.

He turned to the officers, who had settled on the couch, backs rigid, their presence foreign and intrusive in his living room. 'What can I do for you?'

Sergeant Larkin didn't rush, her gaze still drifting to the children, their laughter a backdrop to the brewing storm. 'Professor Bobbins,' she began, her tone measured, 'are you aware that you need a licence to run a childcare centre?'

For a beat, Alex just stared at her, words failing him. Then his face flushed. 'A childcare centre? Here? That's absurd!' He drew himself up, shoulders squared. 'I'm looking after my granddaughter, Sarah. Her friends visit. How does that remotely resemble a childcare centre?'

Larkin's face remained impassive. 'We received reports that several children are dropped off here daily for supervision. That would constitute a childcare service under the law. Concerns were raised, particularly regarding your … situation.'

'My situation?' His voice sharpened, indignation flaring. 'I'm a grandfather caring for his granddaughter. Since when is that a crime?'

The sergeant's face softened, just a fraction. 'No one is accusing you of wrongdoing, Professor. But questions were raised. An elderly gentleman suddenly minding several young children—it's … unusual. People notice.'

Alex's jaw tightened. He felt the heat rising to his face. 'People? Who? Who would be so spiteful as to spread rumours instead of simply asking me?'

Sergeant Larkin's hands rose in a placating gesture. 'The

complaint was anonymous. But concerns were expressed about the nature of this arrangement. Surely, you can see how it might appear unconventional?'

Unconventional? He almost laughed. Was that what they called kindness now? His mind spun, racing back to his confrontation with Adam Hancock last week. Could it have been him? The man had been curt, borderline hostile. Yet Alex had been doing him a favour, looking after Cassie. Why would he complain?

His anger threatened to erupt, but Alex knew better. He drew a deep breath, reining it in. 'Sergeant, my granddaughter Sarah is staying with me while her mother is overseas for work. She invites her friends over. They play. I feed them. I watch over them. That's all there is to it. I'm not charging fees. I'm not running a business.'

Officer Nelson scribbled in his notebook, his face impassive. Larkin's gaze softened, just slightly. 'I understand, Professor. But you can see how this might raise questions?'

~

Sarah was lying on the carpet in the dining room, giggling with her friends as they arranged their dolls in a pretend classroom. She was the teacher, of course—she was always the teacher. Then she heard it. Her name.

Her head snapped up, her curly hair bouncing. Alex's voice sounded … different. Kind of angry. She didn't like it. It made her tummy feel weird. And those police people—she didn't like them one bit. They looked too serious, standing there in their uniforms like they owned the place. Why were they talking to Alex like that?

Without another thought, she pushed herself up from the

floor, brushing crumbs off her dress, and marched straight into the living room. Her friends called after her, but she ignored them. She had to make sure Alex was okay.

She planted herself beside him, pressing close and looping her arm around his. He felt solid and warm, and that made her feel braver. She looked up at the police lady first, then the younger man. They didn't look so scary up close, just … annoying.

'Are you the police?' she demanded, her voice steady and loud, the way the PT teacher had taught her when she was referee on the playground.

The lady officer looked surprised. 'Yes, I'm Sergeant Larkin,' she said, her voice suddenly softer.

'Why are you here? My grandpa didn't do anything wrong. You're making him upset. Aren't you supposed to help people? Not make them angry?'

The two police people exchanged a look. They seemed confused, which was good, Sarah thought. Let them be confused. Maybe they'd leave.

The lady officer crouched down on her knees to Sarah's eye level. 'What's your name, sweetheart?'

'I'm Sarah. And this is my grandpa,' she announced, her chin high. 'He's the best grandpa ever, and you're being mean to him. I don't like you. I think you should leave.'

She saw Alex's eyebrows shoot up. But she didn't care if she was being rude. They were upsetting him. And her.

The lady officer looked a little sad. 'Oh no, honey, we're not here to be mean. We just need to talk to him, that's all. Why don't you go back and play?'

Sarah's eyes narrowed. Did this lady think she was stupid? 'But you're making him mad. I heard him. He never gets upset. But you did make him. Why are you doing that?'

Sergeant Larkin looked at her colleague, who shrugged, clearly out of ideas. She sighed. 'I promise I won't make him angry anymore, okay? We just need to sort out a little misunderstanding.'

Sarah's eyes flicked back to Alex. His face was red, his jaw tight, but his eyes were soft when they looked at her. That made her feel a bit better. 'Okay. But you better not be mean again,' she warned.

She felt Alex's hand on her shoulder, warm and strong. 'It's okay, Sarah,' he murmured, his voice softer now. 'Go play, sweetheart. I'll be all right.'

She looked up at him for a long moment, searching his face. Then she gave the officers one last fierce warning look before turning on her heel and marching back to the dining room.

She sat back down on the carpet with her friends, but her heart wasn't in the game anymore. Her ears stayed sharp, straining to catch every word from the living room. If those police people hurt her Alex, they'd have to answer to her.

~

Alex felt rather pleased at Sarah's intervention, but it did little to assuage his anger with the police and their implicit allegations.

'Look, Officer, if there are questions—I understand. But suspicions? Disgusting! This is nothing more than a grandfather trying to bring some joy to his grandchild's life. If that's a crime, then our world has truly turned upside down.'

'Professor, there is obviously a misunderstanding. But also, a situation which is rather awkward. There is a law that if one is to be a child carer, that is looking after a child or children who are not one's own or a relative's, and if this is done on a daily or regular basis, that would qualify as "child caring", and therefore, this would require a licence.'

Alex began to protest.

Sergeant Larkin interrupted. 'If I may, I understand your situation. And I will offer you a way out. If you continue to entertain Sarah's friends here on a daily or regular basis, then we insist that you have one or more female adults present who are related, in some way, to one of the kids. Does this make sense?

'Please understand, Professor?' Larkin continued. 'We too are in a quandary. The issue has been raised with us. We need to be seen to have taken action. On your part, this relatively simple action will put any further concerns at rest.'

Alex was by now befuddled but still angry and deeply hurt that anyone would even suspect him of child exploitation. If Adam Hancock was indeed the one who had complained, he worried whether Hancock had also been sowing and circulating suspicion about him within the community. He wouldn't put that beyond Hancock, the evil-minded son of a bitch. On the other hand, if it was someone else, he'd never know, and he had to take some kind of action to stifle these vile innuendos.

He calmed himself as he began to see sense in what the sergeant was saying. The murmurings wouldn't go away, however much he protested. On the other hand, what Larkin was proposing wasn't too demanding. However, the proposal they offered was going to complicate his life even further. Bad enough that the children had taken over his life and his house, not that he was complaining anymore—he was actually enjoying it. But now, they were requiring him to have women minders involved as well. In his house. Violating his quiet and privacy.

Why are people's minds so twisted?

'Please don't see this as any reflection on your character, Professor. We think you should be doing this for your own protection.'

~

After the police officers left, Alex sank into his armchair, trying to steady himself. His heart still raced, his mind swirling with disbelief and indignation. It felt cruelly unjust—this cloud of suspicion hanging over him. In over forty years at the university, his reputation had been spotless. Not once had anyone questioned his integrity. And now this?

He exhaled sharply, forcing himself to his feet. The children would soon be clamouring for lunch, and he needed something to ground him, to clear his head. He moved to the kitchen, methodically preparing lunch for the kids. The familiar routine soothed his nerves, each slice and spread helping to ease his frustration. By the time the kids ate, and the plates were cleared with the girls off to their play again, Alex felt a measure of calm return.

But the issue remained, heavy and unresolved. He couldn't ignore the sergeant's warning. The only way forward was to speak to the mothers.

His fingers hovered over his phone as an unfamiliar shame crept over him. How did it come to this? Asking these women to supervise him, as if he were some sort of threat. An old man who only wanted to care for his granddaughter and who, to his own surprise, had come to love the noise and energy these children brought to his once-quiet home.

Yet the idea of another adult—a woman, no less—

invading his space unsettled him. He valued his privacy, his routines. The children were easy; they needed food, safety, and space to play. But an adult presence would be different. She'd have opinions, ideas on menus, suggestions about the house, and might even take over his kitchen. He bristled at the thought.

Luckily, school holidays would end in two and a half weeks. After that, Sarah would be in school most of the day, and the issue would, hopefully, resolve itself. But until then, he needed a solution.

He dialled Alice's mother first. 'Hi, June. Sorry to bother you.'

'No trouble, Alex. Is everything all right? Alice okay?'

'Yes, yes, she's fine. But … well, I had a visit from the police this morning.'

'The police? What on earth for?'

Alex hesitated, still grappling with the absurdity of it all. He explained slowly, each word tasting bitter as he recounted the accusations and the suggestion that he needed supervision.

'That's outrageous!' June's indignation was palpable. 'That someone could even think that of you!'

Alex sighed. 'It's the world we live in. And the police weren't unreasonable. They suggested it would be best for everyone if one of you mothers or a relative was present each day. I … I understand why, even if it hurts.'

June's tone softened. 'Leave it with me, Alex. I know all the other mothers. I'll speak to them, and we'll sort this out. You've been doing us all a massive favour. The girls love it at your place. We won't let this ruin that.'

Relief flooded through him. 'Thank you, June. I really appreciate it.'

After he hung up, he felt a wave of gratitude. June was

just as capable as his own daughter, Kay. It spared him the discomfort of having that conversation with each of the other mothers. Women, he thought, were the true problem solvers—practical, like his late wife, Mabel.

Later that day, his phone buzzed.

It was June again. 'Hi, Alex. I spoke to all the mothers. They're as upset as I am about the complaint. But we've found a solution.'

Alex leaned forward. 'Oh?'

'My aunt, Laura, has volunteered to help out. She has flexible work hours and is more than happy to be there. And when she can't make it, one of us mums will step in. Would that work for you?'

He was surprised at how much he welcomed the idea. 'Absolutely. That's … that's perfect. I met Laura at the park recently. She seemed lovely.'

He also remembered the lively conversation they'd shared about economic theory. The prospect of continuing that discussion brought a spark of anticipation.

'Great! I'll let Laura know. She'll be glad to help.'

Alex ended the call, and his shoulders relaxed. The problem had a solution—one that didn't feel like a punishment. And he realised, with a small smile, that he was actually looking forward to having Laura around. Maybe, just maybe, this intrusion into his world wouldn't be so unwelcome after all.

EIGHT

The professor's fears of women pottering around his house—fussing over things that needed no fussing, rearranging furniture and crockery that were perfectly fine where they were, chatting endlessly, and bombarding him with questions that would keep him from his beloved newspapers and books—turned out to be largely unfounded.

Laura was nothing like he'd imagined. From the day she stepped in, she was all business. Her presence brought structure without intrusion. At first, her arrival was a shock to the girls. They were accustomed to running the show—making their own rules, raiding the refrigerator whenever they pleased, and effortlessly manipulating Alex to cater to their whims. But Laura introduced rules, ones that even Alex had to admit made sense.

On her first day, Laura spent two hours quietly observing. Alex noticed her sharp eyes following every interaction—between him and the children, and among the girls themselves. When he began preparing lunch, she approached him. 'Alex, would you mind if I made a few suggestions about the girls?'

'Not at all, Laura. You've got more experience with kids than I do. I'd appreciate your input.'

She spoke plainly but firmly. 'I think they're taking too many liberties with you, Alex. A little more discipline would be good for them.'

'I've just been careful not to come off as too strict. I don't want to spoil their fun. It is a playgroup, after all.'

'Sure, and it should be fun. But children will always test boundaries. It's in their nature. We don't need to be harsh, just consistent. A few clear rules and consequences will make all the difference. You're already doing a wonderful job—they clearly love coming here. But a bit of structure wouldn't hurt.'

Alex smiled. 'All right, Laura. I'll leave that to you. I trust your judgement.'

Laura's first rule was that everyone would sit together at the dining table for lunch. With a shortage of chairs, she pulled in kitchen stools without a fuss. Alex watched from the sidelines, impressed. Though petite in stature, Laura had a commanding presence. She moved with purpose, her back straight and shoulders square. Her eyes, though warm, were firm, and she spoke in short decisive sentences that brooked no argument. There was no doubt—this was a woman used to being listened to.

'All right, girls,' Laura began once they were settled, six curious little faces turned up at her. 'We come here each day to play with Sarah and each other, right?'

Nods all around.

'And we have fun. But we must remember that this is Alex's house, and we are his guests. That means we need to follow a few rules.'

Some foreheads frowned, the girls wondering what was

coming next.

'I've noticed you've been raiding the fridge whenever you feel like it. That stops today. From now on, we'll have a set snack time and lunch break. No eating in between. The fridge is off limits. If you need something, you ask either Alex or me, and we'll get it for you. Understood?'

A chorus of groans met her declaration, followed by Sarah's protest: 'But it's my house! Why can't I open the fridge if I'm hungry?'

Alex waited, curious about how Laura would handle this. Sarah did have a point.

Laura's gaze softened, but her tone remained steady. 'Sarah, does your mum let you eat anything you want at any time?'

Caught off guard, Sarah hesitated. 'Umm ... no, not always.'

'Well, it's the same here. We're not trying to spoil your fun, but rules are important. Besides the fridge rule, here's another one: whenever you finish playing a game—whether it's Lego, cards, or Play-Doh—you must clean up before starting a new one. That way, we won't have a big mess at the end of the day. Sound fair?'

Heads bobbed in reluctant agreement.

'And,' Laura continued, 'when you use the bathroom, make sure you flush and leave it clean. Understood?'

A few giggles, but they nodded.

'Finally, I've noticed some of you like to play outside without sunscreen or a hat. From now on, everyone must wear sunscreen and a hat when playing outside. I'll keep the sunscreen here on the dining table. Also, whenever you're outside, either Alex or I will be there to supervise. We won't interfere with your games, but an adult always needs to be present.'

This last rule was met with murmurs and a few pouty faces, particularly from Sarah. But Laura remained patient, listening to their complaints and answering their questions calmly, even with humour.

Alex watched, impressed by her ability to strike a balance between authority and kindness. By the end of lunch, the girls had accepted the new rules and ran off to play. Alex was astonished at how quickly they adapted.

~

Life in his house changed for the better. The messes shrank, routines flowed more smoothly, and with Laura managing the structure, Alex found he had more time to relax.

Laura set up her laptop at the dining table, establishing it as her workspace. Alex kept to his usual spot by the window with his books and computer. They took turns supervising the children in the backyard, ensuring their safety without intruding on their games.

During lunch, they resumed their discussions on economics, debating government policies and international trade's impact on the Australian economy. Alex enjoyed these intellectual exchanges. They challenged his thinking and reminded him of his days at the university.

After lunch, they returned to their respective desks, working quietly while keeping a watchful eye on the children. Alex found comfort in the background noise—the girls' playful chatter, Laura's fingers clicking away at her keyboard. It was the sound of life bustling around him, yet he could still lose himself in his research papers, which he continued to review for his former colleagues.

The first few days required minor adjustments, but a rhythm soon developed. They divided the supervision duties, naturally falling into Laura's structured system. They respected each other's quiet time, each focused on their own work without interruption.

Alex was pleasantly surprised that Laura never tried to reorganise his house. She asked questions about where things were kept, but always accepted his way of arranging his space. There was no attempt to take over his kitchen or interfere with his routines. He appreciated that respect for his privacy. Gradually, they grew comfortable with each other. They worked alongside each other in companionable silence, breaking it only when necessary to check on the kids or exchange a thought on a news article or economic trend.

It wasn't until Laura couldn't come one day—her work commitments keeping her away—that Alex realised how much he missed her calm and steady presence. Another mother took her place, but it wasn't the same. The girls sensed the shift in authority and tested the limits, getting away with more mischief. Alex, despite himself, couldn't bring himself to be firm with them. They had, after all, stolen his heart.

That evening, as the house fell quiet, Alex reflected on how much life had changed since Laura entered their world. She'd brought more than just rules and structure. She'd brought balance, a sense of order without suffocating warmth. He realised he not only respected her but also enjoyed her company. She had managed to enter his life without disrupting it, a quiet force that kept the chaos at bay.

Yes, he thought, as he settled down with his newspaper, Laura was indeed perfect company.

~

Late in the week after Laura had begun helping, Alex approached the dining table, coffee mug in hand, curiosity written on his face. It was late morning, not long before the kids' lunch break.

'So, Laura, what's keeping you busy these days?' he asked as he took a seat. Until now, their conversations had mostly revolved around the kids, perhaps the latest political happenings and their economic implications. But Alex was itching to learn more about her work. He suspected it was tied to economic research. Truth be told, he envied her focus and discipline. Even while helping with the kids, Laura remained steadfastly immersed in her work, her laptop always open, her fingers constantly tapping away.

Laura looked up from her screen, a sly smile playing on her lips.

'Why the smile?' Alex asked, his curiosity piqued.

'Because,' she replied, 'what I'm working on wouldn't exactly thrill your end of town.'

'My end of town?' He frowned, genuinely puzzled.

'Well,' she teased, 'being the neoliberal that you are, I assume you're a champion of our bold business leaders and their invaluable contributions to the economy. Am I right?'

Alex chuckled. 'You're not far off. Neoliberalism has brought us game-changing innovations—the iPhone, SpaceX, Uber, Airbnb, and more recently, AI. It's fuelled economic growth and improved living standards. But what does that have to do with what you're working on?'

Laura's eyes sparkled with challenge. 'Your published papers paint you as a staunch advocate for deregulation, privatisation, labour-market flexibility, and globalisation. You argue they foster competition, efficiency, and growth— all for the benefit of the consumer.'

'I couldn't have summed it up better myself,' Alex admitted, leaning back in his chair.

Laura's expression grew serious. 'Alex, while developed economies have seen substantial growth, inequality within these societies—except in the Scandinavian countries—has widened even faster. Would you agree?'

Alex leaned forward. 'The standard of living has also improved, largely due to growth and competition-driven efficiency.'

Laura laughed, a sound both warm and pointed. 'Maybe it's time we both stepped down from our ivory towers and took a good, hard look at reality.'

Without warning, she turned to the kids sprawled on the living room floor, busy with Lego blocks and Play-Doh. 'Hey, kids!' she called out, her voice cutting through their play. Six little faces turned to her, eyes wide with curiosity.

'How about pizza for lunch today?'

A chorus of excited yeahs filled the room, little faces lighting up in delight.

'All right, back to playing now. I'll let you know when it's here.' Laura pulled out her phone to order six large pizzas via Uber Eats.

Alex raised an eyebrow, baffled by this sudden treat. Pizza was not her usual style, but he wasn't complaining. He could definitely do with a slice—or three.

Laura caught his puzzled expression and grinned. 'Be patient, Alex. All will be revealed. But for now, let's set up the table for the kids.'

Twenty minutes later, the doorbell rang. Sarah bolted to the door, followed closely by the rest of the kids, faces beaming in anticipation. The scent of pizza wafted through the house, making Alex's stomach rumble. He followed behind, amused but still clueless about Laura's scheme.

At the door stood a young man with a stack of pizza boxes, his dark complexion contrasted against his wide, toothy smile. Six pairs of eager little hands reached out, but he hesitated, his eyes searching for an adult.

Laura appeared, confirmed her name, and took the boxes, handing them to the kids, much to their delight. 'Put them on the dining table,' she said. 'No opening until Alex and I serve you.' Her voice was firm, leaving no room for negotiation.

She then turned to the young delivery man, who was already making his way back to his bike.

'A moment, please. How much do you earn for a trip?' she asked.

He stopped mid-stride, surprised and puzzled by the question. He paused to reflect and then replied, 'An average of about seven to eight dollars per trip, depending on the distance.'

'I'll pay you twenty dollars if you agree to come in and spend half an hour with us to answer some questions about your job.' She took out a twenty-dollar note and held it out to show she was serious.

He thought for a moment, then walked back to the door, looked at the note, then eyed Laura. Alex saw caution and questions in his eyes. Likely, he was wondering whether this was some scam. Tentatively, with an outstretched hand, he took the note. He then followed Laura to the dining table where the kids crowded around, waiting for their pizza. Alex followed, feeling completely left out of this unfolding drama.

Laura sat the young man on a chair, then, with Alex's help, apportioned the pizzas to the kids.

'Okay, off now, kids. You can sit there on the carpet with your plates. But be very careful not to drop any crumbs on the floor. If I find the floor still clean after you've finished, you'll each get an extra piece. Alex and I need to talk to this young man.'

With that, Laura saw them off and then sat at the table, inviting Alex to do so as well. She placed a slice of pizza on a plate and offered it to the young delivery man. He took it, puzzlement still written on his face.

'How long have you been working at this job?' she asked, as she and Alex helped themselves to a pizza slice each.

'About a year,' he replied, already digging into his pizza. He was young, probably in his early twenties, and slim, with not an ounce of fat on him.

Must be all the bike riding, Alex reflected.

'What's your name, may I ask? I'm Laura. And this is Alex.'

He nodded in acknowledgment between his munches. 'I'm Anand.'

'Do you have any post-school education, Anand?'

'I'm a civil engineer.' Then he added, as if to explain why he was now delivering food, 'I couldn't get a job after I arrived in Australia two years ago. So I had to become a food-delivery man.'

'How much do you earn a day?'

'I make an average of two trips an hour, which is about fifteen to twenty dollars. But often less.'

'So how much a day?'

'I'm lucky if I get one hundred and thirty dollars a day. Depends on the day of the week, the weather, the traffic, and my health.'

'So you're earning an average of seventeen dollars an hour? You realise that's under the minimum wage in Australia?'

Anand smiled patiently. 'Madam, we cannot choose

which job we do. We take what we can.'

'I assume you pay for your own vehicle? What about insurance?'

He laughed. 'None, madam. Too expensive.'

'Any leave?'

'Madam, I'm a contractor. I'm not eligible for any benefits from Uber or Deliveroo, to whom I am contracted.'

Alex got the trend of questioning and was also interested. He joined in. 'What kind of contract did you have to sign? With the delivery platforms?' Interest perked, his questions followed one after another.

Which platforms did Anand prefer and why?

What were his expenses, and which were tax deductible?

Did he own his own vehicle? Which, in this case, was a motorised cycle.

Had he ever asked the company to pay his insurance?

Did the platforms to which he was contracted take any responsibility for his safety?

~

Alex noticed Sarah's gaze flicking over to him and Laura as they engaged Anand with their questions. Curiosity was evident on her face. She was such an observant child. He wondered what was going on in that little head of hers. Probably trying to figure out why Laura had invited the young delivery man inside and even offered him a slice of their pizza.

That was Laura, always thoughtful, always kind. Yet she had her rules, and she made sure they were followed, even by him. Not that he minded. He respected her discipline; it balanced his more easy-going approach. But beyond that, he admired her generosity, her willingness to help him look after Sarah. He didn't know what he'd have done without her these past weeks. And though the mothers pitched in now and then, he realised he preferred Laura's company. She understood him—challenged him, even.

He watched as she spoke with Anand, plying him with questions with genuine interest. He admired how she made the boy feel at ease, how she treated him with such dignity. That was Laura—firm but unfailingly kind.

Alex's gaze shifted back to Sarah, who was now leading her friends to the table, faces earnest as they presented Laura with their spotless clean-up effort and a request for more pizza. A knowing smile tugged at his lips. Laura's rules were taken seriously. The kids clearly respected her, even if they found her strict. He watched Laura rise to check the floor, as thorough as ever. Sarah exchanged a glance with her friends, a smug look that made Alex chuckle inwardly.

As Laura handed out the bonus slices, she turned to Anand, offering him another. 'No, thank you, madam. Can I go, please? I'd like to get more trips in today. I'm running short of money.'

'Yes. And thank you very much for your time.'

She saw him to the front door. Then she returned to join Alex at the dining table.

'So what did you gather from that, Alex?'

'That innovation has given Anand a job when he wouldn't have had any.'

Laura looked at him in amazement. 'Is that all you took from that conversation?'

'Well, not all. However, it made the point that innovation, competition, and labour-law flexibility result in increased jobs and employment. Isn't that great?'

'Alex, that young man is earning a wage below the

minimum required.'

'Well, he's a free agent. He's paid per trip. And he can work for as long as he wishes if he wants to increase his daily wage. You can't compare him to a regular company employee who works on completely different terms and conditions. Anand is an entrepreneur in his own right. That is the beauty of the gig economy.'

Laura shook her head in frustration. 'You don't see that Uber is essentially exploiting that young man and other young people like him? It's taking advantage of his situation to exploit him with less-than-minimum wages, no benefits, no social protections, and no provision for his eventual retirement when he will then become a burden on the state.'

'Well, if he had no job now, Laura, wouldn't he be a burden on the state?'

'Don't get me wrong. I am happy the platforms provide Anand with a job. But can we ask for dignity and equity here? Is this a race to the bottom where companies, in the name of profits, will attempt to get away with the minimum they can pay their employees and contractors? Which is what has been happening increasingly these days. Companies are being discovered to have been underpaying their workers systematically, almost like daylight robbery.'

'Look, Laura, I agree some companies can be exploitative. But does that mean you come down with laws that end up stifling entrepreneurship?'

'I assume you've come across the concept of ESG frameworks being increasingly adopted by companies, taking account of environmental, social, and governance issues in their investing and management.'

'Sure.'

'Do you think that constrains innovation and investments?'

Alex smiled. She was clever. And perhaps she did have a point.

At that moment, they found Sarah at the table, looking worriedly at them both.

'What's the matter, Sarah?' Alex asked.

'You're both snapping at each other. Are you quarrelling? Please don't,' she asked, her eyes pleading.

Alex and Laura burst into laughter.

Laura pulled Sarah to her and gave her a long hug. 'No, dear. We're just silly old adults, thinking we each have the right answer to the world's problems. So we're arguing over them.'

'Please don't. It upsets us.' Alice and Cassie joined Sarah at the table.

Alex and Laura looked sheepishly at each other.

Alex rose, followed by Laura. 'We promise we won't. Let's go and play with your games now. We're both coming to join you.'

NINE

That evening, while getting dinner ready, Sarah said, 'Grandpa, I mean Alex, I thought you and Laura liked each other. So why were you guys arguing today? I don't like it when you snap at each other. Also, you and Mum.'

Alex was taken off guard. He hadn't realised how much she noticed. 'I hate that we upset you, Sarah. Laura and I are friends. And I do love your mum very much. Laura and I were discussing, not arguing.'

'Is there a difference?'

'Well, I hope there is. Though we're friends, we're also economists, and we have different views about economics. So we look at a situation, in this case, the job of the pizza delivery boy, and we exchange our views from an economics point of view.'

'What's economics? You and Laura are always talking about all this stuff I don't understand. Is that all economics? What do economists do?'

Alex had learned the hard way over the last few weeks

that kids always had questions about everything. *Rightly so,* he concluded. *Kids are still in the process of discovering the world, one which is complex and, in many ways, mysterious.*

'That's a good question, Sarah.' His statement bought time while he considered how best to explain economics to a little kid. 'Everything in our lives involves money. The exchange of money. The food we buy, the house we live in, the school you attend, the toys that Mum buys you, and even the Flip Out Park we went to the other day. Everything costs money. Someone sells, like the supermarkets, the school management, the Flip Out owners. And others buy, if they like the product, like us.'

'Does Mum pay you and Laura money to look after us?'

'No, absolutely not. We do it because we love you guys.'

'So not everything involves money, right?'

'Umm, yes, I suppose so. Though it does for most things.'

'But we don't have to pay to go to the park down the road?'

'That's true. Though your mum does pay the government taxes each year, and then the government uses the money to maintain that park.'

'So you and Laura were arguing about how people should use their money? Is it?'

'Not exactly. We were arguing about how much the pizza delivery company which delivered your pizza should be paying the young man who delivered it.'

'Do they pay him a lot?'

'Not really, Sarah.'

'Why?'

Alex was tiring. The questions didn't end. He steeled himself to be patient. 'Let's look at it like this. Your mum needs her garden mowed and weeded. She asks who would be willing to do the job and at what price, and she'll choose the person who's willing to do it for the least amount of money, I guess. Does that make sense?'

'Maybe.' Alex saw her attention waning. 'Anyway, please don't argue with Laura anymore. All of us girls thought you were boyfriend and girlfriend. We liked that. Maybe if you kissed her, you'd stop arguing,' she added.

Alex was aghast. His cheeks flushed. His mouth fell open. His back stiffened. This was turning out to be a disaster. He had to put this fire out before it got out of control. 'Hold it, Sarah. Where in the heavens did you get such an idea?'

'I saw how you look at her, how happy you are when she's here, and how sad you look when she can't come. It's true, right?'

'Don't you dare say such things, Sarah! I've no idea where you got this idea from. Can we just forget about this? I don't want to talk about it again.' Alex became aware that he was trying rather too hard to shut down this line of conversation. He hoped Sarah wouldn't be upset.

'Okay, okay.' She shrugged. 'We won't talk about it. But please, no arguing anymore.'

He agreed readily, nodding. But as he got dinner ready, he thought about Laura. He had indeed become fond of her over the couple of weeks she'd been joining him in the child minding. He wondered where this new interest in the female sex had come from. Ever since Mabel had passed away, his work had consumed him so much that he'd never given a smidgen of thought to getting involved again. At his age, it was neither realistic nor, probably, acceptable to society. But now, confronted with the idea, thanks to Sarah, he didn't think he was averse to advancing the relationship with Laura.

They were munching their dinner and watching a Pokémon show when Sarah paused it and turned to Alex. 'I have an idea.'

'Uh-huh. What?'

'You and Laura, instead of quarrelling about economics, whatever that is, you should work together on a project like I do with my friends. This afternoon, while you and Laura were arguing about economics, we built a tree cubby house in the big tree in the garden out of your spare blankets and towels.'

Alex stood up, almost dropping his bowl. 'You did what?'

'Yes. We forgot to tell you. It's dark now, but we can still see it, if you want. It's cute. And we did it all by ourselves. Together. So why can't you and Laura also do a project together?'

Alex raced to the back door, opened it, and stepped down into the garden. 'Good God! You guys have messed up all my spare blankets and towels.' He surveyed the cubby house they'd built around the tree trunk. The kids had used the low-hanging branches to fix blankets as its walls. Inside, they'd laid out the towels and the pillow.

Looking around it, he suddenly thought, *in fairness, it does look cosy and comfy.* But he'd now have to give all these blankets and towels to the laundry, at probably an exorbitant cost, to get them thoroughly clean again. He bit his lip, shook his head in exasperation, and turned to Sarah, his face tightening.

Tears rolled down her cheeks, and he realised, too late, that he'd allowed his concern about money to mar a child's sense of triumph. He bent over and gave her a long, reassuring hug. Deeply contrite at how petty he'd been, he tried to make up for his irritation. 'It's fabulous, Sarah. You guys are geniuses. How did you think of this? Great idea.'

'You're just saying that to make me happy, right?' she replied between her sobs.

'I'm sorry, Sarah. Here's an example of how our concern for money and the cost of washing these blankets comes in the way of our enjoying your creation. I promise I won't let that happen again.'

Sarah wiped her tears with the back of her hand, somewhat mollified. 'Okay. Then come on into our cubby house and check it out.'

'It's dark, dear. Perhaps tomorrow?'

'But there's enough light coming from the house. Come on.' She disappeared into the cubby house.

Alex sighed, got down on all fours, and groaned. *This is going to be a challenge to crawl into that little cubby house with my huge bulk!* But it was the least he could do to make up for his earlier churlishness.

'So here's the living room.' Sarah pointed. 'That there is the dining room, and that'll be the bedroom when we've finished.'

'You haven't finished yet?' he asked, worried again.

'We need some more blankets. Will you get us some?'

He considered. Maybe he could visit the local op shop and check out whether they had some cheap ones. 'Why don't I see if I can help you guys tomorrow in expanding this cubby house, but with something other than blankets? If I can't, then yes, we'll go and find some more. Okay? Now, let's get inside. It's getting chilly.'

'Okay. Thanks. Now, be careful how you come out, Alex, or you'll pull that blanket down.'

Still on all fours, he crawled carefully. 'Yes, dear. Maybe I need to lose some weight before I can really enjoy your cubby house.'

They both laughed.

At breakfast the next day, Sarah could hardly contain her excitement. 'My friends are going to be thrilled that you're helping us finish the cubby house today!' she exclaimed, her eyes sparkling.

Alex smiled, but felt a pang of resignation. He'd committed himself, and now he had to follow through.

After breakfast, before the other kids arrived with their mothers, Alex and Sarah began scouring the house for materials to make the cubby house sturdier. Alex remembered the old wine cellar he still used, stocked with his favourite vintages. It was down there, in a dusty corner, that he found a stack of empty cardboard boxes from his wine deliveries. They were in all shapes and sizes, depending on the orders.

'Look, Sarah! These should work perfectly,' he announced.

Sarah's face lit up. 'Yes! This is going to be awesome!'

Alex smiled at her use of the word 'awesome'. These days, everything nice was also awesome.

By the time the other kids and Laura arrived, the boxes were stacked in the garden, ready to be transformed. The children buzzed with excitement, bombarding Alex with requests for scissors, tape, and coloured pens. He rushed back and forth, gathering supplies, while Laura leaned against the back door, watching with amusement.

Soon, Alex was on his knees, cutting the cardboard according to Sarah's detailed instructions. She took on the role of lead architect, directing each child on where to place the pieces and how to fit them together. Her vision was clear, and she wasn't shy about giving orders.

Amid the commotion, Alex heard a tinkling laugh. He turned to see Laura grinning, her eyes sparkling with mischief.

'Since when did an emeritus professor of economics become an expert in cubby house construction?' she teased.

Alex smirked. 'Unemployment has its perks. It forces you to dig deep and discover hidden talents.'

Laura laughed again, the sound warm and musical. Then she left them to their work, heading inside to get some of her own done.

All morning, Alex and the kids toiled under Sarah's meticulous supervision. Piece by piece, the cubby house took shape. They managed to replace most of the blankets with sturdy cardboard walls, saving his linens from further exposure to the elements.

Finally, Laura appeared at the back door. 'Time for lunch!' she called.

Covered in dust and sweat, Alex stepped back with the kids to admire their creation. He had to admit, it looked surprisingly cosy and inviting. Sarah beamed with pride, and the other children cheered.

Then, like a herd of hungry animals, they bolted for the house, drawn by the aroma of lunch waiting on the dining table. Alex lingered a moment, gazing at the cubby house and marvelling at how much fun he'd had helping build it.

~

The next day, once Laura had helped him organise the kids' activities, she and Alex retreated to their respective desks to work. But overnight, Sarah's group project to build the cubby house with her friends and her suggestion that he consider working on a project with Laura had kept him awake and thinking.

He ambled over to her desk, coffee mug in hand. She

looked up, surprised. They normally respected each other's quiet time since it was often in short supply due to the kids' needs and interruptions.

'Sarah came up with an interesting proposal last night.'

'Which is?'

'She suggested that you and I, rather than arguing all the time about our economic points of view, collaborate instead on a joint project.'

'Did you say "argue"? I thought we were discussing our points of view.'

'That's what I thought as well. Except, the truth is often in how things are perceived by others. From the kids' point of view, we've been snapping at each other.'

Laura raised her eyebrows. 'That's not good. I'm assuming you agree with me that it's not true, as well.'

'Agreed. But Sarah's suggestion has some merit, don't you think?'

'Could you explain?'

Alex felt she didn't quite take to the idea of a collaboration as he had. He thought there were possibilities. Besides, he would enjoy working with a colleague again. He sorely missed his work at the uni, which was often in collaboration with peers.

He sighed and decided to do his best to persuade her. 'Look, Laura, we both accept that we come to the world of economics from different perspectives. We're not going to change each other's views and convictions anytime soon. In truth, most of those who really give economics a thought and reflect on how the economy is managed fall into the two broad camps that we both represent.

'So what if we collaborate in writing a book, let's say, a polemic, wherein we argue each other's case using current issues? Every economic publication that comes out these days always argues from one point of view or another. What if we say … there is no right or wrong? Here, in this book, we'll provide both points of view and leave it to the reader to decide?'

Laura's eyes widened at his suggestion, signalling her scepticism. 'Look, Alex, first, I'm not an academic. I suppose academics have their role in the world, particularly in universities and teaching the young. My concerns are much more real world, to do with how economic theory impacts on public policy. Which is why I work as an adviser to the Labour Party. So really, I'm not in the least interested in writing another tome for the shelves.'

Her voice softened when she saw the disappointment on his face. 'On the other hand,' she added, 'if you're game to join me in developing a podcast where we debate each other's perspective on economics, sector by sector, issue by issue, and policy by policy, I think that would be something I may be interested in.'

Alex gave it some thought as he sipped his coffee. 'A podcast, eh? Sounds interesting. But I have no experience in doing a podcast. No idea what's involved: what software we should use; what equipment is required; will the podcasts be edited, and by whom? Who'll be the audience? How will we get the podcasts out there? Will a platform accept it?'

'Lots of questions, obviously, Alex.'

He had the uncanny feeling that Laura was enjoying his discomfiture.

'So all the more reason why you should get on with it. Right?' she continued.

'Me?' His eyebrows lifted in surprise. 'What about you?'

'Well, the idea of a project was yours. Right? I'm ready

to help and join in. Maybe we both need to put our heads together to sort this out. But I'm busy with a policy paper for the Labour Party just now. And I also just realised I should be supervising the kids outside in the backyard. So why don't you get on with it?'

'But … but I've never done a podcast. I don't know how to begin.'

'Alex, you've been a teacher for years. You'll have absolutely no problem in doing a podcast.' Her eyes twinkled. 'Think of it as explaining an issue to your students. The subjects will be current policy issues under consideration by the government. Issues that common people are interested in today.'

Alex returned to his desk feeling like a student who'd been told off by his tutor. 'The only way to learn is to dive into it, mate,' had been his tutor's constant advice, and he now realised that he'd have to follow it as well.

He got on with the job. First up, he searched for platforms that would accept podcasts, unsolicited. The answer surprised him: Apple Podcasts, Spotify, Google Podcasts, Amazon Music, Stitcher (whatever that was), Podbean, etc. They all welcomed podcasts, they claimed, on any subject.

Not bad. It appears there is some potential in this.

He was just getting interested in his dive-in when Sarah interrupted.

'Laura said to check with you if you have any more cardboard boxes.'

He sighed and rose. They went together to the wine cellar to search.

'Laura's enjoying our cubby house much more than you are, Alex,' Sarah remarked as they checked out suitable boxes.

He stopped and looked at her, exasperated. 'Why would you say that, Sarah?'

'She's able to get into the house and play "house-house" with us. You're too fat to get in. When are you going to lose weight? I want you also to come in and play house with us.' Then she gave him a mischievous smile that melted his heart.

TEN

It was a Friday evening, and June, Laura, and Alice sat together at dinner. As was their tradition, June and Laura allowed themselves a glass of wine to mark the end of another work week.

'Can we do something different this Saturday, Mum?' Alice suddenly piped up, her voice tinged with longing. 'The week went by so fast. We have so much fun at Sarah's house during the week. Weekends are so boring. Why can't I go to Sarah's house on weekends too?'

June set her fork down, her expression softening as she looked at Alice. 'Because weekends are for family, sweetie. It's our time together. And besides, it's when you help me and Laura around the house—cleaning your room, doing chores. That's what weekends are for.'

Most of their weekends were spent on laundry, cleaning, gardening, and catching up on the tasks that had piled up during the week. June, a firm believer in keeping the household running smoothly, always ensured Alice was involved in the process. For Alice, 'something different' usually meant a day out—a day that would take up hours that they could spend working together.

'But there's only one week of holidays left,' Alice pressed, her eyes wide with pleading. 'Then I'll be back at school. Please? Can I at least go to Sarah's? Cassie will be there too. Besides, my room's already clean, and I've been keeping it tidy. Laura, can you take me to Sarah's house?'

Laura, ever the neutral party, glanced at June with a slight understanding smile. 'Whatever your mum decides, Alice.'

June appreciated that Laura was careful never to usurp her parental authority. It made living with Laura so much easier. When her dad divorced her mum, leaving her for a thirty-year-old, June had invited Laura to come and live with her. It made sense since Laura was also divorced. Laura was a huge help with Alice. And she had flexible work timings.

'Okay,' June said reluctantly. 'Is that okay, Laura? I can ask Alex if she can go over, and you can take her.'

Laura thought for a moment, then brightened. 'What if we went to the Botanical Gardens instead? I'll check with Alex and see if he's willing to bring Sarah and Cassie. That way, Alice can play with them in the gardens rather than spending the whole day at Alex's house.'

June raised an eyebrow. 'That sounds reasonable. But I won't be able to join you. I have chores I need to get done.'

Alice jumped up, her face lighting up with excitement. 'Can you call Alex now, please?' she asked eagerly, her hands clasped together.

'It's dinnertime, love,' Laura reminded her gently. 'I'll call him after we finish, okay?'

June watched the exchange with a soft smile. Laura was truly a gem. Not only was she a highly respected economist involved in numerous social-action groups, but also she had a remarkable dedication to her health. She jogged five kilometres every morning and attended yoga and body pump classes at the gym three times a week. June often wondered if she'd have the same energy and enthusiasm for life when she reached Laura's age. But for now, she admired her aunt deeply.

'Hi, Alex. Laura here.'

Alex's eyes lit up. *What a pleasant surprise.* He hoped she wasn't calling for some problem with Alice. He and Sarah had just finished dinner and had been debating how to spend the weekend. Sarah wanted to go back to Flip Out. Alex was looking for other options.

'Alice wants to come over tomorrow to play with Sarah and Cassie. It's their last weekend before the weekend just prior to school opening. I'm suggesting we take them to the Botanical Gardens for an excursion. How do you feel about that?'

'Laura, you're a saviour! What a fabulous idea. I've been scratching my head about how to keep Sarah and Cassie entertained tomorrow.'

'Would you mind if I checked with the other mothers to see if they and their kids would also like to join? I know sometimes parents struggle with how to keep their kids entertained on weekends.'

'More the merrier, Laura. Please do go ahead.'

It was a pity this marked the penultimate weekend before

school opening. *We should've done this more often*, Laura thought, observing the mothers and children gathering on the central lawn of the Botanical Gardens. Perched on a small hill within the gardens, the lawn offered stunning views of Governor's House and the city skyline, making it a favourite spot for picnics.

On this Saturday morning, families were scattered in various corners of the lawn. Laura claimed a spot near one of the pergolas, conveniently located near the cactus and succulent collection.

The morning felt perfect. The air, crisp and invigorating, filled her lungs with freshness. The sun gleamed brightly off the vibrant-green lawn, while birds serenaded the day with a chorus of trills and melodies. The delicate scent of roses and damp earth lingered in the air, inviting visitors to pause and take in the peaceful surroundings.

Though the pergola stood ready, the kids opted for the open grass. The adults laid out rugs, and soon the food spread followed. But, for now, the kids seemed more interested in exploring the expansive green. They jumped, screamed, ran around, and played tag as if they'd just been released from detention, ignoring the food and goodies. Some of the mothers and carers joined in the general romping around.

Laura and Alex settled on the rugs, though Laura noticed Alex struggled a bit with getting comfortable, his ageing knees making sitting difficult. Thanks to her daily yoga practice, she had little trouble finding her place.

The gardens, with their vast open spaces, gave a sense of freedom, offering room for both mind and body to stretch. Some children, tired from their running, sprawled out on the grass, limbs outstretched, gazing up at the blue sky, imagining life as a bird soaring above. Others darted through the bushes, their laughter echoing as they played hide and seek.

Laura and Alex watched the scene, a comforting sight of carefree joy. Only Sharon Hancock's absence cast a slight shadow on the scene. Laura understood Sharon's situation—she worked seven days a week, with little time for leisure.

What a great place the gardens are for families, Laura reflected as a deep calm descended on her. The garden was a gift from the founders and planners of the city of Melbourne. The city was literally surrounded by expansive gardens and open spaces, ideal for families to take a break, to get some fresh air and enjoy fun family time, particularly on holidays.

Laura glanced down at Alex, who was now flat on his back, having decided it was a better option for his back. She smiled at the sight of his large stomach protruding awkwardly. 'As a neoliberal, I imagine you sometimes question why such beautiful public spaces remain common land rather than being developed by private enterprises.'

Alex chuckled, his smile wry. 'On the gardens, I'm with you, Laura. Sometimes common sense trumps economic theory. Even someone like me can see the wisdom in preserving these grounds for public use.'

'Did you know,' Laura continued, 'that back in the 1860s, this garden was much smaller, with a little zoo featuring kangaroos, emus, and wallabies? Now, it spans thirty-eight hectares and houses eight thousand five hundred species of plants from around the world, but no zoo.'

Alex raised an eyebrow. 'You seem to know a lot about these gardens. Since when did you become a botanist?'

Laura laughed. 'I'm no botanist, Alex. I'm a member of the Botanical Gardens Board. We have experts from various fields—horticulture, science, community engagement. It's an honorary position, but I enjoy it.'

Alex's curiosity piqued. 'What got you involved in that?'

Laura took a breath, her eyes reflecting a recall of memories. 'For years, I worked as an economist in a tech company serving clients like Amazon and Google. The board invited me to join because they wanted someone with industry experience. My background in social issues made me a good fit.'

'Sounds like a significant shift from corporate life. What were you doing in the tech company?'

'I advised on the Australian economy and market trends, helping assess the potential of new innovations. Then …' she trailed off, her tone turning more reflective, 'disillusionment set in.'

Alex leaned in, intrigued. 'You left because you were unhappy with the business?'

'Yes, exactly. I realised that the corporate world, especially in tech, didn't align with my values anymore.' Laura paused, her gaze briefly returning to the children playing, before focusing on Alex. 'Do you remember our conversation with Anand, the Uber delivery driver?'

Alex nodded. 'Yes, what about it?'

'Do you know what percentage of the cost of those pizzas actually went to the restaurant?'

He shrugged. 'I'd guess eighty per cent, with the rest split between Uber and the delivery guy.'

'Closer to sixty-five per cent,' Laura replied.

'Really? I had no idea Uber took such a big cut, thirty-five per cent.'

'Yes,' Laura confirmed, 'despite not being involved in either the production or the delivery of the product. Third-party developers on Apple Store pay that much of their revenues to Apple. Amazon charges similarly to the revenues of authors and publishers. Yanus Varoufakis, the famous or infamous economist, depending on which side of the political spectrum you hail from, terms these tech platforms and the people behind them as technofeudalists. Access to their "digital fief" and cloud comes at the cost of exorbitant rents to producers.'

Alex had heard of Varoufakis and didn't give his economic prescriptions much credence, particularly those he gave the Greek government at the time of its financial crisis. But Varoufakis' take on the role of the tech platforms sounded interesting.

'So you decided you'd had enough of the tech company? Was that it?'

'Yes, Alex. It's bad enough that our Australian economy is now oligarchic in most sectors, dominated by two or three major companies in each sector. The tech companies go further. They themselves don't produce anything. However, they use clever algorithms to extract huge rents from both producers and customers. Every time we use cloud-linked devices like smartphones, laptops, Alexa, Google Assistant, and Siri, we feed money to the Big Tech feudalists. I find this increasingly distressing.'

Alex now sat up from his full supine position and appeared to be getting more interested in her analysis.

Suddenly, urgent calls for Sarah sliced through the air, drawing both their attention. Laura's gaze darted towards the gathering of mothers and children, a flicker of guilt flashing through her as she realised how deeply immersed they'd become in conversation.

There, standing a little distance away, Hanneli and the others repeatedly called out for Sarah. Laura scanned the area—and then the panic set in. Sarah was nowhere to be seen.

With her heart in her throat, Laura sprang to her feet. Alex, now visibly anxious, followed suit, struggling to rise, but driven by worry.

They joined the others, Alex's voice joining in the calls for Sarah, his growing distress evident. Laura saw the panic tightening in his features.

'Take it easy, Alex,' Laura said, trying to keep calm. 'I'm sure Sarah's around here somewhere. Look—there are five of us adults. Hanneli, why don't you stay with the kids? We don't want any more wandering off. Alex, you take the north. The rest of us will cover the east and west.' She turned to the remaining two mothers and laid out a plan. 'Let's reconvene in fifteen minutes. If you find Sarah, shout. Your voice can travel far in the garden.'

They dispersed quickly, and Laura noticed Alex's pace as he shot off in the direction she'd pointed. His semi-jog had an urgency, almost as though he were trying to outrun his own anxiety. Poor man.

Soon, neighbouring families had joined in, alerted by the commotion and echoing calls for Sarah. They ventured into the trees and underbrush, lending their voices to the search.

Fifteen minutes later, Alex returned, looking harried and winded. His cheeks were flushed, his breath shallow from exertion, and his face etched with concern.

The other mothers gathered in a circle, exchanging worried glances. By now, the other kids, too, had become subdued, their earlier energy dampened by the shared uncertainty. The food lay untouched on the blankets.

'Look, she has to be here,' Laura said.' But even as she spoke, a knot of fear twisted inside her. She saw it reflected in Alex's eyes too—the unspeakable worry of what could have happened.

Just as tension began to tighten around them, a voice called from below. 'Hi, everyone! Did I hear my name? I'm here.' Sarah appeared at the bottom of the hill, emerging from the thick trees like a ghost stepping out of the shadows.

'Sarah!' came the collective cry, a rush of relief flooding over them all.

'Where on earth have you been?' Alex asked, rushing to her and enveloping her in a tight hug. 'We were so worried!'

Sarah looked at them, bewildered by their reaction.

Laura, equally relieved but still trying to mask her growing concern, asked, 'Where did you disappear to, Sarah?'

'Down there, in the fern gully.' Sarah pointed towards a lush valley at the foot of the hill, its dense trees forming a green fortress. 'It's Mum's favourite spot, and she always takes me there. Why?'

Everyone collapsed onto the grass, their tension melting into laughter. The kids swarmed Sarah, eager to embrace her. But Sarah remained perplexed by the fuss.

'Do you know you almost gave Alex a heart attack?' Laura said, her voice light, but her smile tinged with genuine concern. 'And the rest of us as well! You know the rule, Sarah—you should always tell an adult before you wander off. We're responsible for you.'

Alex kept holding Sarah's hand, shaking his head and managing a weak smile.

'I'm sorry, Laura. I didn't do it purposely,' Sarah said, her eyes wide with regret.

Then she turned and pointed excitedly down the hill. 'Look for yourself! That's the entrance to the fern gully. You can even see it from here! It's not far at all. Come on, I'll show you. It's lovely.'

And before they protested, she dashed back down the

path she'd just returned from. Alex, Laura, and a few of the other kids followed in her wake.

Laura marvelled at the beauty of the gully. Hidden deep within the gardens, it felt like stepping into another world. The valley's verdant ferns created a rich canopy, softening the sunlight into dappled shadows that danced across the mossy ground. A stream babbled its way through, adding an almost magical undertone to the scene.

'I can see why you didn't hear us calling,' Laura said, her voice soft with understanding. 'This place is like a secret hideaway. The trees and the stream must have muffled everything.'

'It really is lovely,' Alex agreed, his voice filled with quiet admiration as he took in the serene landscape.

But Laura knew it was time to go. 'It's beautiful, Sarah, but we need to head back. The others will be worried again.'

They made their way back up the hill, Alex puffing slightly from the exertion.

'Okay, kids,' Hanneli called, trying to revive the mood, 'let's get back to some games now, shall we?'

Laura watched Hanneli with respect. She admired the woman's energy, her ability to turn any situation into an opportunity for action. She remembered Hanneli's unwavering fitness and communication skills from the gym she attended.

As the other mothers joined in, Alex gamely participated in games that weren't too demanding. It didn't escape Laura's notice that Sarah often pulled him into the activities. He was a good sport, but Laura thought the poor man needed to lose some weight. She'd had that thought a dozen times today already—he was puffing from the slightest exertion.

At long last, lunchtime arrived. The mothers opened the

drinks and snacks, calling the kids to help themselves. After devouring their food, the kids were off again, running around in all directions.

'How about a relay race? Up and down the hill?' suggested Hanneli, and Laura silently agreed. Anything to keep the kids busy and ensure no more wanderings.

'We'll split into two teams—six on each,' Hanneli announced. 'I'll be the referee. Ready?'

The kids cheered, and Sarah and Alice were appointed as team captains. They took turns picking their teams.

Hanneli placed blankets at both the top and bottom of the hill, marking the start and finish lines. The race would begin at the top and end back there, with each runner being tagged by the previous one to start their leg.

The race kicked off with Sarah and Alice leading the way, their small legs carrying them down the hill with shouts of encouragement echoing behind them. Sarah was just ahead of Alice as they tagged the next runners, and soon the race made its way back up the hill and back again.

Alex and Laura were the last remaining runners at the bottom of the hill. Alex had a yard's advantage given to him, but Laura, confident in her fitness, began to close the gap. She was just about to overtake him when, to her horror, she saw him lose his footing and tumble forward, then roll helplessly back down the hill.

She stopped dead in her tracks, ignoring the calls of her team. She raced back, desperate to stop him from rolling further, but as she reached him, she saw he was beyond help—lying at the bottom of the hill, breathless, pale, and utterly spent.

'Just lie still, Alex,' she said, her voice tight with concern. 'Don't get up just yet.'

Hanneli, who'd been watching from the top of the hill, sprinted down, her first aid training kicking in as she took Alex's pulse.

'Stay down, Alex,' she insisted, her voice calm but firm as Alex tried to sit up.

Soon, the kids and the other mothers had gathered around, and Sarah, her face creased with worry, asked, 'Alex, you okay?'

Alex nodded, too winded to speak, but Laura saw his discomfort.

'Let's give him some space,' Laura said, ushering the kids back. 'Let him get some fresh air. He'll recover soon.'

Alex did, gradually. In a few moments, he was able to sit up, his face flushed with the embarrassment at having caused such a scene.

'I'm sorry, Sarah,' he mumbled, his voice hoarse. 'I lost your race. I'm so sorry for making everyone worry.'

They all laughed, the sound tinged with relief. Laura and Hanneli helped him to his feet, and Laura called out, 'All right, kids, let's head back up the hill and relax a little before we pack up.'

She let out a deep sigh of relief as she saw Alex recovering. For a brief moment, when she'd sat beside him at the bottom of the hill, worry had gripped her. She had feared something more serious than just exhaustion.

During their walk back to the cars, Hanneli mentioned she'd come by on Monday to help with the girls. She was free during the day and wanted to keep an eye on Alex. Laura noticed the lingering concern in her eyes.

~

After goodbyes in the parking lot, Alex and Sarah drove home. Alex, still recovering, groaned softly. 'Sarah,' he said, his voice tired, 'I've got no energy to cook tonight. Let's just grab a pizza from the freezer. An easy dinner.'

Sarah, ever the voice of reason, hesitated. 'But didn't Mum say that pizza's not good for your health? Back there, in the garden, you were really not well. Can we have something healthier for dinner?'

Alex sighed. 'You're right. You're right, dear. We'll shower, then I'll make some pasta and veggies. Deal?'

'Yes,' Sarah agreed. 'That's better.'

Alex chuckled inwardly at how Sarah always kept him on track.

'You're worried about me, huh?' he asked, his voice gentle.

'Uh-uh,' she replied, 'I am. But please don't run anymore. I think it's bad for you. I'm sorry for making you do it.'

'No worries, Sarah,' Alex said, squeezing her hand. 'It's my responsibility to take care of my health.'

'But will you ever be strong again, Alex?'

The question caught him off guard, striking him more deeply than he expected. It was clear to him now—she wanted to keep playing, keep having fun with him, but she needed him to be strong enough to keep up.

ELEVEN

Sunday truly deserved its title as the day of rest, Alex mused, sinking deeper into the couch cushions. His body felt like it had been through a storm—battered, bruised, and utterly depleted after his collapse in the garden the day before. Today, rest wasn't just a luxury; it was a necessity.

Sarah seemed to sense that something was off. Her eyes lingered on him, a flicker of worry flashing across her face before she turned to Cassie, who'd come in as usual that morning. Leaning close, she whispered, 'Let's not bother Alex today. He needs to rest.'

Alex overheard and was struck by her maturity. It amazed him how perceptive children were, even at such a young age.

The day had started with pain. Every muscle ached; his limbs felt heavy, and even breathing seemed to require more effort than usual. But it wasn't just the physical discomfort that bothered him. A heavy fog of fatigue and melancholy had settled over him, dulling his spirit. He'd never felt so low, so utterly drained.

'Alex?' Sarah's voice was soft as she approached the couch, her eyes wide with concern. 'Do you want something to eat? Or maybe some juice?' Her little face was drawn with worry, her eyebrows arched, and her lips pressed together.

Alex managed a faint smile. 'Thank you, sweetheart. I'll be fine. We'll have lunch in a bit.'

'I can make it if you want,' she offered earnestly.

'That's sweet of you, but I'm just resting. I'll be all right. Now go on and play,' he said, gently shooing her away.

The girls tiptoed around the house, whispering to each other and playing quietly so as not to disturb him. Alex felt a swell of gratitude for their thoughtfulness.

After a while, he heaved himself off the couch, his body protesting every movement, and shuffled over to his computer. This crushing fatigue worried him. It was more than just soreness from overexertion. He typed his symptoms into Google but found no comfort in the search results. Sleep deprivation? But he'd slept well. Poor diet? Well, he knew he usually overate. Ageing? But Laura was only a little younger than him, and she was bursting with energy.

Frustrated, he abandoned his health search and turned to something more familiar—economics. He began reading up on Varoufakis' theories, which Laura had mentioned the day before. As he read, he found himself nodding. Varoufakis had a point. The tech giants were no longer just players in the economy—they were the puppet masters, controlling both producers and consumers alike. It was no wonder they were the most valuable companies on the US stock market by a colossal margin.

His thoughts drifted to Laura. She was an enigma—a woman who'd walked away from the safety of industry and crafted a new path for herself. Reinventing herself entirely, she'd built a stimulating career that challenged conventional thinking. And she was fit—remarkably so. Clearly, she took care of herself. Alex felt a twinge of admiration, mingled with a hint of envy. There was so much he could learn from her.

The day dragged on, but with Sarah and Cassie's quiet help, he managed to get through it. Their kindness was humbling. As evening settled in, Sarah came up to him, her eyes serious. 'We should go to bed early tonight, Alex. Then we'll both feel better tomorrow.'

Alex felt a lump rise in his throat. How did someone so young have such wisdom? He pulled her close, hugging her gently. 'You're right, Sarah. You're absolutely right.'

~

At breakfast on Monday, Sarah looked up from her muesli, her face thoughtful. Between bites, she asked, 'Grandpa—I mean, Alex—what will you do when my school starts again? This is the last week, you know.'

Caught off guard, Alex paused, his spoon halfway to his mouth. 'Good question, Sarah. What do you think I should do?'

He'd been wrestling with that very thought. Over the past weeks, a new rhythm had taken hold of his life, one that revolved around the children. Their presence had woven itself into his routine, creating a comforting pattern. And then there was Laura. Having the kids around had given him the perfect excuse to see her regularly. Once school started, all of this would change. Would he still have reasons to meet her? And what about the podcast project? It wasn't just a professional interest—it was a chance to collaborate with Laura.

'Weren't you and Laura going to work on a project?' Sarah

asked, as if reading his thoughts.

Alex smiled, impressed by her sharp memory. 'Yes, you're right. She agreed to it but handed all the work to me. Not exactly fair, is it?'

Sarah frowned, her little face serious. 'But she's got her other job, Alex. You don't.'

He stifled a chuckle, shaking his head. How did children manage to cut through everything with brutal logic?

The doorbell rang, breaking the moment. Hanneli had arrived with Anya in tow. For the first time, she'd offered to stay and help out with the kids. Alex was curious about how they'd adjust to each other. Hanneli was always in motion—graceful and efficient, like a dancer moving through a well-rehearsed routine. How would that blend with the chaos of toys and games scattered across his living room?

After settling the kids, Hanneli approached him at his computer table. 'Can we chat, Alex? How about a coffee at the dining table?'

He knew what was coming. It was inevitable. His collapse in the garden had rattled the mothers—and himself. They were worried, and he appreciated their concern, even if he wished they'd leave him alone.

As they sat down with steaming mugs of coffee, he glanced across at Hanneli. She was a striking woman, mid-thirties, with light-brown skin and sharply defined features. Her movements were fluid, effortless, as though she floated rather than walked. She had an elegance about her that intrigued him. Where did she come from? What was her story?

'How you feeling today, Alex?' she asked, her eyes sharp with concern. 'You gave us quite a scare in the garden.'

He laughed, waving a hand dismissively. 'Back to normal, Han. Just a bit embarrassed, that's all.'

'I'd call it more of a wake-up call,' she countered, her voice gentle but firm.

He sighed. 'I know where this is going. You're about to tell me to get into shape. But look at me—I'm sixty-five. It's too late for all that now.' His shoulders slumped as he spoke, resignation weighing down his words.

Without a word, Hanneli pulled out her phone and scrolled purposefully before holding it up for him to see. On the screen was a photo of a woman working out at a gym. Her physique was impressive—toned, strong, radiating vitality. She reminded him of Laura.

'How old do you think she is?' Hanneli asked, her eyes never leaving his face.

Alex squinted at the image. 'I don't know … early sixties?'

'She's seventy-five. She started at sixty-five, just like you are now. Ten years ago, she was out of shape and exhausted all the time.' She swiped to another photo. This one showed the same woman, visibly younger but slouched, pale, and tired. The transformation was nothing short of remarkable.

Alex stared at the images, the contrast so stark it was almost unreal. It was like looking at two entirely different people.

'I hope you don't mind me sharing that,' Hanneli said, her voice softening. 'I won't lecture you, Alex. But if you ever decide you want to feel stronger, more energetic, maybe a little more flexible, let me know. You remember that my husband and I own a gym, right?'

Alex nodded, still staring at the phone.

'All right then, I'll leave you to it. I'm going to check on the kids. I've brought my laptop, so if you don't mind, I'll work at the dining table.' She stood up, her movements graceful, her presence leaving a faint echo of purpose and vitality in the room.

'Thanks, Han,' Alex murmured, his voice distant. 'That's … really interesting.'

He turned back to his computer, but his mind kept drifting to those photos. The woman's eyes in the 'before' picture looked hollow, tired, defeated. But in the 'after' photo, they sparkled with energy and confidence.

The images stayed with him, their contrast haunting him through the next few hours, lingering like a whisper at the back of his mind, challenging his resignation.

~

Early that afternoon, after the lunch dishes had been washed, the kitchen and dining room tidied, and the house had settled into a lazy post-meal quiet, the doorbell rang. Sharp and insistent, it sliced through the calm.

Alex frowned. Not many people visited unannounced, and certainly not with such urgency. Whoever it was, they were impatient. He strolled towards the door, curious but unhurried.

He opened it and froze. Sharon Hancock stood on the threshold, dishevelled and trembling. Her hair hung in tangled strands, her eyes swollen and red from crying. Blood trickled from her nose, and she cradled her jaw with one hand. A harsh purple bruise blossomed across the right side of her face, ugly and angry.

Shock held him still for a heartbeat, then instincts kicked in. He stepped forward, his movements gentle, and took her by the arm. 'Good God, Sharon! Please come in,' he said softly, leading her inside with careful tenderness, as if she might shatter.

The children were playing in the living room, their

laughter fading into stunned silence when they saw Sharon's battered face.

Cassie's scream shattered the stillness. She ran to her mother, wrapping her arms around Sharon's legs, her small body shaking with fear. 'Mum! What happened? Why are you crying? Who did this to you? Was it Daddy again?'

The words hung heavy in the air. Alex felt his stomach clench. His suspicions had been right.

Hanneli sprang up from the dining table, her face taut with alarm. She rushed to Sharon's side, helping Alex guide her to the couch. She gently moved Sharon's hand away from her cheek, revealing the bruise in all its viciousness. Without a word, Hanneli dashed to the kitchen, returning with ice wrapped in a kitchen towel.

'You need to lie down,' Hanneli murmured, her voice low and steady. She pressed the ice pack to Sharon's cheek, her hands firm but careful.

Cassie clung to her mother, her cries raw and panicked. Sharon tried to comfort her, even as her own sobs broke through. But the more she tried to soothe Cassie, the more her daughter cried, the pain in her eyes mirroring her mother's.

Hanneli knelt beside Cassie, her arms encircling the girl, her voice a whisper meant just for her. 'Cassie, sweetheart, your mum is hurt, and she needs us to be strong. If you keep crying, she'll worry even more. Can you help us by being brave?'

Cassie sniffled, her small face streaked with tears, but she nodded, biting her lip to stop herself from sobbing. She held Hanneli's hand tightly, her little fingers trembling.

Alex watched, his heart aching for them both. No child should have to face this. No woman should endure it.

Turning to Sarah, Hanneli spoke softly but firmly. 'Sarah,

can you help? Take Cassie and the other girls to sit on the carpet there. Keep her company while we help her mum.'

Sarah nodded, her face solemn. She gathered the girls, leading them to the rug, where they sat in a circle around Cassie, their faces pale and worried.

'Sharon, just rest for now,' Hanneli urged, sitting beside her on the couch. 'We'll talk later. Alex, could you get her some water? And maybe a coffee afterward?'

Grateful for something to do, Alex hurried to the kitchen. His hands shook as he poured the water, his mind reeling from the shock of seeing Sharon like that. He knew Adam could be difficult, but this ... this was something else. Fury simmered in him, hot and bitter.

When he returned, Sharon was calmer. Her sobs had quieted, her body no longer shaking. She took the glass from him, her fingers brushing his, cold and trembling. She managed a faint smile for Cassie, who sat close by.

Hanneli's voice cut through the silence. 'Okay, kids. Sharon needs some quiet time now. Why don't you go to the play area in the dining room? You can get out your Lego or iPads. But stay inside today, all right?'

She guided them away, her touch gentle but firm, leaving Alex and Sharon alone. Sharon sat up slowly, wincing as she adjusted the ice pack against her cheek. She looked exhausted, hollow, as if the assault had drained every last drop of strength from her.

Hanneli returned and sat beside her. 'If you're ready, Sharon ... can you tell us what happened?'

For a moment, Sharon looked at them, her eyes dark with shame and fear. Then she broke down, fresh tears cutting silent paths down her bruised face. Hanneli placed an arm around her, holding her close.

'It's Adam,' Sharon whispered, her voice raw. 'He was drunk again. When I got home from work, he demanded more money. I refused. He got angry … he hit me. Harder than before.' She took a shuddering breath. 'He's lost so much with his gambling. He's desperate. I was scared … I ran. I didn't know where else to go.'

Alex's hands tightened into fists, his jaw clenched. 'How long has this been going on?' His voice was tight, anger bubbling just beneath the surface.

'Every second or third day,' Sharon confessed, her shoulders trembling. 'But today was worse. He's drowning in debt … and he blames me. I don't know what to do anymore. I thought about … ending it. But I can't. Cassie needs me.' Her voice broke, her anguish piercing.

Alex felt something snap inside him, a white-hot rage rising. 'That bastard,' he growled, his voice low and dangerous. 'How dare he?'

'He's violent, Alex,' Sharon warned, fear flashing in her eyes. 'Please don't confront him. He'll only make things worse.'

A heavy thud rattled the front door. No polite ringing this time—just hard, angry banging. Sharon's eyes widened, her face draining of colour. 'Oh God … it's him. He must have guessed I'd come here.'

Alex stood, his body tense, every muscle bracing for a fight. He glanced at Sharon, saw the terror in her eyes, and felt his anger harden into resolve. 'He's not getting in here,' Alex promised, his voice cold and steely. He turned towards the door, ready to face the man who had done this.

He yanked the door open. Adam Hancock stood there, swaying, his eyes bloodshot and unfocused, the stench of alcohol rolling off him. His face twisted into a sneer as he took in Alex's stance.

They stared at each other across the threshold, the air heavy with tension. Alex collected himself and balled his fists. He wasn't sure how this was going to end, but one thing was certain—Adam was not getting past him. Not today.

Adam stood on the doorstep, swaying unsteadily. He wore stained joggers and a wrinkled shirt that looked like it'd been slept in for days. His hair stuck out at odd angles, his bloodshot eyes were wide and wild, and one of them twitched uncontrollably. His gaze flicked restlessly past Alex, searching the house like a cornered animal looking for escape.

'I'm l–lookin' for my w–wife,' he slurred, his voice jagged and broken. 'You the b–b–bastard hidin' her h–here?'

A hot surge of anger shot through Alex. 'You pathetic coward.' He spat the words with venom. 'You beat your wife, and now you have the nerve to come here looking for her? What kind of man are you?' His voice shook, louder than he intended, words crackling with fury. Alex surprised himself at this spontaneous outburst of anger. He rarely, if ever, got upset. He found uncontrolled anger to be unproductive. He prided himself on his calm and rational approach to everything in life.

Adam blinked, appearing stunned by Alex's defiance. His gaze refocused, as if trying to reconcile the mild-mannered old man he thought he knew with this bristling force blocking his way. But the surprise was fleeting. His nostrils flared, and his chest heaved. He took a stumbling step forward, shoulders angling to shove past Alex.

Alex widened his stance and gripped the doorframe to hold his ground. He wasn't a fighter—never had been. But he'd be damned if he let this brute into his home. They were of similar height, but Alex's bulk made him an immovable wall. Adam pushed harder, his breath reeking of alcohol, his wiry body straining against Alex's unyielding stance.

'You l–l–let me in, you s–son of a b–b–bitch!' Adam's voice rose, spit flying as he hurled the words. 'I know she's in there! H–h–hiding from me with you, you old f–f–fool!'

His voice echoed through the house, and Alex's gut tightened. The kids would hear this. Sharon would hear this. But he couldn't let Adam in, not like this, not in this state.

Then, without warning, Adam's fist shot out, cracking against Alex's jaw with a force that sent him sprawling. Pain exploded in his head, white-hot and dizzying. He hit the floor hard, his vision swimming with flashes of light. He tried to get up, but his body wouldn't respond, heavy and useless beneath him.

Adam staggered past, kicking Alex viciously in the ribs as he went by. A sharp, searing pain tore through Alex's side, leaving him gasping. He watched, helpless, as Adam lurched towards the living room, his voice booming through the house, 'Sharon! Where the hell are you?'

Sharon's scream ripped through the air, raw and panicked. She curled into the couch, pressing herself into the cushions as if willing them to swallow her. The children screamed too, their terror rising in high-pitched wails. Chaos erupted, fear and confusion colliding in a storm of noise. Alex sat up, still on the ground, but feeling helpless.

Hanneli was on her feet in an instant, moving faster than Alex thought possible. She planted herself between Sharon and Adam, feet apart, stance solid. 'Stop right there,' she commanded, voice cold and steady.

Adam's lip curled, a sneer of contempt twisting his face. 'Get outta my way, you b–b–black b–bitch!' He swung at her, a clumsy, drunken swipe meant to shove her aside.

He never saw it coming. Hanneli's right leg shot out in

a powerful arc, connecting with brutal precision between his legs. The impact was sharp and fast, a single, decisive strike. Adam's face contorted, his eyes bulging with shock and pain. He crumpled, collapsing onto his knees.

A guttural moan surfaced from his throat as he curled into a tight ball, hands clutching his groin. Hanneli didn't wait. Her other foot snapped up, striking his head with a sickening thud. Hancock went sprawling, then motionless, groaning faintly.

Alex watched, now sitting on the floor of the foyer. His jaw hung open. He could hardly believe what he'd just witnessed. It had happened so quickly, so effortlessly. Hanneli stood over Adam's crumpled form, fierce and unyielding, her expression hard as stone.

Sharon's eyes were wide, still locked on her fallen husband. The children huddled together, shaking, eyes round with fear and awe. Cassie sobbed, clinging to her mother's leg as if letting go would mean losing her forever.

Hanneli's voice cut through the stunned silence, sharp and decisive. 'Alex, get up. Call the police.'

Alex managed to push himself upright, his jaw throbbing and his ribs burning with each breath. He staggered over to the phone and dialled with trembling fingers.

As he called for help, he watched Hanneli lean over Adam, who was still curled up on the floor, whimpering softly. She didn't touch him, but her voice was low and lethal. 'You're not going anywhere, Hancock. If you even think about moving, I'll make sure you regret it.'

She turned to Alex, her expression softening as she took in his bruised face. 'Are you okay?'

Alex touched his swollen jaw, wincing at the pain. 'I'll live. But … that was incredible, Han. Where did you learn to do that?'

Her lips twitched in the barest hint of a smile. 'I teach self-defence classes,' she said matter-of-factly. She glanced down at Adam, her gaze hardening again. 'No one hurts a woman in my presence and gets away with it.'

Alex looked at her, admiration and gratitude swelling in his chest. He sank into a chair, still dizzy from the blow, but comforted by the knowledge that Hanneli was there, protecting them all.

'I'll look after Sharon and the kids. You sit by this scum till the police arrive.'

Alex pulled up a chair and took a seat near the prone Hancock. He was hoping, though, that Hancock would remain stunned on the floor till the police arrived. He wasn't sure he could handle the guy, and certainly not as Hanneli had done.

Hanneli brought Alex an ice pack for his face and a soft drink bottle. She gave them both to Alex. He looked inquiringly at her.

'Apply the ice. The eye is darkening. You'll look pretty tomorrow. Hold the drink bottle by its neck. If that guy makes an attempt to get up, hit him on the head.' Bending down, she spoke in a steady and determined voice. 'You hear that, Hancock? If you don't want a sore head in addition to the knock you took on your family jewels, I'd suggest you stay put on the floor. We're close by.'

She then took Sharon's hand and led her to the kitchen, calling for the kids to join them at the dining table. She got out some snacks and soft drinks to help calm the kids down and seated them.

Cassie was still crying, holding her mother tight. Sharon, however, had calmed down. She held the ice pack to her face with one hand and had the other around Cassie.

Hanneli looked at the girls. 'Look, girls. Mr Hancock is obviously not well. He has become violent, which is why I had to deal with him the way I did. Alex has called the police, and they will soon be here. There is nothing to be afraid of, okay? Cassie, please don't worry. We'll protect your mum.'

But Cassie held onto Sharon even more tightly, her eyes wide with fear. Voice squeaking, she said, 'My dad is a bad man, Han. He's always hitting Mummy. Please take him away.'

'We will, Cassie. Don't worry, we will.' Hanneli smiled at Cassie and the other children reassuringly.

Alex noted, from where he sat, the set jaw and determined eyes. Han was obviously a woman no man should be messing with.

'Shall I go and help Alex watch over that bad man, Han?' Sarah asked.

Hanneli looked over at Alex. 'You okay, Alex? The police should be here any moment now. Just don't let that guy make a run for it.' Then to Sarah, in a softer voice, 'He'll be okay, Sarah. Your grandpa is a courageous man.'

Alex smiled to himself but kept his watchful eye on Hancock, who was now sitting up, seeming to decide whether to make a run for it.

TWELVE

The doorbell rang, its sharp chime echoing through the tense silence. Alex's pulse quickened. 'Han, I've got this. Keep an eye on him, please, while I open the door,' he called over his shoulder, glancing back to ensure Hancock was still seated on the ground.

Alex moved to the door with uncharacteristic urgency, though every step was painful, his ribs throbbing from Hancock's kick. He opened it to find Senior Sergeant Larkin standing there, her expression unreadable, flanked by Officer Nelson. Alex caught the flicker of surprise in their eyes as they took in his swollen jaw and the dark bruise blossoming beneath his left eye.

'A call came through about a home invasion and assault,' Larkin said, her voice firm but professional. 'May we come in?'

Alex stepped aside. 'Yes, Sergeant. There's been … quite an incident.'

He led them into the living room, where Hancock had risen unsteadily to his feet, his eyes blazing with a wild mixture of anger and panic.

Hancock's hand trembled as he pointed at Alex, his voice a slurred snarl. 'Don't believe a word these b–b–bastards say!' Spit flew from his mouth, his body swaying, his dishevelled appearance more pitiful than menacing. 'That b–b–bitch over there'—he jabbed a finger in Hanneli's direction—'she assaulted me. Kicked me in the b–b–balls and the head. F–f–fucking cunt.'

Alex began to explain just as Hanneli stepped forward to defend herself, but Larkin raised a commanding hand, her voice cutting through the chaos. 'Enough. I'll ask the questions. Professor, take a seat there.' She pointed to a single armchair. 'You'—she fixed Hancock with a steely glare—'sit over there, on that single sofa.' Her tone brooked no argument. 'Nelson, take the children to the backyard. Keep them occupied.' She turned to Hanneli and Sharon. 'Ladies, the couch, please. I'll bring myself a chair from the dining room.'

Her authoritative presence instantly restored order. Hancock stumbled to his seat, still unsteady, his face a mask of defiance laced with fear. As Nelson guided the children outside, murmuring soothing reassurances, Alex's heart sank, wondering how their young minds would cope with this nightmare.

Sergeant Larkin took her seat and turned to Alex. 'Let's start with you, Professor. As the homeowner, tell me what happened.'

Years of teaching had honed Alex's skill for clear, concise communication. He relayed the events as factually as he could, his voice steady despite the lingering sting in his jaw and the throb in his rib cage. Larkin listened intently, her eyes shifting between Alex, Sharon's tear-streaked face, and Hancock, whose twitching eye and jittery limbs betrayed his agitation.

Hancock kept interrupting, his voice growing louder with each outburst. Larkin's patience grew thin. 'Mr Hancock,' she said, her voice hardening, 'you'll get your chance. But if you keep interrupting, you won't be helping your case. So sit down and be quiet.'

Hancock's face contorted with fury. He sprang up, his unsteady legs propelling him towards Sharon. 'You f–f–fuckers don't know how to do your job! I came to take my wife home, and these b–b–bastards assaulted me! And you just sit there talking!'

His hand shot out, aiming to seize Sharon. But Hanneli was faster. Rising from the couch with feline agility, she intercepted his arm, twisting it behind his back in one fluid motion. Her other arm snaked around his neck, locking him in a stranglehold. Hancock's eyes bulged in stunned disbelief as he struggled, only to find himself immobilised by her iron grip.

Hanneli's voice was calm, almost polite. 'Officer, would you like to take over?'

Larkin blinked, momentarily caught off guard by the speed and precision of Hanneli's action. Then her professionalism snapped back into place. She stepped forward, her voice cold and commanding. 'Mr Hancock, I will handcuff you if you don't cooperate. Now, are you going to calm down and sit quietly, or would you prefer to be restrained?' She held up a pair of gleaming handcuffs for emphasis.

Hancock's shoulders sagged in defeat. He gave a jerky nod, his face pale with humiliation. 'Fine,' he croaked, his voice hoarse from Hanneli's chokehold. 'Bitches,' he murmured to himself.

Larkin looked at Hanneli with newfound respect. 'You

can let him go now, ma'am. And your name is …?'

'Hanneli Ghosh.' Her voice was steady, but her eyes blazed with fury as she released Hancock, who stumbled back, rubbing his neck. Her words cut like ice. 'Mr Hancock, if you so much as touch Sharon again, I will emasculate you.'

'That's enough, Ms Ghosh,' Larkin interjected, her tone firm but not unkind. 'Please, everyone, sit down. I'll take your statements one by one.'

With everyone finally seated, Larkin resumed her questioning, her pen scratching across her notebook as she meticulously documented Alex's account. She listened carefully, asking pointed questions to clarify details. Hancock sat sulking, his legs twitching, his fingers tapping restlessly on the armrest.

When it was Hancock's turn, he sneered, his voice dripping with contempt. 'This woman is my w–w–wife. I came to take her back home. This old fart tried to stop me, and that b–b–black bitch assaulted me with her karate shit. Why aren't you arresting them?'

Larkin's eyes hardened. 'Watch your language, Mr Hancock. Mrs Hancock, are you willing to return home with him?'

Sharon's composure broke. She sobbed uncontrollably, her shoulders shaking as she clung to Hanneli. Between gasps, she pleaded with Larkin, describing the abuse she endured— the beatings, the humiliation, the financial control. Alex's fists tightened as he listened, helplessness churning in his gut.

Larkin then turned to Hanneli for her statement. Hanneli's expression turned resolute. After confirming the details laid out by Alex, she added, 'Sergeant, I've witnessed a home invasion, an unprovoked assault, and verbal abuse. I expect charges to be laid against Mr Hancock based on our testimony.'

Her jaw clenched. 'I also intend to assist Mrs Hancock to seek an emergency restraining order on Mr Hancock. My organisation, the Women's Care Centre, will assist her to also apply to the court tomorrow for temporary exclusive use of the family home while she initiates legal proceedings for a divorce. My understanding is that she is the sole owner of her property. What's important is that the police ensure Mr Hancock is kept away from Mrs Hancock, today and tomorrow morning, till we obtain these court orders.'

Larkin raised an eyebrow. 'Women's Care Centre?'

'I'm a volunteer advocate. On my personal time.'

Larkin looked at Hanneli with even more respect, curiosity flickering in her eyes. 'And your regular job?'

'I own a gym. I also run self-defence programs for women on how to handle men … like Mr Hancock.' Her eyes cut to him with cold disdain.

Larkin's lips twitched, almost forming a smile. 'I see.' She closed her notebook and stood, her posture radiating authority. 'Mr Hancock, I'm placing you under arrest for home invasion and assault. You have the right to remain silent …'

As she recited his rights, Hancock's shoulders slumped, defeat sinking into his frame.

Hanneli's eyes stayed locked on him, unblinking, fierce.

Alex looked at her in admiration, his jaw still throbbing, but his heart swelling with gratitude and respect. She had saved them all. And, in the process, revealed a warrior's spirit he hadn't known lay beneath her composed exterior.

Larkin spoke. 'Professor and Mrs Hancock, do you wish to lodge a formal complaint against Mr Hancock, given that you were both attacked by him?'

After a brief, tense pause, and an exchange of glances, Sharon and Alex nodded. Her face was taut with resolve, eyes clouded with the weight of the moment, reflecting Alex's feelings exactly. Larkin then called Nelson in, children in tow.

'Ms Ghosh, could you please take the kids to the dining room while we record Sharon and Alex's complaint statements?' Larkin asked, her voice gentle but firm.

Hanneli guided the children away, and Alex watched, still worried about the impact of this on them. He strained to catch Sarah's voice, tinged with fear. 'What's going to happen now?' she asked, her small face pinched with worry.

Cassie's voice followed, trembling. 'Will my dad come home with Mum and me? I'm scared. He's going to be even angrier now.' Her words quivered, Alex noted with concern.

Hanneli knelt beside them, her voice soothing but steady. 'Listen, kids, the police will take care of everything, okay? Don't be worried. And Cassie, I promise I won't let your dad come near your mum's house again.'

That's a big promise, Alex thought. *I hope she can deliver.*

Larkin finally stood, and her demeanour turned steely as she formally addressed Hancock. 'Mr Hancock, this is the fifth time this year that the police have been called for an assault involving you—not just on your wife, but on other community members as well. This cannot continue. It's now up to the prosecutor and the magistrate to decide the next steps. For now, we're taking you to the station and charging you with assault. You'll appear before the magistrate tomorrow to determine the consequences of this home invasion and the assaults on Professor Bobbins and Mrs Hancock.'

Hancock sprang to his feet, indignation distorting his face. But Larkin was ready. With a speed and precision that belied her age, she snapped the handcuffs on him, her movements swift and decisive.

Turning to Hanneli, Larkin continued, 'Ms Ghosh, if you're assisting Mrs Hancock with the temporary exclusion order, file it first thing tomorrow. Perhaps we can have the magistrate review both cases at once.'

After the police left, Hanneli turned to Sharon. 'We need to visit the Women's Care Centre now. We must draft the emergency restraining order and the temporary exclusion order tonight and file them tomorrow morning. There's no time to lose.'

Hanneli then turned to Cassie, who clung tightly to her mother, small fingers curled desperately around Sharon's arm. 'Cassie, sweetheart, stay here with Sarah and the others. Alex will look after you. I'll call him later to arrange for you to go back to your house, okay?'

Cassie hesitated, her eyes wide and fearful, but she eventually loosened her grip. Alex gently led her to the dining room, his heart aching as he watched her fight back tears. He knew she was trying to be brave. *Too brave for a child her age.*

He distracted them with cookies, arranging them on a plate with hands that shook just slightly from the adrenaline still coursing through him. The throbbing in his jaw and the searing pain around his swollen eye made it difficult to focus, but he forced himself to push through. They needed him.

Just as the children started nibbling on the cookies, the doorbell rang again. Alex's body tensed. Who now? He moved gingerly to the door, each step jarring his battered body.

'Jesus, Alex. You look awful,' Ella Webster exclaimed, her eyes widening as she took in his swollen jaw and bruised eye. 'What on earth happened? I saw the police take Hancock away. Why were you two fighting? What's happening to this neighbourhood?'

Alex fought the urge to roll his eyes. *Not now, Ella. Not now*. He took a deep breath, forcing patience into his voice. 'Ella, I really need your help. The kids are shaken up, and I must call their parents. Can you stay with them for a while?'

Ella folded her arms, her face set in stubborn lines. 'I'm your neighbour, Alex. I have a right to know what happened. The police were here, and I saw them lead Hancock away in handcuffs. I'm glad. Never liked that man. But now I find you with a bruised eye. I assume you both had a fight. That is verging on adolescent behaviour, in my view. Certainly not something I expected from a neighbour.'

Alex clenched his jaw, then winced as pain shot through his face. 'Ella, please. Just this once, can you help without needing all the details? The kids need you. I need you.' His voice cracked, the weight of the evening pressing down on him.

Ella's posture softened. Her eyes flicked to the dining room, where small faces sat around the dining table, eyes wide and anxious. With a resigned sigh, she nodded. 'All right, Alex. I'll help.'

Relief flooded through him when Ella went into the dining room. She immediately wrapped an arm around Sarah and Cassie's shoulders, and whispered words of comfort, her demeanour nurturing.

While Ella watched over the kids, Alex made the difficult calls to each parent, his voice steady but strained as he explained the events of the evening. He reassured them repeatedly that their children were safe and being looked after. Each mother responded with shock and worry, insisting they'd come immediately.

Once the phoning of the mothers was taken care of, Alex made his way to the dining table to join Ella and the kids. For once, Ella didn't seem to have any questions. The kids had probably debriefed her, and in the process, relieved themselves of some of their pent-up tension. They sat together in hushed silence, still munching cookies.

Alex nursed his swollen jaw and black eye with the ice pack Han had given him. The kids watched him, their faces still showing fear and confusion. What had just transpired seemed too much to comprehend. And it had happened so suddenly. One moment, they were deep in the joys of play and make-believe, and the next, the anger and violence of the real world had descended, accompanied by emotional turmoil. Sarah clutched her beloved teddy bear, her go-to when she was worried.

Alex felt deeply anxious for them. Despite his reassurances, their shock persisted. They were usually never at a loss to create their own games. He often envied their carefree spontaneity, their imagination, the delight they created out of play. Now, it seemed to have all evaporated, replaced by a pensive silence, fidgeting and continuous hand wringing. For the first time, they looked to him to find a way to distract them.

'Look, kids, the police and Hanneli are going to look after everything. Okay. Now, shall we get to play?'

But the kids remained fixated on what had happened, and how that was going to affect Cassie and her mum.

'Are they going to send Mr Hancock to prison?'

'When will Mrs Hancock come back home?'

'Will Mr Hancock be able to break out of prison and worry Cassie's mum again?'

'Why is Mr Hancock so angry?'

And on and on it went.

Alex grew desperate. He had to find a way to distract them. 'Do you guys dance? I'll play some music through the speakers, and let's all dance. Okay?'

They looked at him sceptically. Ella stared at him like he was out of his mind, but he refused to be discouraged. He got out his phone, found Spotify, and scrolled to find a happy Abba tune.

'Yuck, Alex. That's old people's music. Here, give me the phone.' Sarah grabbed the phone from Alex and proceeded to scroll down to what she wanted.

These little kids of seven astonished him. Though they didn't own a phone, they operated them so skilfully. They obviously practised on their parents' phones. But they seemed to use them with far more skill than he'd ever mustered.

'Here. Found it. The Zombies. What shall we play?' Sarah asked the others.

'"We Own the Night",' came the spontaneous chorus.

And before Alex knew it, the kids were up and dancing to a catchy tune he'd never heard before.

'Hold it,' Sarah announced. 'I'll put the video on the TV. Let's all go to the living room and dance.'

She brought up a YouTube video on the TV, again showing a skill Alex admired. He found out who The Zombies were: a group of handsome and pretty teenagers, dancing to catchy tunes, with skilled acrobatic moves.

Soon, the kids were immersed in their dance, arms waving, feet stomping, big smiles lighting up their young faces. Some hopped up and down, keeping the rhythm, others held hands and spun in dizzying circles. Squeals and giggles filled the air.

Alex sat back to enjoy their laughter with relief. He continued to nurse his jaw and eye, though the pain was receding. He glanced at Ella and was amused to see her gobsmacked and amazed at this dramatic transformation in the kids.

A loud doorbell brought everything to a standstill again. The kids stood silent, looking at the door, fear again written in their eyes.

Alex went to the door.

It was Laura, the first of the carers and mothers to arrive to pick up their child. 'My God, Alex. What happened to you?'

Laura came in, worry lines creasing her face. She held Alex's chin, then turned his head around to view his injuries from different angles.

He felt embarrassed, and Ella watched with inquiring eyes. The kids looked amused and happy again. They returned to their dancing, while Alex sat with Laura and Ella in the dining room, away from the noisy TV, and explained what had transpired.

Laura couldn't get over the events. But she wasn't in the least surprised when Alex described how Hanneli had handled Hancock. 'Han's fantastic. I attend her classes for women regularly. She's exactly the right person to be here to deal with that. You were lucky, Alex.'

He agreed.

The other mothers arrived to pick up their kids. In Anya's case, it was her dad. Alex found himself repeating the story again and again, with the kids now contributing their views, and in the process embellishing Hanneli's exploits.

~

Later that evening, Alex made dinner for Sarah, Cassie, and himself. Cassie's mum had not returned from her visit with Hanneli to the Women's Centre.

'She's cool, isn't she, Alex?' Sarah asked as he poured the pasta into the sieve.

'Who?' he asked with a furrowed brow. For a moment, he wondered if they were referring to Ella and her solicitousness, for which Alex was grateful.

'Han, of course.' Sarah shook her head and gave Cassie a knowing look, as if it was a silly question.

'Absolutely, Sarah. She saved the day.'

'She saved my mum,' Cassie piped in. 'I love her. I'm going to become like her.'

'We all are,' Sarah confirmed as they high-fived each other to confirm their intentions.

Over dinner, they discussed how they'd become martial arts experts and take on the boys in school to teach them a lesson or two. Alex worried that they were drawing the wrong lessons from the events of the day. But they wouldn't be moved.

Hanneli finally called on the phone.

'Alex, Sharon is fine. We're almost done with the petitions, and she'll submit them to the court tomorrow. I'm calling to ask, can Cassie sleep the night with Sarah? I'd like Sharon to stay with me for the night, for her own safety as well as for convenience. We'll need to leave for the court early tomorrow.'

'No problem, Han. Good idea. Perhaps Sharon can talk with Cassie and reassure her all is well?'

The kids were ecstatic.

Nothing like a sleepover anytime, Alex thought.

Later that night, though, he had to shush them. 'About time you guys go to sleep,' Alex called from outside their bedroom door.

They'd been chatting away nonstop after dinner. That's what sleepovers were for.

THIRTEEN

Alex drove Sarah to school on the first day of the new term.

'Excited?' he asked.

'Nah,' Sarah replied.

'Why not? You'll see your friends again, learn new things. What's not to be excited about?'

'Boys,' she muttered darkly.

That threw him. 'What's wrong with boys?'

'They shout and fight too much. They can't play without pushing and shoving. I hate them.'

Interesting. A strong opinion for a seven-year-old. But right now, he was more excited about getting a glimpse of her school—seeing her classroom, meeting her teachers, and getting a feel for the place where she spent so much of her time.

When they arrived, he parked and instinctively reached for Sarah's hand. He loved the feel of her small fingers curled into his. But as they neared the school entrance, she promptly tucked her hands into her pockets.

Right. He had some unlearning to do. No handholding in the vicinity of school. Not in front of her friends.

Ms Wilson, Sarah's teacher, was a warm, kind-looking woman who immediately put him at ease. She greeted them with a welcoming smile and walked him through the end-of-day pick-up routine.

'No worries, Professor. Sarah will be just fine.'

It seemed everyone still thought of him as 'Professor'. Funny—he'd almost forgotten. A lifetime in academia, and now, just a month into retirement, it already felt like a different world. Though a lot had happened since then.

The Sunday had been a whirlwind of preparations—supermarket runs for lunchbox essentials, a trip to Officeworks for school supplies, uniform washing, and bag packing. Fortunately, Sarah was a remarkably responsible child. Her mother had raised her well.

At lunch the day before, she'd hit him with a question. 'What are you going to do when I start school tomorrow?'

'Good question,' he mused. 'I'll have to think about it.'

'I think you've plenty to do.'

'Oh? And what would that be?'

'You have a project with Laura, remember? Why do you keep forgetting? You can't sit at home and do nothing. You'll get bored. I'm bored on my weekends unless Mum does some activity with me or I have friends over. And you have no friends, right? Except Laura. And she wants you to do that project.'

Right. The podcast. With everything that had happened—the Hancock ordeal, the restraining orders, the court hearings—he'd nearly forgotten. The police had charged Adam Hancock with assault and home invasion. As a repeat offender, he wasn't allowed bail and was awaiting trial. Alex expected to be called as a witness.

The week had been chaotic. Police officers, lawyers, and social workers had been in and out of his house. Sharon had filed for divorce with help from the Women's Care Centre. Through it all, Sarah had been relaying dramatic, wildly embellished accounts of events to her mother in PNG, painting Hancock as a villainous monster and Hanneli as a caped crusader.

Kay, in turn, had bombarded Alex with calls and questions.

'How did you let Hancock in?'

'Why weren't you of more help to Han?'

'Are you sure the kids are okay?'

'Are you even capable of looking after Sarah properly?'

Her calls had gone from daily check-ins to near-hourly interrogations. Frankly, Alex was relieved school was starting. At least now Kay would redirect her anxieties towards Sarah's school experience.

And yes, the podcast. He'd promised Laura. Truth be told, he was probably more excited about it than she was. It gave him a reason to keep in touch with her—a prospect that was becoming increasingly appealing. He suspected she felt the same way.

'And you promised Han you'd go to the gym,' Sarah reminded him.

Jesus! Nothing escaped these kids. That was one commitment he wasn't particularly eager to keep. Gyms intimidated him—all those fit, Lycra-clad young people doing endless, precise movements to sculpt muscles he didn't even know existed. He'd never stepped foot in a gym and wasn't keen to start now.

He hedged. 'Maybe.'

'Maybe?' Sarah gave him a sharp look. 'You promised

Han! A promise is a promise, right?'

'Okay, okay. I'll see when I can make it.'

'But you don't have anything else to do, right? Except the project. And you can't work all day only on that. I get bored if I have to do only one thing a day.'

'Sarah, I'm retired. I worked for over forty years. I have the right to take it easy now.'

She folded her arms. 'Han said you'd drop dead if you don't look after your weight. Then what would I do? Mum's still away. Who's going to take care of me?'

He opened his mouth to respond, but she wasn't finished.

'Also,' she added, softer now, 'I like you. And I don't want you dead.'

That did it. Tough to argue with the logic of a seven-year-old. And impossible to ignore the afterthought.

~

When Alex returned home after dropping Sarah off at school, the house felt hollow. Empty. Which it was. But it wasn't just the silence—it was the absence of warmth, of life, of laughter and chatter. He'd expected to relish the quiet, to put his feet up, sip his coffee, and lose himself in the newspapers stacked by the bay window. Instead, the silence pressed in on him.

It was astonishing how much space a seven-year-old occupied in one's life. And not just Sarah—the past few weeks had been a whirlwind of children running in and out, their voices filling every corner of the house. Now, it was as if the walls themselves were mourning their absence.

Maybe he needed company. A particular kind of company.

He reached for his phone.

'Hi, Laura. Up for a coffee and sandwich at Betsy's? We

can start planning our podcast.'

The reply came quickly. 'I'm working on a paper from home, Alex, but I can take a break. Lunch sounds good. It'll be nice to get away from my desk.'

He wasn't sure, but he thought he detected a note of enthusiasm. That was something to look forward to.

He picked up his newspaper and coffee, but the words blurred. His mind was already at lunch.

~

At Betsy's, for the first time, Alex sat across from Laura with no children to interrupt, no distractions to divert his attention.

He liked what he saw.

She must've been in her late fifties, but her face was remarkably smooth, her bob-cut hair framing sharp-blue eyes that, though kind, were piercing—like she read his thoughts. And judging by the slight smirk that played on her lips, maybe she did.

'You're studying me rather intently, aren't you, Alex?'

Busted. He cleared his throat. 'I was just thinking— this is the first time we've had a conversation without the kids around.'

'Good point. They do keep things lively. But first, let's order, and then we can talk.'

She chose a salad. He went for a steak sandwich with chips. It was time for a treat.

'So,' she began, folding her hands on the table, 'now that your childcare centre is officially closed for the season, what's the plan, Alex?' Her eyes twinkled.

'The centre was as much yours as mine,' he countered. 'You've been a lifesaver. But yes, good question. Sarah thinks I should finally get on with the podcast project we talked about.'

'From children come words of wisdom. So do you look forward to doing the podcast?'

'Absolutely. I've been thinking about topics—productivity, the role of neoliberalism, how governments are becoming more protectionist, the disruptions to global trade—'

'Whoa, slow down.' She held up a hand. 'Answer this first: Who's our audience?'

That stopped him short. He hadn't really thought about it. He'd envisioned debates, the intellectual sparring he missed from university, but … was that enough? Did they even need an audience?

'My first instinct was students—helping them navigate economic theory. But I'm guessing you had something else in mind?'

'Alex, I'm not an academic. My interest isn't in abstract theory—it's in how these policies affect real people. Privatisation, subsidies, public debt, social housing—decisions that change lives. I want to help educate the public so they vote knowledgeably. I want politicians to think about their choices from the perspective of the poor and middle class.'

She leaned in slightly. 'So you need to decide whether you're on board with that. If not—sorry, but I'm out.'

Blunt. No frills. He liked that about her.

Their meals arrived, giving him a moment to process. She wasn't just proposing an academic exercise—she wanted impact. And she was right. He had the time. He had the knowledge. And if he was honest, he wanted this more than she did.

'Okay. If it's going to be about educating the public on important economic decisions that are affecting their lives, how are we going to ensure the podcast reaches them?'

'That, dear Alex, is your homework.' She smiled playfully. 'I've a full-time job. You don't. Except for Sarah, of course.'

There it was again—the unvarnished truth. Once, in his professor days, he might have bristled at being assigned *homework*. But he wasn't *Professor* Alex anymore. Time to let go of the title, the entitlements. Time to start fresh.

'Fair enough,' he conceded.

'Good. Now, let's just enjoy our lunch.' She switched gears smoothly. 'How's Sarah coping after the Hancock incident? And your jaw?'

His hand went instinctively to his face, fingers tracing the still-healing bruise. 'Getting there. Doesn't get in the way of eating.' He grinned, gesturing at his half-devoured sandwich.

Laura's expression softened. 'Alex, we're friends now, right?'

The question caught him off guard. 'Of course,' he said. 'I like you. I want to know you better.'

'Then bear with me while I take some liberties.' She hesitated just a moment before continuing, 'You need to watch your diet.'

He sighed. First Kay. Then Sarah. Then Han. Now Laura. A full-on conspiracy.

'I'm serious,' she pressed. 'I saw what happened to you in the Botanical Gardens. I'm just asking you to think about it. Maybe do a medical check-up—if I'm not mistaken, you haven't had one in years. If ever.'

He had to admit, she wasn't wrong.

'Alex, you're still young. You have a long life ahead—if you *choose* to have it.' She held his gaze. 'I'd like us to be friends for a long time. So please, look after yourself.' She reached across the table and placed her hand over his.

A jolt shot through him—unexpected, disorienting. He

thought he'd left feelings like this behind, tucked away with the memories of a life that no longer existed.

She must have sensed his uncertainty, because she changed the subject with a smile. 'So is Betsy's your go-to lunch spot?'

The rest of the conversation was light—small talk, easy laughter. But when they parted, she gave him a quick, natural hug, and as he walked away, he felt lighter.

Lighter than he had in a long time.

~

As soon as Alex got home, he picked up the phone and called Thomas at the university.

'Alex! Good to hear from you. How's everything going? I assume Sarah's back at school today—my girls are.'

'Yes, Thomas, she is. Which means I suddenly have time on my hands again. I'm working on a new project with a colleague—a podcast examining the pros and cons of neoliberalism in today's society.'

'Sounds interesting,' Thomas said. 'More importantly, it's great to see you back in the economics game. Can't keep a good man down, right? But now you've got me curious. Who's your partner in crime?'

'Her name is Laura Symonds. She's a—'

'An economics adviser to the Labour Party?' Thomas cut in.

Alex raised an eyebrow. 'You know her?'

'Not personally, but I've certainly heard of her. I have a PhD student researching the influence of the Standing Parliamentary Committee on Economics. Laura's name pops up frequently in their archives—her submissions to the committee are sharp, well-argued, and thorough. She's got quite the reputation for cutting through the noise. Sounds like you've got yourself a formidable co-host.'

'Good to hear,' Alex said, though inwardly he was surprised. He'd only met Laura a month ago and had no idea she was that well known in academic circles.

'So tell me,' Thomas continued, 'how can I help? I assume this isn't just a social call.'

'You assume correctly. I know the university runs podcasts for students and has a fully equipped recording studio. Laura and I want our podcast to be an ongoing debate—examining neoliberalism's real-world applications and its impact on government policy. We need a professional studio with recording and editing software. I was hoping you'd help us hire the studio if the facility is available for rent.'

'Got it,' Thomas said. 'Here's what I need from you. Put together a short proposal outlining the podcast's objectives, target audience, format, technical requirements, and distribution platforms. The more polished it is, the better I can pitch it.'

'Of course,' Alex said. 'I appreciate it.'

'One more thing, Alex—frame the proposal in a way that might interest the university. If the department sees value in it, you could get access to the studio for free.'

'That would be fantastic.'

'In fact,' Thomas added, 'this could be bigger than you think. The academic board has been pushing departments to ensure our curriculums better prepare students for real-world employment. Your podcast could be a perfect showcase. If it aligns with that goal, we might even be able to secure funding for you.'

Alex felt a spark of excitement. What had started as a personal intellectual pursuit with Laura could turn into something much larger.

'That'd be great, Thomas.'

'Then let's make it happen,' Thomas said. 'Get me that proposal, and I'll do what I can.'

Alex hung up. This podcast, he realised, might not just be an exercise in debating ideas—it had the potential to influence the next generation of economists. And for the first time in a long while, he felt the familiar thrill of academic purpose.

FOURTEEN

Alex stood among the cluster of parents and carers gathered in the school's receiving area, waiting for the Grade 1 children to be dismissed. He noted and smiled at the now-familiar faces. Some were grandparents like him, and others were mums or dads. He exchanged polite nods and smiles, his gaze settling on June, Alice's mother. He waved but inwardly felt a flicker of disappointment. If June was here, it meant Laura wasn't.

'Hi, Alex.'

He turned to see Hanneli approaching with her characteristic grace. Her presence always seemed to carry an effortless energy. He was pleased to see her, though uncomfortably aware that he had yet to follow through on her invitation to her gym. He had no real excuse—it was in the area where he lived.

'I have a little present for you. I hope you'll accept it.' She held out an envelope.

Intrigued, he took it. 'That's very kind of you, Han. But

what's the occasion? Should I open it now?'

'If you'd like.' Her smile held a hint of mischief.

Curious, he slid his finger under the flap and pulled out the contents. The moment he saw it, an embarrassed grin spread across his face—an annual gym membership.

Hanneli beamed at his guilty expression. 'No more excuses now, Alex. I expect to see you there soon.'

'Han, this is generous, but if I go, I should be paying for it myself.'

'I know you can,' she said gently. 'But this is my way of thanking you—for everything you've done for Anya and me. You've been a huge help. Besides, we're all a little worried about your health. We care about you, Alex. We want you to be well. So whether you like it or not, you're officially my project now.'

Before he protested further, the school bell rang. She gave him a warm hug and moved off in search of her Anya. Alex stood still for a moment, feeling an unexpected warmth spread through him. It was nice—to be cared for, to have this community, all thanks to Sarah.

He watched Han disappear into the crowd of parents and kids. She truly was remarkable. Just last week, after the terrifying incident with Adam Hancock at his home, she'd stepped in to help Sharon Hancock obtain both a restraining order and a temporary exclusion order against her husband. Thanks to Han's relentless efforts, Sharon was now in a safer place than she'd been in years. Adam had been formally charged, denied bail, and was awaiting trial.

'Alex!'

Sarah's voice rang out, bright and exuberant. She barrelled towards him, her school bag—a hulking thing nearly half her size—bouncing on her back. He still couldn't fathom why schools insisted on such enormous, heavy bags. Even empty, they felt cumbersome; once packed with books, a lunchbox, and a drink bottle, they were an unfair burden for a seven-year-old. He reached out and lifted it off her shoulders without a word. She gave him a quick, distracted smile before skipping off to say goodbye to her friends.

Once they were in the car, he asked, 'Did you have a good day, Sarah?'

'Yes! I love Ms Wilson. And guess what? We learned about butterflies today! Did you know some of them taste with their feet?'

He nodded as she rattled on, delighted by her endless chatter. It was one of his favourite times of the day, driving home while she prattled about everything and nothing at once.

Then, suddenly—

'Did you go to the gym today?'

The question jolted him. He sighed internally. This girl was persistent. Here he was enjoying the sunshine, the easy drive, the comfort of routine—and she had to bring up the one thing he was trying to avoid.

'Not yet, Sarah,' he admitted. 'The thing is, I don't have any gym clothes. I have shirts, maybe, but no shorts. So maybe another time.' It was a good excuse. Also, true. He wasn't about to be caught dead in those ill-fitting shorts he'd attempted to wear during their first disastrous outing to the park.

Sarah was unimpressed. 'So why don't you buy some?'

'Maybe I will … sometime.'

'No, Alex! Let's go now. Look, turn up there—Kmart is right ahead.'

'Where?'

'There, can't you see? There on the right. Now turn, quick. They have lots of shorts. I went there with Mum when she bought hers.'

There was no wriggling out of it. Her logic was firm, her determination unwavering. He sighed and surrendered, pulling into the parking lot.

Shopping for clothes was foreign territory for him. He rarely needed new things and preferred to order online when he did. But now, here he was, holding Sarah's small hand (which, without any seven-year-old peers around, was apparently permissible), walking into the bright, bustling store.

Once inside, he was immediately overwhelmed. The men's section sprawled out before him, an endless sea of brands, colours, and styles. He had no idea where to start. Sarah, on the other hand, was undeterred. She spotted an attendant down the aisle and marched up with the confidence of someone on a mission. Amused, the young woman followed her back to Alex and directed them to the gym-wear section.

Then the real challenge began.

Sarah examined the options with the seriousness of a fashion consultant. 'That's too long … that one's too short … ugh, this colour is weird … oh! Look at this one! Yes, this will look good on you.'

And so it went until they finally found a pair that met her strict criteria.

'Now you have to try them on.'

'Oh, come on, Sarah. They look fine. I don't need to try them.'

'Yes, you do,' she insisted. 'Mum always says, "Try it on before you buy it." Otherwise, you'll have to come back if it doesn't fit.'

Reluctantly, he did. Several, in fact, until both Sarah and

he were satisfied. By the time they were ready to find the checkout, he was exhausted. How did people do this for fun?

Then, just as he thought they were done—

'Now we need to get you a gym bag.'

'A what?'

'A gym bag. You can't go to the gym without one.'

'Why not?'

Sarah looked at him as if he had just asked why people needed shoes. 'Because Mum always takes hers! It has her water bottle, her towel, her wipes—'

'Wipes?' He frowned. 'What wipes? I don't need wipes, Sarah. I'm a man, not a woman.'

She crossed her arms. 'Yes, you do. Mum says the gym equipment is full of germs, so you must wipe everything before and after you use it.'

Jeez. This kid had been thoroughly indoctrinated.

In the end, they compromised. He refused the Superman bag she was convinced suited him best, settling instead for a plain black one.

As they left the store, her hand still in his, he realised something. A month ago, he'd never have imagined himself here, shopping for gym clothes with a seven-year-old. But here he was.

And maybe, just maybe, he didn't mind it so much after all.

He was grateful when they finally emerged back into the carpark. Sarah was more excited than him about his purchases. 'They'll all be looking at you in the gym, Alex.'

'That's exactly what I don't want happening, Sarah. Please understand, I don't like people looking at me.'

'That's because you're fat. Once you've lost weight, you'll like people looking. Mum loves people looking at her.'

So much for the honesty of youth.

While they drove back home, he reflected on the last time he'd gone shopping for clothes. Must have been with Mabel more than eight years ago. He smiled at that recollection. Sarah was exactly like her. Maybe it was a feminine thing.

~

The next day, after dropping Sarah off at school, Alex drove to the university. A wave of nostalgia washed over him when he pulled into the familiar parking lot. It felt like months had passed since he was last here, though in reality, it had only been weeks. He stepped out of the car and took a deep breath, enjoying the crisp morning air.

At the campus entrance, he stopped and savoured the sights and sounds he'd missed. Groups of students bustled past, their youthful energy palpable. Laughter rang out as friends jostled each other in camaraderie, couples strolled hand in hand, and others found their way to sunlit lawns, settling into discussions that would shape their futures. It was a scene he'd known so well, yet now he stood as an outsider, an observer rather than a participant. He let the moment stretch, drinking in the sights and sounds he hadn't realised he'd missed.

A wistfulness hit him, but it was swiftly replaced by gratitude. Life had taken a different course—one he hadn't expected, but one that had given him more than he had lost. That morning, watching Sarah skip towards her classroom, her oversized bag bouncing behind her, he'd thought of all she'd brought into his life. His retirement had coincided perfectly with Kay's departure overseas, leaving him to step in as Sarah's caregiver. And through Sarah, he'd met Laura. The thought of her sent a surprising thrill through him. Their bond, still new, yet undeniably strong, had given him a sense of possibility. And then, of course, there was their shared project—the reason he was back here at his old hunting grounds.

He approached the economics department and saw familiar faces lighting up with recognition. Staff, lecturers, and students greeted him with warmth, some pulling him into quick hugs, others firing off rapid questions about his absence. He felt a glow of affection—it was comforting to know that, despite stepping away, he'd not been forgotten.

The commotion must have reached Thomas, because moments later, his old colleague emerged from his office— once Alex's own.

With a hearty hug, Thomas clapped him on the back. 'I got your proposal last night,' Thomas said. 'Great concept. I like it, and I think our students will enjoy what you guys come up with eventually. Whether or not the academic board approves it, the studio is available for rent. Let's introduce you to the studio guy.'

Alex promised to catch up with the others later and followed Thomas across campus to Building 79. He'd spent countless hours here in study groups, conference discussions, and research meetings. But the audio studio? That was uncharted territory.

Inside, they met Noah Saunders, the studio manager.

'Noah, this is Alex,' Thomas said. 'He's got an exciting project in the works.'

Noah extended a hand. 'Nice to meet you, Alex. I've heard of you, but our paths never crossed.'

Alex chuckled. 'I suppose I'm old school. Never ventured into audio or video for my teaching and research. Now I have to, post-retirement. Bit of a paradox, isn't it?'

'Never too late,' Noah said with a grin. 'Come on, let me show you around.'

Thomas bid Alex goodbye while Noah led him into the heart of the studio—a soundproof recording booth. The moment Alex stepped inside, he felt the shift. The outside world faded, replaced by a quiet hum of possibility. Soft lighting cast a warm glow over the space, where a high-quality condenser microphone stood mounted on a stand, flanked by plush headphones and a computer loaded with recording software.

'This is where the magic happens,' Noah said. 'You'll be working with two microphones—one for you and one for your co-host.'

Alex already pictured himself sitting here, Laura beside him, engaged in lively debate. The idea thrilled him more than he'd expected.

Noah led him into the adjoining control room, where a glass partition separated them from the booth. In front of them, a sleek mixing console stretched across the desk, with multiple monitors displaying waveforms and controls.

'This is where the audio engineer monitors the recording, adjusts sound levels, and mixes the tracks if needed,' Noah explained. 'The software is professional grade, so you'll be able to edit and enhance your episodes with ease.'

Alex absorbed it all, his excitement growing. This was real. This was happening.

'What platforms are you planning to upload to?' Noah asked.

Alex hesitated. 'To be honest, I'm still a novice at this. I've done some research, but I haven't settled on the best option.'

'Well, the easiest way to start is with Apple Podcasts, Google Podcasts, and Spotify,' Noah said. 'Podbean is another good option—it's user-friendly and even provides a built-in website for your podcast. When you're ready, I can help you set it up.'

Alex exhaled, feeling a mix of anticipation and apprehension. 'That would be great. This is all new to me, but I'm ready to learn.'

'You're in good hands,' Noah assured him. 'And if you have any questions, just give me a call.'

Alex stepped out of the studio, feeling a familiar sense of purpose settling over him. This was a new chapter—one he hadn't planned for, but one that, just like Sarah and Laura, had found him at exactly the right time. And maybe, just maybe, that was serendipity.

~

During the drive home, Alex settled on the substance of their first podcast. He would make a quick sandwich for lunch, then immerse himself in the task until it was time to pick up Sarah later in the afternoon.

He'd just started preparing his meal when his phone rang. Laura. His spirits lifted instantly. 'Hi, Laura. How's it going?'

'Hope I'm not disturbing you, Alex. I just wanted to bounce some ideas off you for a paper I'm working on.'

'Of course. What's on your mind?'

'How should Australia manage its transition from a fossil-fuel-based energy sector to one driven by renewables? And should the government lead the charge?'

Alex chuckled. 'Is this a trick question?'

'Not at all. I genuinely want to hear your take—as a neoliberal economist. I assume you agree that this is now a national priority?'

He hesitated. She was leading him somewhere, but he wasn't sure where yet.

'There are two key aspects to consider,' he said. 'Policy and financing.'

'I'm not sure those are separate issues,' Laura countered. 'But go on.'

'Ideally, the transition should be market driven, with private enterprise leading the way. Investment should be guided by market forces rather than government intervention, ensuring the most efficient and cost-effective solutions emerge naturally.'

'So no government involvement at all?'

'Not necessarily,' Alex conceded. 'The government has a role in shaping policies that influence the energy sector—creating a regulatory environment that encourages competition, innovation, and investment in renewable energy. But beyond that, it should let market dynamics play out.'

But Laura didn't seem to want to let him off that easily. 'Even if that means falling behind while the rest of the world races ahead? Governments everywhere are actively supporting clean energy—China, the UK, the EU, even the developing countries. Are you saying Australia should just sit back and wait?'

Alex exhaled. 'You're right. We don't live in an ideal world. Other governments are offering massive subsidies, picking winners and losers in the fight against climate change. The playing field isn't level anymore.'

'Exactly. And if Australia is at a disadvantage because of that, should our government still sit back and rely on the market?'

He sighed, laughing despite himself. 'I knew you were trying to corner me. You're being mischievous, Laura.'

'I'm being serious, Alex. This isn't just an academic debate. It's about the future—Sarah's, Alice's. They're the ones who'll be left to deal with what's already happening: catastrophic fires every summer, relentless floods in Queensland and New South Wales. Entire communities are now uninsurable. And yet, we're still waiting for market forces to catch up.'

Alex fell silent for a moment. She had a point. 'So … are you saying the government should take the lead in renewable energy investment?'

'I'm saying that's exactly what's happening globally. If we don't act, we'll be left behind. In fact we're already being left behind.'

Alex chuckled again, shaking his head. 'You know what? Maybe this should be the first topic for our podcast.'

FIFTEEN

Alex looked at himself in the mirror and sighed.

This is ridiculous.

He scrutinised his reflection with a critical eye. The old T-shirt clung unflatteringly to his torso, but it was the shorts that truly unsettled him. His generous gut wobbled rebelliously over the waistband, making him feel both exposed and absurd. Athletic wear had never been part of his wardrobe, and now he understood why.

He turned to examine himself from different angles, but there was no escaping the truth. He looked like a man far removed from the world of gyms and fitness routines. But a promise was a promise. He'd told both Sarah and Han that today would be the day, and he wasn't about to back out now.

Sarah, ever the strategist, had even begged him to wear his gym clothes when dropping her off at school—probably to ensure there'd be no turning back. But on that, he had stood firm. Some lines, however arbitrary, were not to be crossed.

Now there was no more delaying. He stepped outside,

already feeling self-conscious.

'Jesus Christ! Am I seeing right, or is this an illusion?'

Alex groaned. Ella Webster. Of course, she had to be in her garden at precisely the wrong moment.

'No need for the biting sarcasm, Ella,' he said, narrowing his eyes at her. 'Why must you always be lurking around just when I least need an audience?'

But Ella was clearly enjoying herself. She let out a delighted chortle. 'Wait till I tell the sewing group what I saw this morning! Agatha Wallum and Joan Chester, in particular, will be tickled. Like it or not, Professor, you look sexy.'

Alex rolled his eyes. 'Yes, yes, I look like a clown. Which is exactly why I need to do something about it.'

Ella's mirth softened into something kinder. 'Jokes aside, Alex, I admire you. I heard what happened in the gardens. We all want you around for a good long while, so good on you for taking this step.'

He nodded, appreciating the encouragement more than he cared to admit. With a wave, he set off on foot towards the gym, per Han's advice. It was a half-hour walk at most— enough to serve as a decent warm-up.

The morning was crisp and bright. The scent of freshly mown grass drifted in the air, mingling with the distant sound of birdsong. Alex inhaled deeply, allowing a small flicker of optimism to settle within him. Despite his apprehensions, there was something satisfying about taking charge of his own well-being. And though he wouldn't say it out loud, he also wanted to present himself better—especially now that things with Laura were beginning to bloom.

He arrived at the gym's entrance.

BODYWORKS GYM.

Interesting name, he mused. Han had told him that she

and her husband, Arun, had started it from scratch. Alex had always admired entrepreneurial grit. Arun, a mechanical engineer, and Han, a physical education teacher, had arrived in Australia six years ago only to find their qualifications unrecognised. Instead of being defeated, they had hustled, taking on odd jobs until they secured a loan and could open this gym. A bold, risky step—but immigrants, Alex thought, always found a way.

Taking a deep breath, he pushed open the glass door and stepped inside.

He was instantly gobsmacked.

The gym was a symphony of motion and sound. The rhythmic clanking of weights, the steady pounding of feet on treadmills, and the hum of conversation filled the air. Bright fluorescent lights illuminated row upon row of gleaming exercise machines—treadmills, rowing machines, cable stations, free weights, and all sorts of exercise machines. He recognised only a couple; the rest might as well have been medieval torture devices.

People of all ages and fitness levels spread throughout the space. Some lifted weights with intense focus, others jogged steadily, earbuds in place. A few were deep in yoga poses, and personal trainers guided clients through their gruelling routines.

Alex's economist mind kicked into gear. The equipment alone must have cost at least two to three hundred grand. Add in rent, insurance, trainer salaries ... what kind of return on investment were they seeing?

'Hi, Alex! Finally made it, I see.'

Han approached, her face lighting up with a warm smile. She hugged him—a brief, friendly squeeze—and he noticed how fit and toned she was.

'This is an impressive setup,' he said.

Han beamed. 'A bit ambitious, maybe, but we've been at it for two years now. Slow but steady growth. Let me introduce you to Arun.'

Arun, a lean, tall man in his thirties with clean features and a prematurely receding hairline, greeted him with an easy smile. 'I've heard a lot about you, Alex,' he said. 'Thanks for helping with Anya. And welcome. We're glad to have you.'

'All right, Arun, he's all yours,' Han said with a grin before heading off.

Arun led him to a quieter corner, where a water fountain stood—no sofas, Alex noted. No coffee machine either. Fitness first, clearly.

'Let's chat about your goals,' Arun began. 'What you want to achieve, and how do we make it happen?'

Alex laid it out: his struggles with weight, his sluggish energy, the creeping stiffness in his joints, his lack of stamina leading to breathlessness after any atypical exertion. He needed to regain some control over his body before it betrayed him completely.

Arun studied him, eyes sweeping up and down. Alex felt like a pumpkin being assessed at the supermarket.

'At your age, Alex, showing up is half the battle. Hats off to you.' Arun's voice held genuine respect. 'Now, I won't sugar-coat it—it won't be easy. But we'll start simple: treadmill, rowing machine, dumbbells.' He explained the basics: cardio to build stamina, rowing for full-body engagement, weight training to counteract muscle loss.

'After thirty, we all lose muscle mass. After sixty, it accelerates. Strength training isn't optional if you want to avoid becoming frail.'

And so, Alex thought, *it begins.*

The first few minutes were brutal. He was out of breath, sweating profusely, and convinced he might collapse. After fifteen minutes, he was sorely tempted to call it quits. But he pushed through, reminding himself that both Han and Arun were counting on him. Slowly, the movements became more manageable. Before he knew it, an hour had passed.

Arun debriefed him before he left. 'Expect soreness tomorrow, but don't skip. Just adjust the intensity. See you soon, Alex.'

On the walk home, Alex reflected on how much he had to report back to Sarah. And to Laura.

~

He arrived at the school early enough to secure a prime parking spot. With twenty minutes to kill, he decided to walk around the block—a suggestion from Han and Arun. He rounded a corner and spotted a familiar figure ahead. He quickened his pace.

Laura.

She must've heard his heavy breathing, because she turned, startled. 'What are you doing out here?' she asked, amused.

'Same as you,' he replied with a grin. 'Getting some exercise while waiting for the kids.'

'So, you're really taking this seriously.'

They walked together as Alex updated her on his day.

'We need to sit down and plan our first podcast,' she said. 'How about tomorrow after school drop-off?'

'Actually, can we make it later? I plan to hit the gym first.'

Laura raised an eyebrow. 'Wow! I'm impressed. Han's really done a job on you. That's great. I also use her gym, though for the body pump classes she runs three times a week.'

'What's body pump?'

'It's a fifty-minute weights-aerobic group exercise regimen, to which I owe my fitness and good health. Have been doing it for years. Han's a great trainer. We may see each other in the gym from time to time. But yes, coming back to meeting tomorrow. We should meet perhaps at Betsy's for a light lunch and plan the session.'

He couldn't explain it, but he was mightily pleased about the arrangement. Somehow, things were falling into place.

SIXTEEN

On the way home from school, Sarah leaned forward from the back seat, her voice bright with curiosity. 'Did you get to the gym, Alex?'

He grinned but didn't answer right away.

'What? Yes or no?' she demanded, impatient as ever.

'Yes, I did.'

She beamed and reached forward to pat his shoulder. 'Well done, Alex! Did you meet Han? Did she teach you any martial arts moves? You need to learn those for the next time Mr Hancock attacks you. And you can show me. But actually, I'd like to learn from Han. I like her.'

'Yes, I did meet Han, and she asked about you. She runs a really impressive gym. I should take you there sometime.'

Sarah nodded approvingly. 'Are you going every day now?'

'That's the plan. Han even gave me a one-year membership—very generous of her.'

Sarah stared out the window, her expression turning thoughtful. Then, almost hesitantly, she said, 'You know, I had a fight with some boys in my class today.'

Alex's grip on the steering wheel tightened. 'What happened? Did they hurt you?'

'They called Anya a blackie. It was really mean.'

A sharp wave of anger surged through him. 'What did Anya do?'

'She told them she liked her colour,' Sarah said, her voice brimming with admiration. 'But she wouldn't complain to the teacher. So I did.'

Alex exhaled slowly. 'And then?'

'The boys got mad at me. They started teasing me instead.'

'Good for you, Sarah,' he said, his chest swelling with pride. 'You did the right thing standing up for Anya. If they keep bothering you, let me know. I'll talk to your teacher. Maybe even their parents.'

Sarah huffed. 'No need. I'll just join the gym and get strong. And Han will teach me martial arts. Then, when those boys act funny and tease me, I'll take them down—just like Han did to Mr Hancock!'

Alex nearly laughed but caught himself. 'Whoa, hold on there, warrior. We don't solve problems with fights. We talk things out. Maybe those boys just need to understand why it's wrong to make fun of someone's skin colour.'

'But Han didn't talk to Mr Hancock. He was bad, and she took him down.'

'That was different,' Alex said patiently. 'Mr Hancock was drunk and violent. Han had no choice. But with your classmates, you do have a choice. If they bother Anya again, try explaining to them why what they're saying is hurtful.'

Sarah crossed her arms, her small face set with frustration. 'Alex, boys are dumb. You can talk all you want, but they won't listen. That's why I hate them.'

Alex glanced at her in the rear-view mirror, startled by the emotion in her voice. Her lips were pressed into a firm line, her eyes dark with anger.

This was a tricky one. Kids could be brutally cruel, and at their age, reason didn't always win out over instinct. He sighed inwardly. How do you teach children fairness in a world that often wasn't fair?

The next morning was the most painful in Alex's memory; every muscle in his body throbbed, every movement sent fresh waves of soreness rippling through him. He barely managed to swing his legs over the edge of the bed, wincing as he stood. There was no way he was making it to the gym today. Hell, he could hardly make it to the bathroom.

Still, he had responsibilities. Sarah had to get to school, and that meant dragging himself through the morning routine, no matter how much he wanted to collapse back into bed.

As he fumbled with her lunchbox, Sarah, ever the taskmaster, shot him a disapproving look.

'You're moving so slowly, Alex. We're going to be late!'

'Okay, okay, girl.' He groaned. 'This bloody exercise is killing me.'

Sarah gasped. 'Don't say words like that! Mum would be mad if she heard you.'

'Right, right. No complaints. Let's just get on with the job and get ma'am to school on time.'

'Now you're teasing me.' She huffed, crossing her arms.

'Sorry, sorry,' he said with an exaggerated bow. 'Let's hurry to the car and get you there in time for the school bell.'

Hurrying, however, was easier said than done. Every step felt like an ordeal, but he powered through, dropping Sarah off just as the first bell rang.

Back home, he collapsed into a chair. A major decision loomed. Should he go back to the gym? Han and Arun had both said consistency was key, but right now, all he wanted was to crawl under the covers and forget fitness existed.

Still, his pride was on the line. He wasn't about to quit at the first hurdle.

With a groan of determination, he forced himself to get ready. The idea of walking to the gym felt insurmountable, but he told himself he'd take it slow. Step by step, he made his way there, and surprisingly, by the time he arrived, the stiffness had eased a little.

'Hi, Alex! Great to see you,' Arun greeted him with his usual enthusiasm.

'I almost skipped,' Alex admitted, rolling his shoulders gingerly.

Arun chuckled. 'I wouldn't have blamed you. The soreness is normal, but as you keep going, it'll get easier. Today, let's focus on stretching to help with recovery.'

Stretching, it turned out, was its own kind of torture. Every position felt like medieval punishment, his body resisting at first, then grudgingly easing into each hold. The pain was sharp, but the longer he held the stretches, the more bearable it became.

'You watch,' Arun said encouragingly. 'Once you push through this first week, it'll be a breeze. You won't even need me around.'

Alex snorted. 'Doubt that.'

'Trust me. After these stretches, we'll do some light treadmill work and dumbbells—nothing too intense, just enough to activate muscles you didn't use yesterday.'

It was brutal, but by the end of the session, something surprising happened. Alex actually felt better. Not just physically, but mentally. The fog in his head had lifted, the fatigue replaced by a quiet sense of accomplishment.

'Thanks, Arun,' he said as he headed out. 'See you tomorrow.'

He walked home, finding himself looking forward to lunch with Laura.

~

Laura spotted him first. 'Hey, Alex! Over here!'

She'd already claimed a quiet corner table, perfect for a focused conversation. He assumed he'd arrive before her, but, of course, she was ahead of him, efficient as ever.

As he approached, he felt an odd rush—almost like an adolescent meeting a crush. He shoved the thought aside. This was business. He wanted to make this podcast project work, and Laura was the perfect partner.

Still, he noticed how radiant she looked—navy blue dress, bob cut framing her face, eyes bright with energy.

'Hi, Laura. Nice table. You ordered?'

'No. Let's do that first, then get down to business.'

They both ordered salads.

'I'm impressed, Alex. You're taking this weight management thing seriously.'

He grinned. 'Arun's been putting me through hell, but I'm sticking with it.'

'Good,' she said approvingly. Then, without missing a beat, she changed gears. 'So this university studio you've found—do we have to pay for it?'

He'd been growing more excited about the studio, picturing the two of them in the recording booth, diving into discussions, debating energy policies, editing the audio together.

'As of now, yes. And if we have to, I'll look after it. But it's possible we'll get it free.'

'How?'

'Thomas—my successor as head of economics—thinks that if the academic board likes our first episode, they might sponsor us.' He leaned back, pleased with the revelation.

But Laura's expression hardened. 'Hold on, Alex. I've said this before—I don't want this podcast turning into an academic debate on theory or ideology. If the university wants that, fine, but that's not what I'm here for. Are we agreed on that? Even if it means losing their support?'

Alex hesitated, then nodded. 'Okay, I agree.' He saw she needed to take the lead on this, to feel as invested as he was.

'Our target audience isn't academics,' she pressed on. 'It's everyday people—how they see and struggle with economic issues. Right?'

'Agreed. I told Thomas that. And he still thought the university might be interested.'

'That's their business,' she said firmly. 'Ours is making this useful to ordinary people. If the university likes it and helps distribute it, great. But that's secondary.'

He admired her conviction. She wasn't just saying the right things—she truly cared about making the podcast relevant.

Their salads arrived, and as they ate, Laura pulled out a notebook. 'I've been thinking about topics. We could start with the energy transition, like we discussed yesterday, but the more I thought about it, the more I think we should open with housing affordability. It's what's keeping young people up at night.'

'Hmmm. Maybe you're right,' Alex said.

'Governments talk a lot but do nothing,' she continued. 'Developers care about profits, not solutions. I want us to give community groups, unions, and charities practical ideas—things they can use to pressure politicians.'

'Makes sense.'

'Another possibility is the issue of productivity,' she added. 'Every time economists talk about it, they blame workers, as if labour is the only factor influencing productivity. But what about managerial efficiency? Innovation? Business investment?'

Alex nodded. 'I'm with you.'

'And let's not forget stagnant wages …'

On and on they went, selecting topics, debating angles, outlining objectives.

After an hour, Laura leaned back with a satisfied smile. 'This is good. I'm actually excited about this.'

Hearing that was more gratifying than Alex expected.

'So,' she said, 'when can I see this studio? I want to check it out before we record.'

'Maybe next week,' he said. 'This week, I'm tied up with the prosecutor's office. Preparing my testimony for the Hancock trial.'

Her brows lifted.

He explained. 'Apparently, I'm a key witness—one of Hancock's victims.'

Laura leaned forward, her expression serious. 'When's the case being heard?'

'The prosecutor wants it scheduled as soon as possible. The government is pushing hard to fast-track domestic violence cases. They want the message out there—loud and clear—that they're taking this seriously.' Alex sighed. 'Political pressure has a way of making the wheels of justice spin faster.'

'About time they did.' Laura frowned. 'Even so, this is fast. Hancock was charged just a couple of weeks ago, wasn't he?'

'Yes, but given his record, there's no need to drag it out. The prosecution says it'll be a straightforward case. He's been a repeat offender for years—numerous complaints, multiple police reports. The trial shouldn't last more than three days.'

'Is he out on bail? How's Sharon coping?' Laura asked.

'He wasn't allowed bail. The police have had it with him. But here's the interesting part—he didn't even ask for it. Turns out his debts have skyrocketed, and his creditors are breathing down his neck. Jail is probably safer for him than the outside world.'

Laura gave a short, humourless laugh. 'Poetic justice. But Sharon must be relieved?'

'She is. With Han's help, she got an emergency restraining order against him, plus a temporary exclusion order. Since she owns the house, Hancock has no legal claim to return. Not that he'd want to—not with those debt collectors waiting for him.'

'Good. Han's quite a force of nature.'

Alex nodded. 'She's been a godsend. She'll be one of the key witnesses, too. With luck, Hancock will be put away for a long time.'

Laura exhaled, shaking her head. 'I'm so relieved this is going forward. I've known Sharon a little over the years— Alice and Cassie go to the same school—but I had no idea what she was going through. I always sensed something was off, though. She's always seemed … anxious. On edge.'

'This whole issue of domestic violence seems to be cropping up everywhere lately,' Alex mused.

Laura's eyes flashed. 'Not lately,' she corrected. 'It's always been there, Alex. Women have been dealing with it forever. It's just that now, people like Han won't let it be ignored anymore. They shine a light on it, drag it into the public eye, and force action.' She paused, then added, 'Which reminds me—we should cover this on our podcast.'

Alex hesitated. 'But isn't this more of a social issue? Our focus is economics.'

Laura scoffed. 'The economic impact of domestic violence is enormous: lost income, stalled careers, homelessness, healthcare costs, financial dependence, intergenerational trauma. This isn't just a social issue—it's an economic crisis.'

She leaned in, her voice steady but charged. 'If I remember correctly, one study estimates that three-quarters of a million Australian women report domestic violence each year. The cost to the economy? Between twelve and fifteen billion dollars per year.'

Alex let out a sceptical laugh. 'That's a huge number, Laura. I have a hard time believing it. Where did you get those figures?'

Laura's expression darkened. 'Typical. The cynical male response.'

'Now, hold on,' Alex said, suddenly defensive. 'All I'm saying is that the economic impacts of what I consider a social and often highly personal issue cannot be anywhere near what you indicated.'

'I see your scepticism. Just a characteristic male reaction, and I'm not surprised. I tell you what, I'd like to make this the first subject of our podcast debate, namely, the impacts of domestic violence on the economy.' Laura's chin firmed.

'Come on, Laura. As I've said, I agree it's a huge social issue. More perhaps than I'd realised. But I doubt this should figure on the list of economic issues we debate, and certainly not as the first. Besides, I don't think those figures you quoted are credible.'

'Your scepticism, Alex, makes it all the more reason why it's ripe for our debate. Tell me, what solution does your neoliberalism, and its free markets and deregulation, offer to address a factor that impacts the economy so heavily? Nothing. You just shove it into the "social issue" basket and conveniently forget about it.'

'Hold on now, you're jumping to conclusions. It's not just—'

'Fifteen billion dollars, Alex.' Her voice grew sharp. 'That's the impact. And next week, when you're in court, you'll see it firsthand. Sharon will lose wages for taking time off. Han will miss work. You'll lose time, too. That's just three people. Multiply that by the hundreds of thousands of cases happening every year.'

She exhaled, trying to steady herself. 'Look, I'll send you the studies. If you find the sources are credible, do you agree to make this our first podcast topic?'

Alex hesitated. He saw how much this meant to her, how fiercely she believed in it. And maybe—just maybe—she had a point. 'All right, Laura. If your numbers hold up, we'll do it.'

Laura nodded, satisfied. They left the restaurant, but Alex found himself still thinking about domestic violence—an issue he'd never given much thought to before. Now, it wouldn't leave his mind.

SEVENTEEN

A week later, Alex drove Sarah to school with her brimming with curiosity, her questions coming like rapid fire.

'Will the judge be wearing one of those wigs like they do on TV?'

Alex smiled. 'No, and there won't be a judge. It'll be a magistrate.'

'What's a magistrate?'

'Well, a magistrate is like a judge, but—'

'Then why don't they just call him or her a judge?'

He chuckled at her persistence. 'Sarah, there are different levels of courts in Australia. The Magistrates' Court is the lowest one. Judges preside over higher courts. And yes, sometimes in those courts, they do wear wigs.'

Sarah considered this, then fired off another question. 'Will they bring Mr Hancock in chains?'

Alex laughed outright. 'They don't use chains anymore, sweetheart.'

'But what if Mr Hancock gets drunk and tries to hit the

judge? Like he did to you and Mrs Hancock?'

'He won't be drunk, Sarah. He's been in prison since that night. The magistrate refused him bail.'

'What's bail?'

Alex took a breath, glancing at her eager face. 'Bail is when a magistrate allows someone accused of a crime to stay free until their trial.'

'What's a trial?'

'A trial is when the court hears evidence to decide whether someone is guilty of a crime.'

Sarah frowned. 'But everyone already knows Mr Hancock is bad. Why can't they just put him in prison forever? He hit you and Mrs Hancock! And he tried to hit Han, too! He often hits Cassie as well. He is a bad, bad man.' Her small face was fierce, her conviction unwavering.

Alex marvelled at how she was getting a crash course on the justice system. But they were out of time—the car had pulled up in front of the school gates.

She stepped out of the car reluctantly, still brimming with questions. 'You'll be here to pick me up at three thirty, right?'

Alex saw the worry in her eyes and softened. 'Of course, dear. Don't worry.' He watched as she disappeared into the school building, then let out a slow breath.

But he, too, was uneasy.

He was stepping into unfamiliar territory. Lately, there'd been too many unknowns for his liking. He'd never testified in court before, never stood in a witness box to be cross-examined. The prosecution lawyer had spent the past week preparing him, assuring him that everything would be fine. And yet, a knot tightened in his stomach at the thought of facing Hancock again.

Then his thoughts turned to Sharon. If he was nervous,

he imagined how she was feeling.

~

Alex walked up the few steps from the street to the entrance of the court. His hands were clammy, and his heart beat faster than usual. He'd never set foot in a court before.

The room was solemn and imposing, with high ceilings, polished floors, and rows of wooden benches. A few people sat on the audience benches. He'd been told theirs was the first case to be heard that day.

He walked to the front row, passing what he thought was a group of local news reporters with their notepads and iPhones. This concerned him. The last thing he wanted was for Hancock's crash into his house to become a news item. It was already the talk of the local precinct in which he lived.

A raised desk at the front of the room dominated the scene. The magistrate's, he assumed. Two flags, the Australian and the Aboriginal one, flanked it. Next in the row, facing the magistrate, were two desks, one on the left and the other on the right of the centre aisle. The lawyers, he gathered.

Then he spied the lawyer from the prosecutor's office, who'd been preparing him for the trial. She sat at the desk on the left side of the room. Behind her desk sat Sharon and Han on the first row of benches. On the right-hand side, he spied Adam Hancock, who sat in the defence section of the dock. Today, he was well dressed and staring straight in front, not making eye contact with anyone. Two stern-looking policemen stood behind him.

Nearer to the magistrate's raised podium was a box placed with the magistrate to its left and the audience to its right. The witness box, he assumed.

Further down the left side of the room, on the first bench behind the prosecution, sat Sergeant Larkin and Officer Nelson. They nodded at him. He nodded back.

Han saw him and gave him a wave. She whispered to the lawyer, who immediately rose and guided Alex to his seat. He smiled at Sharon and Han as he took his seat next to them. Sharon looked nervous, her eyes blinking rapidly and her hands held tight together. Han was a reassuring presence, as usual, her arm wrapped protectively around Sharon.

The call of an officious-looking man seated at a slightly lower level than the magistrate cut the low murmur of conversation sharply—the bailiff, Alex assumed. His voice echoed through the room, calling the court to order.

A moment later, the doors swung open, and in walked the magistrate. She was a senior woman, her hair streaked with silver, her features sharp and unwavering, and her posture regal in flowing black robes. Her presence commanded the room immediately. She took her seat, and the echo of the gavel striking down reverberated with authority, silencing the whispers. The business of the day was about to begin.

The clerk beside the bailiff read aloud the charges with clinical precision. Three charges. An assault on Mrs Sharon Hancock in her own home. A home invasion at Professor Alex Bobbins' residence. A second assault on him. The date of each occurrence followed, delivered with an emotionless tone, but Alex felt the weight of those words. The events, now officially in motion, were a blur of emotion and reality, but hearing them spoken out loud made them all too real.

The magistrate addressed the court in a short but direct introduction. Her voice was steady with an unmistakable firmness. She emphasised that she would weigh all evidence impartially, uncover the truth, and ensure a fair judgement was reached. The room felt heavier, the air thickened with the seriousness of the moment. She then turned her gaze towards the press seated in the back.

'I caution the members of the press present,' she announced with unwavering gaze, 'that this is a case of domestic violence. As such, the names of both the victim and the perpetrator are to remain confidential. Any information that could lead to identification is to be suppressed. Additionally, no personal details—such as occupation or address—are to be reported. Witnesses are not to be interviewed without the court's express permission.'

A ripple of murmurs spread through the press. Some appeared disgruntled, their heads shaking in silent protest, but the magistrate's gaze held firm, silencing any objections.

Alex let out a breath he hadn't realised he was holding. The press was now aware of his presence in the courtroom, and the thought of them following him—of the story being dragged into the public eye—made his stomach tighten. He feared what they might do with his testimony, how they might invade his privacy. He had no desire to see his home, his life, splashed across the papers.

Once the magistrate had finished addressing the press, she gestured for the prosecution to begin. The prosecutor rose, her demeanour as sharp as her voice. She outlined the events leading to Adam Hancock's arrest, presenting the charges with meticulous detail.

The prosecution's words filled the air, and Alex's mind raced. He'd lived through the events, but hearing them described with such chilling clarity made everything feel even more real, more suffocating.

The magistrate then invited the defence to enter a plea of guilty or not guilty.

Alex waited expectantly. The defence lawyer rose. Alex wondered if Hancock had money to hire the lawyer or if the lawyer was offered to Hancock by the state. The defence lawyer stated that his client pleaded not guilty to the three charges. He would show that Mr Hancock had suffered severe abuse as a child. This had created post-traumatic stress disorder as well as severe ADHD in Mr Hancock. This, in turn, affected his ability to get and maintain a job.

The lawyer went on to explain that the occasional impulsive and violent behaviour Mr Hancock sometimes exhibited was entirely involuntary and simply manifestations of his chronic mental illness. Consequently, he was unable to keep a job due to such illness and resorted to gambling, from time to time, to help the family's finances. The defence maintained that Mr Hancock had every right to take his wife back to his house from Professor Bobbins' house on the date mentioned, that she was being forcibly kept there by Professor Bobbins, and that the professor had attacked Mr Hancock, who had then resorted to self-defence.

Alex was astounded when he heard the case for the defence. He leaned over to the prosecution lawyer to protest what he saw as blatant lies. The lawyer shushed him, suggesting he keep calm. There would be an opportunity to refute this version of events.

The prosecution was then invited to bring on her witnesses.

The prosecution began by bringing on Sergeant Larkin, followed by Officer Nelson. With their help, she established the facts of the case, the sequence of events, the injuries that they had both witnessed on Sharon and Alex. It was authoritative testimony, given confidently by officers who obviously were familiar with court proceedings and giving testimony before.

The defence was given the opportunity of cross-examination. But aside from a few clarifications, the defence was unable to poke any holes in the police account of events.

The prosecution next called Sharon Hancock to the witness box. She approached it nervously, biting her lower lip, clutching her handbag tightly, and looking back at Han for reassurance. After she'd taken her oath, the prosecution lawyer began questioning her. The prosecution handled her gently, lobbing questions accompanied with assurances that she takes her time to respond. It was distressing to hear all she had gone through. It was also obvious she was still emotionally distressed. Alex knew part of her story. But as she now described it in even more detail, he was astounded by how a woman coped as patiently as she had done for so long.

'How often did Mr Hancock assault you?' the prosecution lawyer asked.

'Almost every day.'

'What was the nature of the assaults?'

'Adam would return to the house each evening, always drunk. He would demand food immediately. If the food hadn't been prepared, he'd be upset and hit me on my body. He usually tried to avoid hitting my face so that no visible marks were seen by anybody the next day.'

'But when you arrived at Professor Bobbins' house on the day in question, he found you with a bleeding nose and a large bruise on your jaw. So this was not typical?'

'On the days when he was either very drunk or very angry, he seemed to forget to take care where he hit me. On that day, he was both very drunk and very angry.'

'Why was he so angry?'

'It was payday. I earn about two thousand dollars each fortnight. He knows the day I'm paid and demands that I give him half of that amount.'

'So a thousand dollars each fortnight of the two thousand you earn?'

'Yes. That's right.'

'Do you give it to him?'

'I have no choice. He beats me if I don't. And if I still refuse, he then threatens to beat Cassie as well. I simply cannot tolerate that.'

'So if you gave half your salary to him that day, why was he still so angry, and why did he beat you so badly?'

'That day, he wanted more. And I couldn't give it to him.'

'Why did he want more?'

'He said he had to pay his debtors a minimum amount, or his life was at stake.'

'Did you give him what he wanted?'

'No.'

'Why?'

'I must manage the family's needs on half my salary, which is already basic. I was unwilling to give him more than the one thousand dollars. I need to feed my daughter well. She's growing.'

'You manage the family's needs on half your salary?'

'Yes.'

'Does Mr Hancock do any work to assist in the family's expenses?'

'He used to work when we married eight years ago. But he lost his job within a year of our marriage and has never worked since.'

'Do you know who these debtors are?'

'No. He would never tell me. All he wanted was the money.'

'How did he incur these debts?'

'He once told me he gambled on horses. But in general, he doesn't tell me anything about his gambling. He's very secretive.'

'Do you know how much he was indebted for?'

'No. But I think his repayments are in arrears and now amount to something substantial. He's been getting increasingly nervous about his debtors.'

'So you live in fear of threats and beatings every day?'

'Not just me. My little daughter Cassie as well. Life has become impossible. I feel like committing suicide, but my little girl will have no one to look after her. I must live and cope with him for her sake.' She broke into deep sobs.

The prosecution lawyer waited for her to calm down. 'Why do you not divorce Mr Hancock if life with him is so difficult?'

'We live in my house. The one I've inherited from my parents. I want to leave it to my daughter. If I file for divorce, it's possible I'll have to sell the house and give him half the proceeds. I'm not willing to do that. Cassie deserves her full inheritance.'

Alex had been intently listening and glancing at Adam Hancock from time to time. He saw that Hancock was increasingly uncomfortable with Sharon's revelations of their personal life details. While he stoically continued to stare in front of him, his hands grew restless; his left eye blinked furiously. He began perspiring, frequently wiping his forehead with tissues. The absence of any alcohol support must also have been telling.

Sharon's was a damning account of Hancock's multitude of transgressions as a husband and father. Alex looked around, noting everyone's stern faces; he saw no sympathy for Hancock anywhere in the courtroom.

The prosecution's questions continued, further detailing Hancock's abuse and how he traded his family's finances and happiness to feed his alcoholism and gambling.

Once the prosecution lawyer finished questioning Sharon, the magistrate invited the defence lawyer to cross-examine her. Alex saw fear in Sharon's eyes, knowing she would now be the target of an attack.

'How long have you been married to Mr Hancock, Mrs Hancock?'

'Eight years and two months.'

'Have there been times when Mr Hancock was a loving husband and kind to you?'

Sharon hesitated. 'Yes, there were times in the past,' she admitted, 'especially in our early years of marriage. He used to be charming then. But not now.'

'So why has he changed since then?'

'I don't know. I do know that he now drinks heavily, and this always makes him violent.'

'Was he like this when you married?'

'No.'

'Then something has happened for him to have become like you claim he is now.'

'Yes.'

'Do you criticise him daily for not having a job?'

'I do ask him to try to get one, since my income is barely adequate to keep us going. And keeping up with his debt repayments has become impossible.'

'So you've been criticising and harassing him on this issue all the time?'

The prosecution lawyer rose. 'Objection, Your Honour. The defence is insinuating behaviour on the part of the defendant.'

'Sustained,' the magistrate declared. 'The defence is warned not to imply behaviour on the part of the witness.'

'How often do you ask Mr Hancock to get a job?'

'I only do so when he asks for money for his gambling,' Sharon answered defensively, colour rising to her cheeks.

'Do you realise that he gambles to try to get money for the family?'

'I don't think so. In any case, he never gives me money if he has won any.'

'So you don't support him when he tries to get money for the household?'

'Sir, I have no more money to give. Please understand this. I am on a little more than a minimum wage, and I have to look after the whole family. As it is, I give him half of that wage.'

'So, instead, you badger him to get a job. You raise your voice in anger when you demand why he doesn't get a job, right?'

Sharon looked uncertain. Her face then morphed into a mix of defiance, anger, and resentment. She hesitated in her response.

'Do you or do you not?' demanded the defence lawyer.

'Perhaps, sometimes,' she admitted in a low voice, her eyes darting to the prosecution lawyer, hoping for some intervention.

'Do you realise that, with his mental illness, Mr Hancock is in a very fragile state of mind?'

'I don't know what this mental illness is you're talking about ...' Sharon's anger and impatience surfaced. Her eyes narrowed, and she bit her lip in an attempt to stay in control.

'Do you know, Mrs Hancock, that Mr Hancock suffers from severe post-traumatic stress disorder?'

'I don't know what that is,' Sharon replied, genuinely puzzled by the term.

The defence looked at the magistrate triumphantly, then continued, 'Mrs Hancock, do you realise that you should be Mr Hancock's primary emotional support for the severe mental illness he suffers from? Instead, we find that you do not even care to understand what this mental illness is.'

Sharon shook her head vigorously, shrugging her shoulders and opening her hands in an appeal to someone to come to her defence against the unfair accusations.

The defence's cross-examination continued in the same vein, trying in various ways to paint Sharon as an unfeeling, unsupportive partner, and implying that Hancock was the actual victim here.

Alex wasn't convinced the defence had achieved this objective. Sharon's account of Hancock's ongoing violence had been detailed and persuasive. Her pain came across patently; he was certain that it'd touched the heartstrings of those listening.

At the end of the cross-examination, the magistrate signalled Sharon could return to her seat. She did so, relief written on her face.

Then it was Alex's turn. He approached the witness box more nervously than when he'd entered the courthouse. An empty feeling gnawed at the pit of his stomach. His hands were clammy again, and trembling. He calmed himself, deciding it was now up to him to confirm what a cad Hancock was. He gave his oath, and the prosecution began her questions.

The defence then took the floor for cross-examination. Alex felt more confident and in control. But he held the edge of the witness box tightly to give himself reassurance.

The defence lawyer looked Alex up and down. Alex

thought he saw a sneer in his eyes. He prepared himself mentally for the onslaught that he knew would come.

'Professor Bobbins, I understand Mrs Hancock is a frequent visitor to your house. Is that correct?'

The question was completely unexpected.

Alex cleared his throat and answered. 'She did come regularly to drop off her child, Cassie, during the recent school holidays. Her child is a close friend of my grandchild. They played together every day during those holidays.'

'Is it correct to say that you have become her confidante?'

'I don't know what you mean, sir.' Alex wondered where this was leading.

'Are you not a close friend of hers, in whom she regularly confides her problems and with whom she enjoys spending time?'

Alex was appalled by what the defence lawyer was implying. His face reddened, and his lips tightened. 'Sir, if your sick and dirty little mind is in any way implying that Mrs Hancock and I are in some kind of relationship, let me remind you, I'm old enough to be her father and old enough to be yours as well.'

'Professor,' the magistrate intervened, 'please control yourself. Just answer the question.'

Alex had lost his nervousness. He was apoplectic. 'Your Honour, I have not come here to be insulted by this little punk.'

'Professor, please. I remind you, it's your duty to simply answer the question.'

Alex made an effort to bring his emotions under control. He shut his eyes. Then, after a moment, he opened them, and he went on. 'On one occasion, and only ONE, about a month and a half ago, did Mrs Hancock and I have a personal conversation. She came to ask me if she could leave her child at my house to play with my grandkid. The kids were on holidays, and she couldn't afford the childcare fees. She is the only breadwinner for the family, and her wages struggle to cover school childcare in addition to all their basic expenses. I asked why her husband didn't work and earn to help. She replied he was a drunk and an abuser. Does that answer make you any happier, sir?'

The magistrate had a slight smile.

The defence lawyer continued. 'So if Mrs Hancock felt confident enough to share this private family detail with you, does this not mean you two have been close for some time now? After all, you both live a few houses apart on the same street?'

'I have known Mrs Hancock's parents for a long time. I knew her from when she was growing up in the neighbourhood. We had a nodding acquaintance. So let me repeat, for your benefit, the first time she entered my house was a month and a half ago, and it was with the request I have just described.'

'Are you saying, Professor, that each time Mrs Hancock dropped and picked up her child, except for the one occasion, she didn't spend time with you in conversation and sharing confidences?'

'That is correct,' Alex answered. 'And if you can prove otherwise, I shall gladly reward you with an ice cream after the court session.'

There was laughter among the audience. The magistrate frowned. The defence lawyer looked uncomfortable. But Alex had made his point.

The defence lawyer continued his cross-examination. 'Professor, did you not insult Mr Hancock when he showed up at your front door, seeking his wife?'

Alex tried to remember. He wanted to recount the event accurately. 'I was surprised to see Mr Hancock at my front door. He was shabbily dressed and very obviously drunk. I told him quite bluntly that his wife, who was in my house at the time and in the company of Ms Ghosh and the children, didn't want to see him,' Alex answered after some thought.

'But you didn't first ask Mrs Hancock if she wanted to see her husband, who had come to find her, out of concern for her.'

'You're living in another universe, my friend,' Alex replied, getting irritated again. *Take control,* he quietly reminded himself. Taking a deep breath, he continued, 'May I remind you, sir, that Mrs Hancock had just arrived at my house, bleeding and bruised, complaining about being physically attacked by Mr Hancock? She came asking for refuge. Would you, in your right mind, have allowed Mr Hancock to enter?'

The cross-examination went on. Alex grew in confidence as he fielded the defence's questions. At the end, when he stepped down from the witness box, the prosecution lawyer, Sharon and Han, smiled and nodded approvingly. *I did my best for Sharon,* he thought, feeling vindicated.

~

'So did the magistrate then put Mr Hancock in chains?' Sarah asked in an eager voice as he debriefed her in the car on the way home that afternoon.

'Not so fast, Sarah. We have a second day of hearing at the court. They still have other witnesses and experts to testify. Then lawyers for the prosecution and defence will make their final closing arguments. Only then will the magistrate decide.'

'But we all saw what Mr Hancock did on that day. Why is it taking so long for the magistrate to decide?'

'Our justice system requires that Mr Hancock is also allowed to defend himself properly, Sarah,' he explained patiently. 'Tomorrow, it's his turn to bring witnesses.'

'Does that mean you have to go back again tomorrow?' Sarah didn't seem very happy with the idea.

'Yes, dear. But I'm hoping the court hearing will be finished by tomorrow, and the magistrate will give her decision.'

'I hope he'll be sent to prison,' Sarah said. 'I'm worried about Cassie. She and her mum don't want Mr Hancock back. I hope he gets sent to prison forever and ever.'

'I'm not sure for how long, Sarah. But I think he will go to prison if the magistrate is fair. We'll see.'

'I'll become a magistrate and be much stricter with men like Mr Hancock.'

'That's a good idea. But for that, you're going to have to study hard, dear.'

EIGHTEEN

That evening, after Sarah had gone to bed, Alex turned his focus to the research Laura had sent him about the economic impacts of domestic violence. She seemed intent on making it the first topic of their podcast. Alex wasn't so sure. He doubted the economic toll was significant enough to be considered an issue of economic importance. It was undeniably a major social concern, but he needed to handle the debate with Laura carefully. For that, he needed to have his facts straight.

The first source Laura cited was a report from the Department of Social Services of the Australian Government. As he read, his eyes widened in disbelief. What she'd said was true—this was an officially published report. It had to be accurate.

He continued reading, his shock deepening. The cost of domestic violence to the Australian economy in the previous year was estimated at $15.6 billion. This was more than the government's $11 billion stimulus package and more than three-quarters of the budget allocation for the Building Australia Fund.

Still sceptical, Alex delved deeper into the cost breakdown of that $15.6 billion. The report detailed both direct and indirect costs. Among the direct costs, some were immediately obvious: lost productivity when victims missed work, the wages they lost, and the direct healthcare costs. He suspected that Sharon hadn't sought mental health care, and most of her injuries had been treated at home. But there were others for whom state healthcare was crucial. Then there were the costs Alex himself was experiencing—the costs of bringing perpetrators like Adam Hancock to justice. The criminal justice system, the witnesses, and the victim all incurred costs.

The indirect costs were just as staggering: poverty, homelessness, premature mortality, and reduced tax revenue when victims couldn't earn their full wages. Social isolation and the gradual erosion of the social fabric were equally troubling.

The question that now haunted him was how widespread domestic violence must be to trigger such a report and generate these massive estimated costs. His research led him to a report from The Australian Institute of Health and Welfare, which found that more than one in four women—27%—experienced domestic violence and abuse. On average, one woman a week was murdered by her current or former partner.

The numbers staggered him. He realised he'd lived in a bubble—his home, the university, and a few close friends. Before the Hancocks, he'd never directly encountered domestic violence. He'd read about it in the papers occasionally, but hadn't realised how widespread it was. People like him often remained blissfully unaware of the violent conflicts happening behind closed doors, sometimes literally next door. These conflicts didn't just impose punishing costs on the victims;

they also affected the children involved and their futures, eroding social peace and stability over time.

That night, Alex went to bed troubled by something deeply wrong with Australian society. Why were men so often violent? Was it biology—perhaps high testosterone levels? He would need to check if non-violent men also had high testosterone or if there were violent men with low levels. Surely, someone had studied this?

Or was it something about the way Australian society raised its boys? He thought of Sarah and her aversion to boys because of their aggression. Or was it simply cultural? He thought of the violent nature of sports like rugby and Australian football, which promoted aggression so openly.

Whatever the reason, the statistics on domestic violence and its economic impact were astonishing. Yet policymakers seemed to do little about it. The image of Sharon Hancock, bleeding, bruised, and sobbing as she entered his home, flashed before him. What a miserable life she'd endured. If it weren't for Sarah's playgroup, he would never have known. Yet he lived just a few doors away, and on the surface, everything seemed perfectly normal.

The disturbing thoughts churned in his mind. He couldn't sleep. Finally, he got up, went back to his computer, and decided to dig deeper into the issue—socially and economically.

~

The next day, Alex entered the court in a calmer state of mind. His testimony was over, and his active role in the case was done. But the exhaustion from a sleepless night still lingered. His mind remained consumed by the issue of domestic violence and its economic impact. He was eager to see what the magistrate's decision would be by the end of the day, hoping for a substantial prison sentence for Hancock, for Sharon's sake.

He greeted Sharon and Han warmly. His empathy for women and their struggles had grown significantly over the past few days. Sharon seemed calmer today.

The defence called its first witness: a bespectacled grey-haired man who stepped into the witness box with an air of solemnity. He adjusted his spectacles and cleared his throat after taking his oath.

'Dr Sondheim, what is your area of expertise?' the defence lawyer asked.

'I'm a psychiatrist with over twenty years of experience treating patients with childhood trauma and other mental health issues,' Dr Sondheim replied.

'Can you explain how childhood trauma affects adult behaviour?'

'Childhood trauma can profoundly impact adult behaviour. It can lead to mental health problems, such as PTSD, depression, and anxiety. These conditions can make it difficult for individuals to manage their emotions and behaviours in a healthy way.'

'And how does childhood trauma specifically lead to violent behaviour in men?'

'Trauma can disrupt the development of brain regions like the prefrontal cortex, which controls impulse regulation and emotional responses. This makes it harder for men who've experienced trauma to manage their anger and aggression, often leading them to lash out violently in response to perceived threats or stress.'

The witness paused, cleared his throat, and continued, 'Childhood trauma can also affect the amygdala, the part of the brain responsible for processing fear and aggression. An overactive amygdala leads to heightened reactions to perceived threats. Additionally, trauma can alter the balance of hormones and neurotransmitters in the brain, such as serotonin, which plays a role in mood regulation. Low serotonin levels are linked to a higher likelihood of violent behaviour.'

'Thank you, Dr Sondheim. Can you now explain, in simpler terms, how childhood trauma leads to what we term "violent episodes" in adults?'

'Certainly. In short, men who've experienced childhood trauma may struggle with impulsivity and have difficulty thinking before acting. They're also more likely to overreact to anger or frustration from others. This increases the risk of violent outbursts, even when the intent isn't there. Moreover, such men are more prone to violence because of an inability to control their emotions, which stems from their traumatic pasts.'

He cleared his throat, then continued, 'Men who have experienced childhood trauma are also more likely to abuse drugs and alcohol. Substance abuse can impair judgement and increase the risk of violent behaviour.'

'In your professional opinion, Dr Sondheim, can childhood trauma explain Mr Hancock's violent behaviour as described earlier?'

'It can.'

'Are there specific circumstances that can trigger this post-traumatic stress and lead to violent behaviour in Mr Hancock?'

Dr Sondheim paused thoughtfully. 'Research suggests that when an individual is accused, particularly in an angry manner, it can act as a trigger for the trauma, leading to violent responses.'

'So if the defendant's wife was persistently and angrily confronting him,' the defence suggested, 'could this provoke violent reactions?'

'Yes, it can.'

Alex recognised where the defence was headed. The lawyer had failed to undermine the testimonies from Sharon, Han, and him regarding the events of that day. Now he was attempting to introduce expert medical testimony to present a mitigating explanation that could potentially reduce the inevitable sentence.

The magistrate nodded and invited the prosecution to cross-examine the witness.

'Dr Sondheim, you've testified that childhood trauma can account for violent behaviour in Mr Hancock. However, is it not true that many men who have experienced childhood trauma do not exhibit violent behaviour?'

'Yes, that's correct. Not all men with a history of childhood trauma engage in violent behaviour. However, men with such histories are statistically at a higher risk of exhibiting violent tendencies.'

'So are you implying that Mr Hancock is not responsible for his actions because of his childhood trauma?'

'No, I'm not saying that,' Dr Sondheim clarified. 'What I'm stating is that childhood trauma may explain the behaviour, but it does not absolve him of responsibility.'

'Good,' the prosecutor responded, 'so you're confirming that, if he chooses to, Mr Hancock can indeed control his violent reactions?'

'Possibly,' Dr Sondheim replied cautiously. 'But I can't say for certain, since Mr Hancock is not my patient.'

'Mr Hancock appears to lead a relatively normal life outside of his domestic environment, doesn't he?' the prosecutor continued. 'We haven't heard any reports of violent behaviour in other contexts, have we?'

Dr Sondheim shrugged. 'I don't have sufficient information to comment on that.'

The prosecution turned towards the magistrate. 'Your Honour, it seems from the available information that Mr Hancock can control his emotions in other areas of his life. Yet in his domestic relationship, he seems unable to do so. It's almost as if the alleged childhood trauma conveniently resurfaces during certain times.'

A murmur spread through the courtroom.

The magistrate raised her hand for silence. Dr Sondheim looked distinctly uneasy.

'You've heard the testimony about Mr Hancock's drunken and violent behaviour at home,' the prosecutor said. 'Would you agree that, based on your own testimony, such behaviour is inflicting childhood trauma on his seven-year-old daughter, Cassie?'

Dr Sondheim hesitated, clearly caught off guard by the question. Alex nodded to himself, impressed by the prosecutor's strategy.

'I would need to examine the specific details of Mr Hancock's behaviour in his home environment before I make such a determination,' Dr Sondheim said carefully.

'But if such behaviour is occurring,' the prosecutor pressed, 'would it not create conditions for childhood trauma in Mr Hancock's daughter?'

Dr Sondheim paused before responding, clearly uncomfortable. 'All I can say, without more detailed information, is … perhaps.'

'Thank you, Dr Sondheim. No further questions, Your Honour.'

The defence proceeded to present more evidence through witnesses, attempting to establish Mr Hancock's traumatic childhood as the cause of his PTSD and ADHD behaviours. By lunchtime, the defence had rested its case.

The magistrate then informed the court that she would need time to consider the evidence and would deliver her verdict the following Monday morning at 10:00 am. The court was dismissed.

On his way out of the building, Alex caught sight of Adam Hancock deep in conversation with his defence lawyer. Alex waited, hoping for some form of eye contact, but Adam deliberately looked away.

Alex, Sharon, and Han made their way to a nearby café, discussing the day's proceedings.

Han seemed the most confident. 'I don't see how the magistrate can come to any conclusion other than guilty. The defence couldn't disprove the facts—Sharon's bruises, the assault on you, Alex, and the home invasion. I think they've accepted a guilty verdict is inevitable, and now they're just focused on mitigating the sentence.'

Alex nodded, agreeing with Han. Sharon, however, remained tense and anxious.

Finally, Alex asked the question that had been on his mind. 'Sharon, I know you've missed work these last couple of days. Would you like some help with money until you get back on your feet?'

Sharon's eyes welled up with tears. 'Thank you, Professor. You've already been so kind to me. But I'll be fine. I'm lucky I don't have a mortgage, and the school helps with Cassie's meals. We're managing, somehow. What worries me now is if they let Adam go free.'

Alex placed a reassuring hand on her arm. 'Sharon, I

agree with Han. We'll have a verdict on Monday, and I'm confident he'll be sent to prison. I don't know for how long, but you'll be free of him for a while. Let's wait for Monday and talk then.'

NINETEEN

It was a quiet Saturday morning, the start of the weekend.

'Alex, how many more days until Mum comes home?' Sarah asked, her eyes wide with anticipation.

During Kay's first month away, she'd called regularly, but as her travel schedule in the provinces of Papua New Guinea grew more demanding, her calls grew less frequent. The poor phone connections didn't help. Sarah waited eagerly for each call, a feeling of longing building up as the days passed. With the time for her mother's return approaching, Alex sensed her anticipation bubbling over. He paused for a moment, reflecting on the deep, irreplaceable bond between mother and child.

'Two more weeks, Sarah,' Alex replied gently. 'Now, tell me, have you been enjoying your time here with me?'

'Loved it, Alex. Can I come for sleepovers after Mum gets back?'

Alex chuckled, pleased by the thought. 'Of course. Why not? I've got an idea. How about you start making a special welcome-back card for your mum?'

'Yes! I'll start today!' Sarah said, her face lighting up. Then her curiosity shifted. 'Alex, when's Mr Hancock going to prison? Everyone at school's been asking Cassie, but she doesn't know.'

A pang of sympathy struck Alex. It was deeply unfair that someone so young, like Cassie, had to bear such a heavy burden. 'I think the magistrate will give us the verdict on Monday.'

'And then will Mr Hancock go to prison?'

'If the verdict is guilty, and the magistrate sentences him to prison, yes, he will. We'll know soon enough. Personally, I do think he'll be found guilty. In my view, he certainly should be.'

Sarah pondered this for a moment before asking, 'But why does Mr Hancock beat Mrs Hancock and people like you, Alex? It's like the boys in my school, always wanting to fight.'

Alex hesitated, searching for the right words. 'I've been wondering about that too, Sarah. I'm not sure I have the answer yet.'

'It's like what we see on TV,' Sarah continued thoughtfully. 'Men are always fighting and hurting people. Why do they do that?'

Alex smiled gently, brushing a lock of hair from Sarah's face. 'I'll tell you when I find the answer, sweetheart. But for now, let's think about what we can do this weekend. We haven't planned anything yet. You choose—zoo, aquarium, or maybe a boat ride down the Yarra River?'

Sarah bit her lip, considering the options. 'I'd love to go on a boat ride. I've never been on a boat. Mum's taken me to the zoo a lot, and once to the aquarium.'

'All right then, we're off to the river.'

'Can I invite Alice and Cassie too?' Sarah asked, her excitement growing.

'If their mums say it's okay, sure,' Alex replied with a grin.

'Yippee! Alex, you're the best grandad I could have!'

Alex chuckled. 'Well, I'm your only one, I think. So you'd better make the most of it, girl. Let's call Alice's mum, June, and Sharon to see if they can come.'

Sarah's enthusiasm bubbled over. 'Maybe we can go to the aquarium on Sunday?'

She looked almost guilty for suggesting another outing, but Alex, with a hug, reassured her. 'Sure, why not? I only have two weeks left with you, and I'll miss you when you're gone.'

Alex soon found himself as excited about the trip to the river as the girls. June couldn't make it, but suggested that Laura accompany Alice as her chaperone. Sharon, busy catching up on hours lost during the court hearings, was grateful to Alex for looking after Cassie over the weekend.

The plan was to meet at Southgate Mall, right on the Southbank, familiar ground for Alex. His daily commute to the university took him over the river, and he often passed by Southgate on his way home, sometimes stopping to grab a meal if he hadn't eaten at the university.

~

Laura drove towards the Yarra River with Alice sitting quietly in the back. 'Are you excited about today's outing, Alice?'

'Yes, Laura, yes! It'll be fun to be with my friends on the boat. I've never been to a river or been on a boat before. Have you?'

'I've been to the Yarra River, but like you, Alice, I've never been on a boat ride. It should be fun.' Laura smiled.

'Alex is fun too,' Alice added brightly. 'Since he's been looking after Sarah, we've had the best time ever!'

Laura smiled warmly. 'You should tell him that sometime, Alice. He'll love to hear it.'

While driving, Laura reflected on Alice's words. Alex was the catalyst that brought this group of kids and their families together. They all seemed to click, to gel, naturally supporting each other in ways she hadn't anticipated. The events surrounding the Hancocks had drawn them even closer. Laura suspected that Alex didn't realise the positive role he was playing in all their lives, a quiet force holding them together.

'Sarah says her mum will be back in two weeks,' Laura said thoughtfully. 'I hope we can still have these outings when she's back, but we'll have to make sure Alex still joins us.'

Alice nodded. 'Yes, please.'

Laura, reflecting on their shared bond, realised that she'd come to like Alex more than she'd expected. When they first met, he'd been immersed in his world of economics, struggling to relate to the world of children. But then she'd watched, amazed, as Sarah had slowly coaxed him out of his academic cocoon. Now he was a happy, jolly grandfather who'd earned the affection of those around him.

She was glad to have met him, albeit by chance, that time on the playfield. While she disagreed with some of his economic views, she admired his willingness to listen to opposing perspectives. Men like him—intellectual, yet open-minded—were rare.

She was also looking forward to their podcast project. Initially hesitant, Laura had warmed to the idea, seeing its potential to demystify complex economic theories for ordinary people. It was intellectually stimulating, and challenging Alex's neoliberal stance required her to reconsider her own views. Unexpectedly, she'd grown fond of their collaboration, both professionally and personally. Beneath his serious exterior, Alex was a kind soul, and Laura found herself warming to him more and more.

Finally, they arrived at the Southgate Mall's car park and stepped onto the promenade.

Alice squealed in excitement. 'Yippee, it's the river, and there's Alex with Sarah and Cassie!'

Alex and the two girls stood about fifty metres away, and Alice dashed off like a rocket to meet up with her friends. The children greeted each other with hugs, their eyes wide with wonder as they ran to the guardrail to peer out at the boats. Laura smiled, sharing in their excitement. It had been a while since she had visited the riverbank, though she often passed by it in her car. There was something different about seeing it from the ground, right next to the water.

The morning was bright, the sun shining down on the river, not a cloud in the sky. It felt wonderful to be out in the open air on the river's edge. A gentle breeze, cool and refreshing, stirred the air, adding to the beauty of the day. The river shimmered, which was rare for the Yarra. Its usually muddy waters were a shining blue today, inviting them for a boat ride.

Alex seemed unusually relaxed that morning. He wore a brightly coloured shirt—a striking departure from his usual muted attire. He also looked fitter, leaner, a result of his new exercise routine, she suspected. Not by much, but enough to suggest he was on the right track. Laura noticed the difference and made a mental note to ask him—on another day— whether he liked his new exercise regime, as well as how his court testimony had gone and how Sharon was holding up. But today was for the kids.

'Alex, Laura, are we going in this long, big boat or one of the small ones?'

Several small boats bobbed on the river, each carrying between two and six passengers. Along the bank, near where they stood, a couple of large glass-roofed tourist boats were waiting to take on crowds of sightseers.

Alex glanced at Laura, deferring to her.

'You seem to know more about this than I do, Alex. You choose,' she said, deciding she'd simply go with the flow today.

Alex turned to the kids. 'Look, kiddos, the big boat takes lots of tourists at one go, and I can't promise you a window seat. But if we walk down to that little wharf'—he pointed to a dock about two hundred metres away—'we can hire a smaller boat just for us. That way, everyone gets a window seat. What do you say?'

The vote was unanimous—small boat, no question.

They strolled towards the wharf near Queensbridge Street, and Laura was struck by how much Southbank had changed. A decade ago, the last time she was here for a Labour Party conference at the exhibition centre, the area had been far quieter. Now it was buzzing with life.

The children skipped ahead while Laura walked beside Alex, the riverside path shaded by rows of plane trees that lent the embankment a holiday feel. Restaurants and bars spilled over with patrons, their laughter and conversation blending into a lively hum. It wasn't noon yet, but some places were already noisy enough that she wondered how people managed to hear each other. Then again, for the younger crowd, the louder, the better.

At the small boat wharf, the kids practically bounced

on their toes, brimming with excitement. Alex paid for the rental and secured life jackets for each child, then he and Laura helped them buckle in, while the operator ran through a safety briefing and showed Alex how to handle the tiller.

At last, they were off.

Laura watched the kids' faces light up, their squeals of delight filling the air. At first, they were content to lean over the edge, dipping their fingers in the water and splashing each other. Then their attention turned upward to the gleaming skyscrapers towering above them.

The questions came in a rush. 'How tall are those buildings?'

'Are they the tallest in Australia?'

'How long is the river?'

'How deep?'

'Are there crocodiles or fish in it?'

To her mild surprise, Alex answered most of their queries with ease. His knowledge of the city was impressive. Before long, the kids lost interest in the adults and turned to chatter among themselves.

Laura took a deep breath, feeling utterly content. The gentle sway of the boat, the glistening water, the laughter of children—it was all unexpectedly perfect.

'Laura, I've been checking some of the sources you gave me the other day on the economic impact of domestic violence—'

'Alex,' she interrupted gently, looking at him with warm amusement. 'Can we leave all that for another day? This is too beautiful a moment to waste talking shop. I'm enjoying myself far more than I expected. Thank you for this gorgeous outing.' She reached forward and gave his hand a quick squeeze.

Alex looked momentarily flustered, then smiled, his expression softening. She had to admit, he was quite a sweet man under that gruff academic exterior. It was a pity he'd buried himself in his work for so long. Watching him with Sarah over the last few months, she felt certain that, in making her happy, he was rediscovering parts of himself that had long been locked away.

They floated beneath Princes Bridge, emerging on the other side, where Alice's eyes widened. 'Alex, what are those little houses along the river?'

'Those are rowboat sheds. That's where the rowing clubs store their boats.'

'You mean little boats like ours, but with row handles? Like those?' She pointed at two rowboats gliding up the river ahead.

'Exactly. Those don't have engines, just oars. Some are rowed by one person, some by two, and others by as many as eight. They even have rowing races here. I once was a participant in a race.'

'You mean you actually rowed in one?' Sarah piped up, smirking. 'You must have been much younger and thinner then.'

He let out a laugh. 'You cheeky little shrimp. But yes, I was younger, when I was in university—and a lot leaner.'

Laura smiled, enjoying the easy camaraderie between them. They shared an intimacy now, a warmth that hadn't been there before. She felt happy for both of them. From what she'd gathered, Alex's relationship with his daughter Kay had always been distant. But with Sarah, things were different.

They drifted past the Rod Laver Arena and the MCG, and then the Botanical Gardens came into view. Laura reminded the kids of their recent picnic there, and their excitement reignited.

Every kid wanted a hand on the tiller. Alex patiently

allowed each in turn to sit by him. They found it fascinating that moving the tiller to the left made the boat turn right. And vice versa. He tried hard to explain, then finally said, 'Look, when we get home, I'll draw the tiller's link to the rudder and show you how they work.'

The boat rental lasted an hour and a half, so at the Morell Bridge near the gardens, they turned back.

On the return journey, the girls peppered Alex with new questions about the city's skyline.

'Why are there so many high buildings here but not where we live?' Cassie asked.

'Because this is where all the big company offices are. If you get a job in one of them when you grow up, you'll probably come here every day.'

'I'd like to work up there.' Sarah pointed at the top floor of Shell House on the corner of Flinders and Spring Streets.

This sparked a lively discussion about their future careers. Sarah confidently announced she'd be a magistrate, impressing the others as she explained what that meant. Alice and Cassie still felt they'd follow Han and become martial arts experts. Then Sarah changed her mind. Yes, it would be martial arts for her too. And maybe a magistrate as well.

Alex guided the boat back to the dock. 'So did you all enjoy that?' he asked with a grin.

'Yeah! Can we do it again?'

'Kiddos, it's past lunchtime. Aren't you hungry?'

Sarah clutched her stomach. 'Starving!'

And just like that, their minds shifted from grand career plans to the more immediate and pressing concern—food.

Alex suggested they grab lunch at the food court in Southgate. 'Then perhaps a stroll along the riverbank before heading home?' He glanced at Laura for confirmation.

She smiled and nodded. 'Sounds perfect.'

Over lunch, the relaxed atmosphere lingered. The children were absorbed in their meals, their chatter punctuated by bursts of laughter. Seizing the moment, Laura reached across the table and lightly clasped Alex's hand.

'Alex, I want to thank you for today. It's been the most enjoyable day I've had in a long while. You're a wonderful man—so many talents hidden under a bushel. I hope we get to know each other better.'

For a moment, Alex looked utterly flustered. A deep blush crept up his face, and instead of responding, he sputtered into his sandwich.

Laura chuckled and decided to ease his discomfort. 'As promised, let's talk about our podcast on Monday.'

Alex recovered quickly. 'If I'm free, Laura,' he replied, though his expression darkened slightly. 'The magistrate is delivering her verdict on Hancock that morning.'

'Oh! I'll be keeping my fingers crossed for poor Sharon. Call me and let me know what happens.'

'I will.'

~

On the drive back home, Cassie suddenly piped up from the back seat. 'Alex, will my dad be sent to prison next week?'

Sarah turned to look at her friend. She felt sad for Cassie. Not having a father at all seemed better than having one like Cassie's—a man who hurt her mother and sometimes hurt Cassie too.

She waited for Alex's answer.

He sighed, taking a moment before responding. 'Cassie, sweetheart, would you want him to go to prison?'

'Yes,' Cassie said firmly. 'I don't like the way he beats my mum. And he takes all our money, so we have nothing to eat. We'd be happier without him.'

Sarah reached over and squeezed Cassie's hand. 'Don't worry, Cassie. I don't have a dad, and it's not so bad.'

Alex cleared his throat. 'Let's wait and see what the magistrate decides.'

~

Once home, Alex left them to play while he settled at his computer. The weekend had flown by, and he needed to prepare for his meeting with Laura. They had serious planning to do for their first podcast.

Later that evening, after Sharon picked up Cassie, Alex and Sarah ate dinner together. They were washing up when the phone rang.

'It's Mum!' Sarah squealed, dashing to answer.

Alex listened in the background as Sarah's voice rang out, triumphant. 'Mum! Tomorrow they're sending Mr Hancock to prison! Cassie and her mum will finally be free!'

Alex sighed, pondering how this would shape Sarah's understanding of the world. The Hancock case had been a harsh introduction to life's darker realities. It was only a matter of time before she started questioning what kind of man her own father had been.

Sarah's excited voice pulled him from his thoughts. 'Mum, I've decided—I'm going to become a karate champ like Han!'

Alex imagined Kay's reaction. He heard the inevitable back-and-forth as mother and daughter debated the wisdom of a martial arts career, neither willing to concede defeat.

Finally, he took the phone, bracing himself. As expected,

Kay launched into a barrage of rapid-fire questions. He smiled to himself. The cross-examination was worse than the grilling he'd endured in court during Hancock's trial.

Eventually, Kay's concerns were assuaged. Before hanging up, she promised to call again the next day to hear the verdict firsthand.

Alex set the phone down, exhaling. He had a feeling the next few days would bring even more questions, more discoveries—for all of them.

TWENTY

Monday morning arrived with tension in the air. Alex gripped the steering wheel as he navigated the streets, his stomach a nest of nervous butterflies. Today was the day. The magistrate's ruling on Adam Hancock loomed ahead like an unavoidable storm.

From the passenger seat, Sarah huffed in frustration, her arms crossed defiantly. 'Why can't I take the day off school and come with you to the magistrate's office?' She'd been badgering him about it since breakfast.

'Because,' Alex replied with practised patience, 'unless you're sick, you're supposed to be in school.'

'It's not fair! Sharon and Han don't have to go to work. Why should I have to go to school? I want to see Mr Hancock in chains.'

'For the last time, Sarah, we don't use chains these days. Only handcuffs.' He sighed. 'And no one knows what the magistrate will decide. Maybe he'll be sent to prison. Maybe not.'

'Then I want to tell the magistrate what I saw! She'll believe me and put Mr Hancock in chains!'

The argument carried on through the drive until they reached the school gates. With a reluctant sigh, Sarah climbed out of the car, her face a thundercloud. She turned back with a glare. 'I don't like you. But you better be here to pick me up this afternoon.' Then she spotted her friends, and just like that, Alex and Hancock were forgotten.

Watching her scamper off, Alex chuckled to himself. She was a firecracker, fierce and full of conviction. He admired that about her.

~

The courthouse buzzed with a hushed anticipation. Conversations were whispered, gazes flitted from face to face, and the weight of expectation pressed down on the room. Alex slipped in and found Sharon and Han seated together, speaking in low tones. Across the aisle, Adam Hancock sat rigidly beside his lawyer, his expression unreadable, though his left eye twitched involuntarily.

The courtroom fell silent as the bailiff called for order. The magistrate entered, taking her seat with a measured gaze sweeping across the room before settling on Sharon and then Hancock.

She began with the formalities—reciting the charges, detailing the events, naming the victims and the accused. Then, with composed breath, she launched into her ruling.

'Ladies and gentlemen, the case before us concerns allegations of persistent domestic violence. It has been stated that the accused, Adam Hancock, subjected his wife, Sharon Hancock, to repeated physical assault, coercively controlled her finances to fuel a gambling addiction, and inflicted emotional and psychological torment upon both his wife and child. Furthermore, it has been alleged that he unlawfully entered the home of Professor Bobbins, where his wife had sought refuge, and proceeded to violently assault the professor before attempting to forcibly remove Mrs Hancock.

'The defence has not provided substantial grounds to dispute these events. Instead, it has argued that Mr Hancock's behaviour stems from severe childhood trauma, a claim that, while not dismissed outright, does not absolve him of responsibility.

'I find this argument disingenuous. While our past informs who we are, it does not excuse our actions. We are all accountable for the choices we make. To allow childhood trauma to serve as justification for violence would be to erode the very principles upon which justice stands.

'I also wish to address, specifically, the matter of domestic violence. Too often, both society and the justice system have turned a blind eye to this insidious crime. It is a violation that breeds fear, helplessness, and isolation. It fractures families, leaves scars that span generations, and undermines the very foundation of our community.

'Domestic violence is particularly heinous because the victim is often rendered powerless, trapped within the confines of their own home. Perpetrators wield unchecked control, their victims at their mercy. This must end. Society needs to call a halt to this plague.'

She paused, her eyes sweeping across the room, letting the weight of her words settle. 'The accused, Mr Adam Hancock, has shown no remorse. Instead, he has sought excuses. This, to me, is indicative of an individual unlikely to change without intervention.'

She turned her full attention to Hancock. 'Mr Hancock, I find you guilty of all charges against you: domestic violence and assault against your wife and child, unlawful home invasion, and the assault of Professor Bobbins. There are no mitigating factors in this case. You have demonstrated no accountability, no remorse. It is my belief that you require time in prison to reflect upon your actions and to undertake the necessary steps towards change. I hereby sentence you to twelve months in prison, with an additional requirement that you participate in a behavioural change program under the supervision of the prison authorities.'

A sharp sob escaped from Hancock, and his head bowed. If he'd hoped for leniency, he'd received none. Alex felt no sympathy. Justice had been served.

The magistrate's voice softened slightly as she turned to Sharon. 'Mrs Hancock, you are not alone. I see that you have strong people standing beside you. I commend them. I urge you to find strength, to seek the support available to you, and to rebuild your life. The government offers assistance programs for those in situations such as yours. You have demonstrated remarkable courage and resilience in the face of adversity. I wish you the best in your journey forward.'

She closed the file in front of her. 'The court is dismissed.'

Sharon let out a choked sob as Han pulled her into a firm embrace. Alex joined them, his arms wrapping around them both in solidarity. Across the room, uniformed officers approached Hancock. He remained still, his head hung low, hands clenched together in his lap. The officers, to their credit, handled him with unexpected gentleness, lifting him to his feet before clicking the handcuffs into place.

Sharon didn't look up as he was led away.

She, Han, and Alex turned instead to the prosecution

lawyer, shaking hands, murmuring thanks. Officers Larkin and Nelson approached as well, offering their congratulations. Sharon nodded at them in gratitude, her voice barely above a whisper.

Han gave Alex a meaningful look, and together, they guided Sharon out of the courthouse into the crisp morning air—towards a future that, finally, held the promise of freedom.

'I think it's best we just get away from here as soon as possible,' Han suggested.

Alex nodded. 'Bring her to my house. We'll have a coffee, and I'll rustle up some lunch. Then you can take her to her place to settle back in.'

Han agreed.

~

At his house, Alex set down two steaming cups of coffee in front of the women before turning to the kitchen counter to prepare lunch. The rhythmic sounds of slicing bread and spreading butter filled the air as he worked, occasionally glancing towards Sharon. She seemed calmer now, more centred—no longer the trembling, overwhelmed woman from the courthouse.

Sharon wrapped her hands around her cup, as if drawing warmth from it. 'Thank you again, Professor. I wouldn't have gotten through this ordeal without you and Han.'

She still called him 'Professor', despite his repeated requests to use his first name. He smiled but let it go.

'So, Sharon,' he said gently, 'what happens now?'

She hesitated, stirring her coffee absently. 'Truthfully, Professor, I haven't dared to think about it.'

Han leaned forward, her tone firm but kind. 'Alex is right,

Sharon. You need to take stock. That nightmare is over—at least for now. You have a chance to rebuild your life.'

Sharon let out a short, bitter laugh. 'Is it really over, Han? Twelve months. That's all he got. What happens after that? Maybe they'll even let him out earlier.'

'Which is exactly why we need to talk,' Han said. 'You need a plan for your life after Adam. So let me ask you—do you intend to file for divorce?'

Alex saw it then—the flicker of hesitation in Sharon's eyes. A hesitation that surprised him. After everything, why?

Sharon exhaled slowly. 'It wouldn't be fair to Cassie,' she murmured. 'For her to grow up without a father.'

Alex hesitated. Should he tell her? Was it his place? But then he thought of Cassie—her small voice in the car, her quiet but certain truth. Sharon needed to hear it.

'Sharon, when I took Cassie and Sarah to the river the other day, she asked me if the magistrate would send her dad to prison. I asked her how she felt about that.'

Sharon's entire body tensed. She was listening now.

'She didn't give me a simple yes or no,' Alex continued. 'But she did say this: "I don't like the way he beats my mum. And he takes all our money, so we have nothing to eat. We would be happier without him."'

Silence. The weight of Cassie's words settled over them. Sharon sat still, absorbing it. Han, too, remained quiet, understanding this was a decision Sharon had to make for herself.

Finally, Sharon lifted her gaze. Alex saw something new in her eyes—a quiet determination replacing uncertainty. 'Yes,' she said. 'I think I will proceed with the divorce.'

Han let out a breath, relief evident in her expression. 'The Women's Care Centre will help you. In my opinion, it'll be an open-and-shut case. We've already secured you sole possession of the house—though temporary, for now. That can be made permanent.'

Sharon bit her lip. 'But what if he comes after me when he gets out?'

'He won't get the chance,' Han assured her. 'The court can issue a permanent protection order. Legally, you're in a strong position. You're free to live the life you want now, Sharon.'

Tears welled in Sharon's eyes again, but this time, they weren't just from pain. They held something else—hope. 'I don't know how I can ever thank you both,' she whispered.

Alex leaned against the counter. 'The best way to thank us,' he said, 'is to do exactly what Han said. Focus on rebuilding your life—your home, your finances, your peace. And if the legal fees are too much, don't worry. I'll cover them. You're not alone in this. We've got your back.'

He placed the sandwiches on the table with a small grin. 'I won't claim to be the world's greatest cook, but I hope these will do for now.'

After lunch, Han reached for her bag. 'Come on, Sharon. I'll take you home. We'll set up a time for your visit to the Women's Care Centre.'

Sharon turned to Alex, then, without a word, wrapped her arms around him in a long, grateful hug.

Moments later, he stood at the doorway, watching as they drove away, hoping—just hoping—that this was truly the beginning of something better for her.

~

Alex checked his watch. He still had time before picking up Sarah, so he poured himself another coffee and settled into the bay window seat overlooking his garden. The afternoon light slanted through the trees, casting long shadows on the grass. A quiet moment. A rare one. Time to think.

His mind circled back, again and again, to the raw reality of domestic violence—no longer just a statistic in a report or a passing headline, but something he'd seen up close. Something that had shaken him.

He'd always known it existed. The news was full of it. The government had even launched a national inquiry, alarmed by its growing scale and devastating social costs. But until now, he'd placed it—conveniently, as Laura had pointed out—into the broad category of 'social issues'. Not his concern. Not something for an economist like him to dwell on.

But there was no looking away now. He'd seen its brutality, its relentless grip on the lives of women and children. He'd witnessed its financial and emotional toll, the impossible choices it forced on its victims. Sharon had been fortunate— if such a word was at all appropriate—to have inherited her house and to hold a steady job. What of the women who had neither? Those without income, without assets, with nowhere to go? Homelessness, destitution—how could that be acceptable in a modern society?

A hard question formed in his mind, one that unsettled him. Did neoliberal policies—the very economic principles he'd long championed—contribute to domestic violence?

He'd always believed in a level playing field, in minimal government intervention. Neoliberalism insisted on personal responsibility, on the freedom of individuals to navigate their own lives. But did that ideology, even unintentionally, allow domestic violence to remain hidden behind closed doors? It assumed equality between partners. But equality was a myth in cases like Sharon's.

There was no comparison between Adam and Sharon. He was physically stronger, socially dominant, the self-proclaimed 'head of the family'. He had leeched off her, lived in her home without contributing, drained her finances—and, worst of all, controlled her through violence and fear.

A true neoliberal argument would say that Sharon had the agency to leave. But did she? She couldn't walk away from her own home—it was her inheritance. Divorce wasn't a simple escape, either. If she filed, Adam would fight it. He might retaliate with more violence. And if the court got involved, they might force her to sell the house and split the proceeds with the very man who had abused her.

Alex exhaled, staring out at the garden, but seeing none of it. Neoliberalism wasn't just failing to solve this problem—it was making it worse. By insisting that domestic violence was a 'private matter' to be settled between equals, it ignored the power imbalance, the lack of real choice for women like Sharon. And in doing so, it allowed dysfunction to fester. Dysfunction that had real economic costs.

This wasn't just a social issue. It was his issue.

For the first time, he questioned his long-held scepticism about government intervention. Maybe some public issues weren't just policy debates. Maybe they were moral imperatives.

A sharp glance at his watch jolted him out of his thoughts. Damn. He'd lost track of time. Sarah would be waiting.

Grabbing his keys, he rushed out to the car.

~

When he arrived at the school, the playground was nearly empty, the afternoon light fading into soft gold. Sarah sat alone under a tree, her small figure hunched, eyes scanning the street.

The moment she spotted him, she jumped to her feet and ran to the car. Guilt pressed against his chest.

'Alex! What happened?' she demanded as he opened the door. 'I thought they'd taken you to prison too!'

He laughed, hugging her. 'No such luck. Come on, let's get you strapped in, and I'll tell you all about it.' Alex drove off, bracing himself for the inevitable barrage of questions.

'Did they put him in chains?' Sarah asked immediately, skipping past formalities.

'Handcuffs.'

'And did they take him to prison?'

'Yes.'

'Yippee!' she squealed. 'I'm so happy for Cassie and Mrs Hancock! Now they can live happily ever after, right?'

'I certainly hope so.'

'What did the magistrate say?'

'She didn't approve of Mr Hancock hitting his wife and attacking me. So she sent him to prison—where he belongs.'

'Was she angry?'

'Magistrates don't show anger, Sarah. They try to be as objective as possible.'

She frowned. 'What's "objective"?'

Alex hesitated, realising how difficult that was to explain.

'Never mind,' she said quickly. 'How long will he be in prison?'

'Twelve months.'

'And after that?'

'I don't know,' he admitted. 'Han and I are hoping Sharon will file for divorce and get a court order to keep him away.'

'I hope she does,' Sarah said firmly. 'Like my mum did with my dad, right?'

'Yes, but at least you still get to see your dad sometimes.'

Sarah shrugged. 'He doesn't really have time for me. But that's okay. We can do without him.' She was quiet for a moment, then added softly, 'But I wonder sometimes what it would be like to have a dad.'

Alex's chest tightened. Life was cruel to some kids.

Then, as if shaking off the thought, she turned to him with sudden authority. 'By the way, you haven't been to the gym in ages,' she said accusingly.

He laughed. 'Sarah, I've been dealing with the court case since last week. And let's not forget—you made me take you out both days last weekend.'

'Okay, okay. But you'll go back to Han's gym tomorrow, right? Promise?'

'Yes, yes.' He sighed. 'You're like a mother to me, you know that?'

Sarah giggled, delighted by the thought.

Alex glanced at her in the rear-view mirror. In a world where fathers could be absent and husbands could be dangerous, it was comforting—at least—to have someone looking out for him too.

TWENTY-ONE

Alex pushed himself hard at the gym, his muscles burning as he powered through his routine. It was Tuesday morning, the day after the verdict and sentencing. Hancock was behind bars, at least for a while, and Alex felt a deep, weary relief. The ordeal was over. Or so he thought.

After dropping Sarah at school, he'd driven to the gym, where Han greeted him at the reception desk.

'Hi, Han. How's Sharon holding up?'

Han sighed. 'She's got a lot to work through, poor thing. But the Women's Care Centre is guiding her through it step by step. It's not going to be easy, but she's in the right frame of mind now.'

'Glad to hear that.'

'And glad to see you back, Alex.'

He grinned. 'Well, my little minder insisted. I was given no choice.'

They both laughed.

'Where's Arun? I don't see him around today.'

'Offsite training. We offer free exercise classes to some of the underfunded aged care homes that can't afford instructors. He'll be out all day.'

This couple always impressed Alex.

'If you need anything, call out,' Han said.

He nodded and moved to his usual spot, starting his workout. By the time he got to the exercise bike, sweat dripped from his brow. He was deep in rhythm when his phone rang. He kept it nearby, just in case the school needed to reach him about Sarah.

Dismounting, he retrieved the phone. The number was unfamiliar.

'Hello?'

'Hi, Professor.'

Alex frowned. 'Who's this?'

The voice was calm and unsettlingly measured. 'You don't need to know my name, Professor. But you do need to know that my colleagues and I have been following the Hancock case closely. You're the guy who called the cops on him, aren't you? The one who started all this?'

Alex stiffened. 'I don't know who you are or what your interest in Hancock is, but if you have an issue, I suggest you take it up with the police. Goodbye.'

He ended the call and exhaled, shaking off the unease. Probably a reporter looking for more details now that the trial was over. He was about to get back on the bike when the phone rang again. He hesitated, then answered.

'I'd advise you not to hang up on me again, Professor. You and your grandkid will be very sorry.'

Alex froze. His stomach clenched. 'Who the hell are you?' he demanded, his voice tight.

'That doesn't matter. What matters is that you listen. You

love your little grandkid, don't you?'

The world seemed to stop. A wave of nausea washed over him. 'Excuse me? What are you talking about?'

'If you want her to stay safe, you'll pay attention. Understood?'

Alex's hands trembled. His breathing quickened.

'Are you the one who called the cops on Hancock?' the voice pressed.

'Yes. He assaulted me. He broke into my home.'

'And you testified in court against him?'

'A lot of people testified, including the police,' Alex said defensively.

The caller snorted. 'It was your testimony that sealed the deal. And now, Professor, you're going to pay for it. Hancock owed us over twenty grand in gambling debts.'

Alex's pulse pounded in his ears. So that was it—the debtors and the debt. 'I've nothing to do with Hancock's debts. This has nothing to do with me.'

'Oh, it has everything to do with you. Because you're the reason he's behind bars. And we're not waiting twelve months for our money. So now, it's your problem.'

'I don't have twenty thousand dollars!' Alex sputtered. 'Leave me alone.'

'Don't lie to me, Professor. We know you. We know you keep twenty-five grand in your current account. So don't play games. Now listen carefully.'

Alex gulped, his mouth dry.

'At three thirty this afternoon, you'll pick up your grandkid from school like usual. Then you'll drive straight to your bank. We'll be watching. By three forty-five, you'll withdraw twenty thousand dollars. Then you'll take it home and wait for our next call.'

Alex remained silent, his mind racing.

'And don't even think about calling the cops. We'll know. If you do anything stupid, things will get a whole lot worse for you and your grandkid. Especially your grandkid.'

A sickening dread settled in Alex's gut. His hand gripped the phone so tightly his knuckles turned white.

'Do exactly as you're told, Professor, and you and your grandkid will be safe. Fail, and I promise—you won't like what happens next.'

Alex couldn't bring himself to agree.

'I repeat, don't dream of calling the police. Once we get what is rightfully due to us, you and your grandkid will be safe to go on with your lovely lives. Tread carefully, Professor.'

The caller rang off.

Alex staggered to the nearest chair and collapsed onto it, his head in his hands, his body trembling. He wasn't afraid for himself. It was Sarah—the mere thought of her being in danger sent waves of panic crashing through him. His mind refused to function rationally. How did they know so much? About him. About Sarah. Her school. Her pick-up times. His bank account.

The steady hum of the gym carried on around him, indifferent to the storm raging inside him. The clang of weights, the rhythmic pounding of treadmills, the faint buzz of conversation—it all seemed distant, unreal. His stomach churned. He thought he might throw up.

He'd heard stories of gambling syndicates—their ruthlessness, their unrelenting pursuit of debts, the terrifying lengths they would go to reclaim their money. And now, he was tangled in their web. Trapped. Helpless. A fly caught in a spider's grip.

A voice startled him. 'You okay, Alex?'

He jerked upright, blinking.

Han stood before him, concern etched across her face. Her hand rested gently on his shoulder. 'Was the workout too much for you?' she asked.

He shook his head. Words failed him. He couldn't tell her. If he did, he feared it would set something in motion— something that couldn't be undone. He clenched his trembling hands into fists, willing himself to stay composed.

But Han had noticed. She pulled up a chair beside him, her gaze unwavering. 'Alex, talk to me. I don't like the look on your face. Your hands are shaking. Something's happened. What is it?'

'I can't tell you, Han. It's dangerous. Dangerous for Sarah.' His voice was hoarse, edged with desperation.

Han's concern sharpened into determination. 'I saw you take a call, Alex. And now you're like this. I'm sorry, but you're going to tell me what that was about. You and Sarah mean too much to us. There is no way I'm letting you walk out of here without knowing what's going on.'

Alex met her gaze. Her jaw was set, her lips pressed into a firm line. There was no evading her. He felt his resistance crumbling. Tears welled in his eyes as Sarah's face flashed through his mind. *Oh, dear God, no.* Nothing should happen to her.

Han moved her chair to face him, gripping his forearms. 'Alex, I need to know.'

He shook his head weakly. 'It could put you in danger too, Han. It already has for Sarah and me.'

'Someone has threatened you?'

Alex hesitated. 'Look, Han, it's … it's fine. I just need to pay them. Then it will be over.'

Han's eyes narrowed. 'It's never "fine" to give in to

extortion. Tell me everything.'

His shoulders sagged in surrender. In a halting voice, he relayed the chilling call—the link to Hancock, the threats, the demands, the explicit instructions. 'Please, Han, promise me you won't tell the police,' he pleaded. 'They're watching me. If they suspect I've gone to the cops, Sarah—' His breath caught. 'I'll just pay them. It'll be over.'

Han's expression hardened. 'Alex, I can guarantee no one in this gym is spying on you. But outside? That's possible. However, you're safe in here. Now, let's go over this again.'

She made him recount every detail, pressing for clarity, ensuring nothing was missed. When he finished, she pulled out her phone.

'I know how to handle this,' she said firmly.

Alex's pulse spiked. 'Han, please, don't—'

She cut him off. 'Detective Lewis is a regular here. Also a friend. He helps with the self-defence classes we run for women. I'm calling him. Right now.'

'Han, no.' Alex's voice cracked with urgency. His palms opened in a desperate appeal. 'They said not to go to the police. Sarah's safety—'

'I don't care what they said. It's possible they've tapped your phone. That would explain how they know your bank balance. But my phone? It's clean. They won't know we've spoken to Tim.'

Alex wavered. He didn't want to agree, but fear had robbed him of alternatives. His throat was tight, his breath shallow. Finally, he gave a reluctant nod.

Han placed the call on speaker. 'Tim, it's Han. I've got a situation. Urgent.'

She introduced Alex, then had him recount the call once more. His voice trembled as he spoke.

Detective Lewis listened calmly. Then, in a steady, measured voice, he said, 'Alex, stay put. I'll be there in thirty minutes. I'll come in through the back door. Han, leave it open for me. We'll take it from there. Trust me.'

Alex exhaled shakily. He and Han locked eyes.

'I know you think I've just made things worse,' she said. 'But Alex, you have to trust me on this. If I thought going to Tim would put you or Sarah in more danger, I wouldn't have done it. You can't just give in to them. They won't stop.'

Alex wished he could believe that. But his nerves were shot, his body still buzzing with fear. Had he just made everything worse?

Han stood and returned a moment later with a cup of coffee. Alex blinked at it in confusion. There was no coffee machine in sight. But he didn't question it. His hands wrapped around the warm cup, and he gulped it down, hoping—praying—it would steady him.

As promised, Detective Tim Lewis arrived in under thirty minutes.

He was an imposing figure—well over six feet, broad-shouldered, built like a man who knew how to handle himself. His ruddy, handsome face bore a look of quiet confidence, but his eyes—kind, yet keen—assessed Alex with practised scrutiny.

He strode up to them and gave Han a quick hug. Clearly, they knew each other well.

Alex sat frozen, gripping his coffee cup, watching as the detective pulled up a chair.

'All right,' Lewis said, his voice calm and steady. 'Let's get to work.'

Alex couldn't stop sweating. His shirt clung to his back, and his hands felt clammy. He was a mess. What if the caller or his men had seen Lewis enter? He was doing exactly what they had warned him not to—bringing the police into it. Was this a terrible mistake?

Meanwhile, Lewis radiated an air of confidence and calm, his presence steadying like an anchor in a storm. 'Professor, can I call you Alex?'

'Yes, please do.'

'All right, Alex. Here's the plan.'

Lewis laid out his strategy step by step. Alex listened intently, his pulse still racing, but a small part of him— somewhere deep beneath the fear—began to settle. At least Sarah's safety was at the centre of the strategy. He barely cared what happened to him, as long as she was protected.

'Now, I need your address,' Lewis continued.

Alex gave it to him.

'Do you have a neighbour you trust?'

'Yes. Ella Webster. She lives next door.'

'Does she have a front yard garden?'

Alex managed a weak smile. 'That's where she spends most of her daylight hours.'

'Perfect. Call her. I need to speak with her.'

Alex hesitated. 'Are you going to tell her everything?'

Lewis placed a reassuring hand on his arm. 'Trust me, Alex. We know what we're doing.' He handed Alex his phone. 'It's on speaker. Just tell her I need to talk to her.'

Alex dialled, his mind racing. Was he digging himself deeper into a hole? The more people who knew, the greater the risk. But Lewis had a plan, and for now, he had to trust it.

'Hello, is that Ella?'

'Yes, it is. Is that you, Alex?'

'Yes, it's me—'

'Then why aren't you calling from your own phone? What

are you up to now?'

'Nothing, Ella. If you'll just allow me to explain—'

'Okay. But it better be a good explanation. I don't like people calling from a number that's not theirs. It's suspicious, you know.'

Alex sighed. 'Ella, please, just listen. I have Detective Lewis here with me. He needs to speak with you.'

A sharp intake of breath. 'A detective? Oh dear. I *knew* this would happen. I *knew* you'd land in trouble again, now that you're not working and Sarah's back in school.'

Alex closed his eyes briefly, pinching the bridge of his nose. 'Ella, please, just hear him out.' He handed the phone to Lewis.

'Hello, Ella. I'm Detective Lewis.'

'How old are you, Detective?'

Lewis blinked. 'I—don't see how that's relevant.'

'Then kindly refer to me as *Ms Webster*,' she replied primly.

Lewis smiled, unfazed. 'Of course, Ms Webster. My pleasure.'

Alex marvelled at the way Lewis handled people, adapting effortlessly.

The detective kept his explanation minimal, revealing just enough to secure her cooperation. There was a potential threat, and he needed to station two undercover officers in her garden—posing as landscapers. They wouldn't interfere with her day, but would help keep an eye on Alex's house.

'You'll get a free afternoon of gardening help out of it,' he added, a touch of charm in his voice.

Ella hesitated. 'Will this put me in danger? Or my house? That Hancock was bad enough. Now you're talking about some others creating problems. What is this neighbourhood coming to?'

Lewis gently reassured her. All was under control. This was only a safety measure. And just in case. She would be absolutely safe. Besides, she'd be getting some gardening help.

'Are they strong enough to help with my weeding?'

'Absolutely, Ms Webster,' Lewis assured her.

A pause. Then, grudgingly, 'Fine. But they'd better not trample my marigolds.'

Lewis thanked her warmly, then ended the call.

Alex exhaled. *This might actually work.*

Lewis reached into his pocket and pulled out a small, round device attached to a thin chain. 'This,' he said, holding it up, 'is a duress alarm.'

Alex took it, frowning. It looked like a pendant.

'I want you to wear it under your shirt at all times,' Lewis said. 'See this button in the centre? If you're in danger—if anything happens—press it. It will alert us immediately, and we'll know where you are.'

'How fast can you get to me?'

'Ten minutes. Tops.'

Alex swallowed. He'd have to survive for ten minutes if something went wrong.

Lewis handed another alarm to Han. 'Yours is linked separately—don't mix them up.'

Alex glanced at Han, who nodded grimly as she slipped it over her head.

'Ten minutes is a long time in a fight,' Alex muttered.

Lewis grinned. 'Which is why I brought you this as well.' He reached into his jacket and pulled out a small canister. It looked like a deodorant or bug spray.

'This is a pepper spray,' he said. 'Normally, civilians can't carry this in our state, but I'm making an exception. Use it only if you've no other choice. And *never* show it to anyone.' He demonstrated the grip and motion without actually spraying.

Alex accepted it hesitantly. *God, I hope I never have to use this.*

Lewis clapped a reassuring hand on his shoulder. 'You're not alone in this, Alex.' Then, with a firm nod to Han, he slipped out through the back door and out of sight.

TWENTY-TWO

After Lewis left, Han turned to Alex. 'Are you okay with all of that?'

Alex nodded, though the weight of the situation pressed heavily on him. 'I think so, Han. I don't know if it'll work, but the alternative is to give the extortionists what they want. And as Tim pointed out, there's no guarantee they'd stop there.' He exhaled sharply, trying to steady himself. 'At least Sarah's safety is being carefully considered. That's what matters most. I can't thank you enough, Han.'

Han waved off his gratitude. 'No worries, Alex. But before you leave, there's something we need to do.'

Alex looked at her curiously. 'What's that?'

'I'm going to show you some basic self-defence techniques. If you're attacked, you'll need to hold your own until help arrives.'

Alex let out a laugh, shaking his head. 'You can't be serious, Han. Look at me—I'm an old man, out of shape, spent my life behind a desk. And now you think you can turn me into some kind of fighter in half an hour?' He grinned despite the gravity of the situation, but Han's expression remained firm.

'I'm serious. You need to defend yourself for at least ten minutes—maybe more—until backup gets there, assuming the duress alarm works. Those ten minutes could be the difference between life and death. Whether you like it or not, we're doing this. Now, up. Let's move to a more private space.'

With a reluctant sigh, Alex got to his feet and followed Han into an adjoining room. The space was large, with wooden floors and exercise mats. In one corner stood two life-sized dummies, rigid and expectant. Han guided him to the centre of the room.

'First, take a boxer's stance.'

Alex obeyed, albeit sheepishly—left foot forward, left hand leading, right hand poised behind. It felt like stepping back into his student days when he'd dabbled in boxing, though it had been decades ago.

'Good. The stance is similar to that of martial arts. You lead with one side of your body, hands up, ready to defend.' She circled him, assessing. 'Which hand is stronger?'

'Right,' he answered.

'Show me how you'd hit an attacker.'

Alex hesitated, then dropped his hands and slumped his shoulders. Frustration creased his face. 'Han, this just isn't me. I don't fight. I can't do this.'

Han's expression hardened. 'Neither is this situation, Alex. But here you are, in real danger. You have to adapt. I am determined to teach you how, so get past your doubts. Now, show me.'

Realising she wouldn't back down, Alex squared his shoulders and attempted a punch. It felt clumsy, foreign, almost ridiculous at his age.

Han observed carefully before speaking. 'First principle: speed. You need to land a hit before your attacker does—catch them by surprise. A direct punch is far more effective than the wide, sweeping blow you just attempted. That takes too long and telegraphs your move.'

She demonstrated. Alex watched, transfixed. Her movements were fluid, efficient, powerful. A blend of grace and deadliness.

'Second principle—are you paying attention?'

He blinked, forcing himself to focus. 'Yes.'

'Use the heel of your hand or a closed fist. Never an open hand. Like this.'

She struck the air with precision, and Alex nodded.

'When you punch, drive from your whole arm, not just your hand. From your shoulder. Execute it straight—like an arrow.'

She repeated the motion, her strikes crisp and controlled. Alex tried to imitate her, feeling a flicker of his old athleticism stir within him.

'Third principle: target the most vulnerable areas—the nose, throat, and groin. The eyes are an option too, but go for what you can reach quickly. Use the heel of your hand for the nose and throat. A direct, forceful kick to the groin is another option.'

Alex remembered her textbook take-down of Hancock.

She gestured towards the dummies. 'Let's practise.'

Alex followed her, still sceptical. The dummies appeared to be made of a resilient synthetic material resembling body muscle. They stood silent, seemingly watchful, but ready for punishment. He sighed. 'Han, this is beyond my pay grade. Don't you understand? Fighting isn't who I am.'

Han's voice sharpened. 'This isn't about fighting. It's

about survival. There's a difference. You realise you have little option if you're attacked? And there's every likelihood you will be. You can try to wish it away. But it's a distinct possibility.'

He exhaled, absorbing the gravity of her words. She was right. He owed it to Sarah—and to himself—to try. Steeling himself, he watched as Han delivered rapid, decisive strikes to the first dummy, then pivoted effortlessly to the second. The sheer force of her attacks made him flinch. The dummies rocked under the impact of her blows, but remained anchored to the ground. They probably had been weighted to ensure they remained in place.

'The goal is to strike where they least expect it and disable them quickly. Now, your turn.'

Alex hesitated, but then threw a punch. It was awkward, but better than he'd expected. Something within him awakened—a distant memory of a younger, stronger self. Encouraged, he tried again, this time with more force. His confidence grew. He threw one punch, followed by another and another, with Han encouraging him along.

Han then demonstrated the kick. 'Keep it sharp, quick, direct—no wasted motion.'

He mimicked her movements, and with each repetition, the fear he'd carried for the past hour began to fade, replaced by something new: resolve.

Han left him to practise as she tended to other work. Half an hour later, by the time he finished, sweat dampened his shirt, and exhaustion weighed on his limbs. He wiped his brow and prepared to leave.

Han said bye and gave him a reassuring hug. 'Just remember the duress alarm, and decide never to succumb. Also, Alex, remember that the mind is equally important. Keep cool, focus, and ensure each blow you deliver has maximum impact.' Then she gave him a thumbs-up.

He stepped out and scanned the surroundings, hyper-aware of every movement, every parked car, every pedestrian passing by. Paranoia crept in—were they watching him? Most certainly they were. Did they already know he'd contacted the police? He hoped not.

The walk home was torture. He felt like he was under a microscope. They were surely there, somewhere. But they wouldn't touch him now. They just needed to make sure he followed their directions.

When he reached home, he spotted Ella Webster in the garden, directing two young men dressed as landscapers. That was fast. Lewis must have sent them immediately after he left the gym. The men, clearly undercover officers, barely acknowledged him but remained alert.

Ella simply waved. No questions. That, too, had to be part of the plan. Alex felt a surge of relief at their presence.

~

Inside his house, Alex collapsed onto the sofa with a weary sigh. Just that morning, everything had felt normal—Sarah had been her usual chatty self, excited about Kay's homecoming. They'd made plans to clean and restock Kay's house. He'd been looking forward to reconnecting with his daughter.

Then, in a single phone call, his world had shattered. A faceless threat had yanked him into a nightmare.

Would Lewis' plan work? He didn't know. The only comfort was knowing Sarah would be protected. As for his own safety—well, that remained uncertain. He had to drive from school to the bank and then back home. Anything could happen. Though the danger lay mainly once he'd withdrawn the money.

The idea of defending himself in a real fight still seemed absurd. He'd never understood violence, had always believed in reason over brute force. And yet here he was, trying to convince himself he could last ten minutes against a professional criminal.

He stood up and threw a few more punches, practising what Han had taught him. But he tired quickly. Who was he fooling? He wasn't a fighter. He never would be.

He sank back onto the couch, rubbing his eyes. His chest tightened. Fear gnawed at him, insidious and relentless.

Then, slowly, determination took root. He had to try. He had Sarah to protect. Ten minutes. That's all he needed.

Surely, he could manage ten minutes.

TWENTY-THREE

At precisely 3:00 pm, Alex stepped out of his front door, casting a quick glance at Ella's garden, before heading to his car. The landscape gardeners were still at work, their tools scraping against soil and stone, the rhythmic sounds blending with the afternoon heat. He slid into the driver's seat, shut the door, and exhaled sharply. Every nerve in his body was taut. He scanned the street, his senses on high alert. If they were watching him, this was the start of the end game—Sarah's school pick-up. She was the pressure point, the sword hanging over his head.

At the school, he retrieved a small bag from the back seat and strode towards the waiting area, slipping into the throng of parents and carers. He spotted Han, exchanged a subtle nod, then inched his way towards her, careful, deliberate, unobtrusive. When they finally stood side by side, they engaged in idle chatter, masking the undercurrent of tension between them. Everything had to appear normal.

The closing bell rang, interrupting the fragile calm. The

schoolyard erupted into chaos—children spilling out of classrooms, shrieking, laughing, darting past each other in a whirlwind of energy. Alex seized the moment, his movement swift and precise. He slipped the bag into Han's hands, barely a motion, a breath of exchange.

Then he heard her.

'Alex!' Sarah barrelled towards him. He caught her, hugging her tight, surprising even himself. She usually wriggled free, reluctant to display affection in public. This time, she didn't pull away.

Her eyes flickered to Han. 'Hi, Han.'

'Hi, Sarah. Lovely to see you. Oh, there's Anya!' Han gestured as her daughter came bounding towards them.

Alex took a breath, steeling himself. 'Sarah, I have a surprise for you. How about a sleepover at Anya's tonight?'

Sarah's brow furrowed. The unexpected offer flummoxed her for a moment. Then her face lit up. 'Really? That'd be awesome! But ... what about you?'

He forced a grin. 'I'll be fine. Han has your bag with everything you need. I've got an urgent meeting, so she'll take care of you. She'll drop you off at school tomorrow, and I'll see you here at three thirty.'

Before she questioned him further, he pulled her in for another hug. Then, without another word, he melted into the shifting crowd, weaving his way back to his car. He didn't turn around. He couldn't. He had to trust that Han and Sarah were already slipping away, unnoticed.

Once inside his car, he gripped the steering wheel, his fingers tightening. If they were following him, they'd soon realise Sarah wasn't with him. Would they notice immediately? Would they care? He didn't know. Or perhaps they had concentrated forces at the bank, given the money was their focus.

He drove to the bank. Parked. Walked inside.

Ten minutes later, he emerged, a large envelope clutched firmly in his hand. He moved with purpose but not haste, careful to appear unbothered. His heartbeat told a different story. Sliding into the driver's seat, he placed the envelope beside him, its presence a silent taunt.

Then he checked the rear-view mirror.

Crunch time.

If they wanted the money, this was their window—here or en route home. He flexed his fingers around the wheel, inhaled deeply, exhaled slowly. His pulse pounded, but his mind was clear. The duress alarm around his neck. The pepper spray in his pocket. Han's self-defence training as a backup. He wasn't helpless.

But Sarah.

Had they realised she was missing? Had they backtracked, tried to work out who he'd handed her to? He could only guess. Yet with the money now visibly in his possession, he hoped their focus had shifted.

The drive home was a study in vigilance, a journey on tenterhooks. He watched the mirrors, checked parked cars, noted every pedestrian. Each turn brought new tension, new possibilities. But nothing happened. No sudden pursuit. No unexpected detour. No sudden confrontation and a snatching of the all-important envelope.

Too quiet.

He pulled into his driveway, parked, and stepped out, envelope in hand. His gaze flicked to Ella's garden. The two gardeners were still at work, their bodies slick with sweat, labouring under the relentless sun. Ella stood nearby, watching them. Alex felt a twinge of relief. A normal scene.

No threat here.

He climbed the steps, unlocked the door, and stepped inside.

The moment he shut the door, a chill ran down his spine.

Something was wrong.

He stilled, listening. The air moved unnaturally. A faint, unfamiliar draft. His stomach tightened. Every time he left, he made sure the house was locked, the windows shut. So why this draft of wind?

Slowly, cautiously, he moved through the foyer into the living room.

The bay window. Open.

His breath caught. He had closed it. He was sure of it.

Then—a movement.

A figure rose from behind the couch.

The intruder stood with the light from the window behind him, casting his features in shadow. But Alex saw enough. Young. Solid build. Cap pulled low. Joggers. Late twenties. The kind of man who wouldn't hesitate.

'G'day, mate.' The voice was gruff. Flat. No nonsense.

Alex froze. His muscles locked. His heart pounded wildly, a drumbeat of fear. How had this man gotten the bay window open? How had he got to the backyard? The fence was high. Perhaps higher than the height of a normal person. Had he somehow vaulted in from one of the neighbour's gardens? But how had he got through there without being noticed? Had he been waiting all along? Watching? Planning?

Alex's mind raced, but the man's next words hit him like a punch to the gut.

'Put the envelope on the table. NOW. Nice and quiet.'

The tone left no room for argument.

'And where the fuck's the kid?'

A jolt of ice shot through Alex's veins. His palms turned slick, his breath shallow. He fought the tremor in his hands.

Sarah.

They were still looking for her.

He swallowed hard. No. He couldn't lose control. Not now. He had to stay calm, had to keep her safe. At all costs.

Somewhere in the back of his mind, he registered a terrifying realisation. The man in front of him wasn't acting alone. Someone else had been watching. Tracking. Communicating. They knew Sarah wasn't with him. Which meant …

They were still searching for her.

The game had just changed.

The man stepped around the sofa, moving deliberately towards Alex. 'Envelope on the table, mate. NOW!'

He pulled a switchblade from his pocket, the blade glinting in the afternoon light streaming from the windows. His grip was steady, his movements cautious.

Alex's breath caught in his throat at the sight of the knife. A surge of panic rose. Then, belatedly, he remembered the duress alarm. His free right hand crept to his chest where the alarm pendant hung. He pressed it, hoping it worked.

The man caught the movement. His eyes narrowed. He charged towards Alex, head down, and lunged into his midriff, sending Alex sprawling to the floor. The impact knocked the wind from Alex's lungs. Pain flared in his ribs. Before he recovered, the man was on top of him, fingers clawing for the envelope still clenched in Alex's left hand.

Survival instincts took over. With every ounce of strength, and remembering Han's instructions, Alex jabbed his right hand upward and hard, striking the man's nose with the heel of his palm. Straight as an arrow. Powering from the shoulder.

Han would be proud, he thought fleetingly.

The man let out a muffled curse, his head snapping back. Blood trickled from his nostrils, but he didn't let go of Alex's hand holding the envelope. With a final wrench, he tore the envelope from Alex's grasp.

Scrambling to his feet, the attacker delivered a savage kick to Alex's side. A searing jolt of agony ripped through him. Alex cried out, pain and panic mingling in his voice. Was the knife next?

The front door crashed open.

The man whipped around, surprise flashing across his face. He turned to flee, leaping towards the bay window, envelope in hand. He never made it. Two young officers tackled him in mid-air, sending all three sprawling onto the living room floor.

One officer pinned the man's face to the hardwood, pressing down with his full weight. The other twisted the attacker's wrist, forcing him to release the knife. The blade clattered to the floor. The envelope tumbled free, landing near the coffee table.

Handcuffs snapped into place. The officers hauled the man to his feet. His nostrils flared, blood still trickling down, his chest heaving, but he didn't resist further.

Lewis burst through the door, breathless.

Alex groaned from the floor, curling around his midsection, holding his tender ribs. What was it that made his ribs such an attractive proposition for his enemies? Lewis knelt beside him. 'You okay? Any stab wounds?'

Alex grimaced, sucking in air. 'Just bruised, I think.'

Ella Webster appeared in the doorway, her face a picture of scandalised disapproval. 'Honestly, Alex, you're creating a lot of trouble.' She sniffed. 'Certainly more than one would expect from an educated neighbour. Mabel would never have tolerated this. Why are you sitting on the floor? And who is this man my gardeners are holding? Where did he come from? I didn't see him entering from the front door. Have you been in a fight with him? Oh goodness, is he an intruder? Merciful heavens, where did he come from?'

Consternation spread across her face. She walked up to examine the guy, now in handcuffs. 'Did you come in over the backyard fence? Mother Mary, none of us are safe here anymore. It's you, Alex, right? You're responsible. First Hancock. Now this character. You're attracting all the wrong sorts.'

Alex was in too much pain to respond. The others ignored her. Lewis helped Alex onto the couch, then turned to the officers. 'Take him to the station, Sam. Bag that knife— carefully. I want no extra fingerprints on it. I'll stay here in case there's follow-up from his mates.'

The officers nodded and escorted the attacker out. Ella, still muttering, finally allowed Lewis to guide her back to her house.

Alex exhaled sharply, the worst of the pain ebbing. Lewis returned and handed him a glass of water, which he drank greedily. His throat was parched.

'Alex,' Lewis said after a pause, 'we got played. Twice.'

Alex stiffened. 'Twice?'

'One, they must have planted this guy in your backyard shortly after they called you. Maybe even while we were at the gym. He probably climbed in from a backyard neighbour's property. I should've thought to secure the yard. I didn't realise your bay windows made for such an easy entry point. That's on me. But at least your alarm worked, and we had officers nearby.'

Alex swallowed hard. 'And the second mistake?'

Lewis's expression darkened. 'We only caught one of them. This crew doesn't work alone. There were likely others watching you at the bank, maybe planning to intercept you on your way home. I have unmarked cars patrolling, but so far, no sign of them. They're careful. If they saw the cops, they might have held back.'

Alex's pulse quickened. 'So they're still out there? Still a threat?'

Lewis nodded grimly. 'And by now they know their man has failed. He hasn't checked in, hasn't delivered the cash. The real question is—what's their next move? Speaking of which—where's the money envelope that I asked you to carry?'

'The last I know, the attacker ripped it from me when we were on the ground.' Alex remained on the sofa, nursing his midriff.

Lewis rose and went searching. He finally found the envelope on the floor near the bay window where the intruder had dropped it when grappled to the floor by the two police officers. Lewis picked it up with a handkerchief and brought it to the centre table. He then removed a brown paper bag from his back pocket, dropped the envelope into it, and laid it down carefully on the centre table.

'May be useful for fingerprints,' he remarked. 'I'll keep it here for the time being. Do you mind if I sit here at your dining table and take stock of the situation with the officers I have in place in the neighbourhood? I need to make those calls quickly.'

'Be my guest,' Alex said. 'I'll get some ice to calm down this tenderness that idiot gifted me.'

He went off to the refrigerator, got an ice pack, and sat down on the sofa in the living room to ice his midriff. On the centre table lay the envelope in Lewis' brown bag, still safe. If only the thugs knew it was empty. Lewis had told him not to withdraw any money but to exit the bank with the large envelope.

The envelope had served its purpose. A honey pot to entrap the bees. But apparently, some were still at large. This worried him. He hoped Sarah was safe.

Half an hour later, Lewis suddenly stiffened to attention. Then stood up. 'Shit, it's Han. I have to go. You okay here alone, Alex?'

'I'm coming with you, Lewis. I'm worried about Sarah.'

'Alex, you're injured. Please stay here.'

'I'm fine.' Alex winced with pain but rose from his seat, holding his side, and followed Lewis hurriedly to the front door.

If Han was in trouble, then Sarah would be as well.

TWENTY-FOUR

Han drove with deliberate caution, her fingers gripping the steering wheel a little too tightly as she guided the car through the familiar streets. She didn't think anyone had seen her pick up Sarah, but certainty was a luxury she couldn't afford. Her eyes flicked between the road ahead and the rear-view mirror, scanning for anything out of place. Most of the drive took them along the main road cutting through the suburb, but as she turned onto the quieter residential streets, her senses sharpened. These streets, with their neatly lined houses and sleepy driveways, offered both refuge and risk.

The children chattered away in the back seat, oblivious to her tension.

'You okay, Sarah?' Han asked, keeping her tone light.

'I'm good, Han. But why did Alex run off like that? He never did that before. Was he sick and didn't want to tell me? He always tells me everything.'

'He's fine, sweetheart,' Han said, glancing at her in the mirror. 'Something urgent came up, and he couldn't take you.'

'Is it about Mr Hancock? Has he escaped from prison? I hope the police catch him quickly before he goes to Cassie's house. And Alex shouldn't be chasing after him. He can't run very fast. You know that, Han.'

Despite the tension, Han smiled. 'No, dear. Mr Hancock remains in prison. Please don't worry. As I said, Alex had something urgent. And I promise you'll have fun at our place. Have you stayed over anywhere?'

'Once. Anya and I slept over at Alice's. That was fun, right, Anya?'

Anya nodded enthusiastically, and the two girls launched into excited plans for the evening.

Han pulled into her driveway and parked. She stepped out first, scanning the quiet street. Nothing seemed amiss. No idling cars. No shadowy figures lurking in doorways. So far, so good. The handover had gone unnoticed—at least, she hoped. But her thoughts drifted to Alex. He'd be walking out of the bank about now, carrying the envelope Lewis had instructed him to retrieve. The extortionists would be waiting. She swallowed her worry. He was strong. But was he strong enough for this?

'Okay, girls, grab your bags and head inside,' Han said, keeping her voice even. She didn't want to be encumbered in case someone suddenly emerged from one of the parked cars. She regularly drilled it into her students in the women's self-defence course she taught at her gym. Never take anything for granted.

As Han approached the front door, the children in train behind her, her training kicked in again: check, recheck, and always listen. Never assume safety. The front door creaked as she pushed it open, her muscles taut. She stepped in first, scanning for signs of forced entry. Everything appeared undisturbed.

'All right, inside, and take your bags to the dining room. I don't want them in the foyer,' she said. 'Anya, show Sarah the washroom and your room upstairs. I'll get something ready for you both to eat.'

'Okay, Mum,' Anya replied. The girls dashed upstairs, leaving their bags in the foyer.

Typical, Han thought, rolling her eyes before picking them up and carrying them to the dining room. She wanted no encumbrances in the foyer if there was going to be a forced entry.

She moved through the routine motions of unpacking lunchboxes, washing them, and preparing snacks, but her mind remained elsewhere. Alex. The Hancock attack had been bad enough. Now this. The man didn't deserve it.

An hour passed in a haze of chopping and stirring, then the doorbell rang. A sharp, urgent sound.

Han stilled. Her stomach clenched.

Now what?

She approached the door cautiously, her instincts alert. 'Who's there?' she called.

'The police. We need to talk.'

Her heart pounded. The police? Was this about Alex? Had something gone wrong? She unlatched the door, her mind already racing through worst-case scenarios.

The door exploded inward.

It struck her forehead with brutal force, sending her staggering backward, nearly falling. Before she recovered, two men pushed their way inside and banged the door shut behind them.

Pain flared across her face, but she forced it down, stepping back, recalibrating. The extortionists had found them. The handover hadn't been clean. These men weren't amateurs.

The leader was massive—square-jawed, his forehead almost bulging, his beady eyes cold and focused. Behind him, the second man was lean and wiry, a layer of stubble shadowing his angular face. One hand was buried in his pocket. Armed, Han guessed.

The big one spoke, his voice a gravelly rasp. 'Listen, lady, we don't want trouble. We just want the professor's grandkid. We know she's here. Stay put, and you won't get hurt. We're gonna search the house.' He stepped forward to grab her.

Rookie mistake.

In a flash, Han's leg shot forward, her foot connecting with his groin in a vicious, precise strike. She felt the sickening crunch through her shoe. He let out a strangled howl, his face twisting in agony as he crumpled, clutching himself, his breath coming in ragged gasps.

One down.

The wiry one reacted, jerking his hand from his pocket. The glint of steel caught the light—a switchblade, already open, held with practised ease.

Knife boy, she thought grimly. They always worked in pairs: muscle and blade. At least it wasn't a gun.

He levelled the knife at her, his eyes gleaming with sadistic pleasure. 'Hold it,' he snarled. 'Do what I say, or I'll cut you up so bad your own mother won't recognise you. And don't scream if you want to keep breathing.'

Han held his gaze, unmoving, her mind calculating angles, distances, weaknesses. He advanced, the knife steady in his grip, moving sideways to shield his groin. Smart.

She feinted left. He lunged—predictable.

She stepped back nimbly, pivoting on her toes, and spun to the right, her leg arcing high like a dancer's. Her foot connected with his throat in a lightning, devastating strike. A sickening crunch followed.

Not good.

The knife went flying, clattering to the ground. The man dropped instantly, both hands clutching his throat, his body convulsing as he struggled for air. She'd seen this before. A crushed larynx, fractured trachea—potentially fatal. But there was no time for guilt.

The first man was stirring, groaning as he fought to his feet, his hand darting to his belt. Another weapon.

Han's fingers moved subtly to her neckline, pressing the tiny duress alarm Lewis had given her. She needed help *now.*

But she wasn't counting on it. Not yet. Not when her child and Sarah were still upstairs, waiting. Not when she was still the only thing standing between them and these men.

She readied herself, feet planted, muscles coiled.

Round two.

Han noted how well-armed these men were. Or perhaps knives were just standard tools of their trade. Either way, she was grateful they weren't carrying guns.

She backed towards the living room, keeping her eyes on the leader. The slim one on the floor was no longer a concern—she knew she'd hurt him badly. He wouldn't be getting up anytime soon.

The leader, his small, beady eyes now bright with fury, stalked after her. His movements were slower, more deliberate. He wasn't going to underestimate her again.

'What do we have here? A black martial arts bitch, is it?' he said with a sneer. 'I've dealt with your kind before. You had your chance, cunt. Give up now before you get yourself hurt. I told you—we've no problem with you. We just want the old man's grandkid. Though, on second thoughts, I owe you after that vicious kick in the balls. I'm going to make you pay. Dearly. You don't mess with the likes of me and get away scot-free.'

She felt the intensity of his anger. It must have felt humiliating to have been floored by a woman, a black woman at that, in front of his colleague.

Han didn't dignify his comment with a response. She focused instead on her strategy. He was fully alert now, tense as a coiled spring. This would be harder.

They circled each other like fighters in a ring, each waiting for the other to make the first mistake. She feinted left. He adjusted. Then right. He followed. Always advancing. Always watching. Then she suddenly looked up and waved towards the door. 'Tim, here!' she called.

His head flicked around, just for a fraction of a second. That was all she needed. On her toes again, she swung her right leg forward in a sharp, flying kick, smashing into his jaw. His head snapped sideways, and he crumpled, arms flailing, as the knife skittered across the floor.

Han wasn't about to give him a second chance. She delivered another swift kick to his jaw, ensuring he stayed down. It was brutal, but necessary. The lives of two children depended on it.

~

Lewis' car screeched to a halt outside Han's house. He was out in a flash, his bulk moving with surprising speed. Alex followed, still clutching his injured side, hobbling behind.

Lewis charged up the few stairs to the front entrance, then through the front door—and stopped dead in the foyer. His mouth fell open.

Alex caught up, breathing heavily, wondering why Lewis had stopped. Sarah was in danger, and they needed to hurry. Then he, too, came to a full stop. His eyes widened. His mouth too fell open at the sight before him. Han sat calmly in a chair, watching over two groaning figures sprawled on the floor. In one hand, she held a soft-drink bottle by the neck, ready for use should one of the prone figures rise to attack again. Two knives lay discarded nearby. One man clutched his jaw, the other his throat, both writhing and moaning in pain. No blood, but plenty of damage.

Lewis let out a low whistle. 'A textbook demonstration of women's self-defence, I assume?' he mused, as if discussing the weather. 'Bet they never saw it coming. Well done, Han. I'll call in the troops to clean up.'

Han gave him a small smile but didn't take her eyes off the men. Lewis knelt down and slapped handcuffs on them. Not that they resisted—one was still gasping for breath, the other barely able to move his jaw.

Alex stood and looked in bewilderment. How had she managed to floor two armed men, assumedly practised criminals, one of whom was huge? He had a hundred questions to ask. But perhaps he'd leave that for another time.

The backup officers arrived shortly after. They too must have been connected to his and Han's duress alarms. The officers worked with practised efficiency. A photographer documented the scene. Gloved hands bagged the knives as evidence. Two officers hauled the injured thugs into a sitting position. Han frowned at the one she had kicked in the throat. He was still struggling to breathe.

'Tim, that guy needs medical attention,' she said quietly. 'Urgently. I kicked his throat hard. I had no option.'

Lewis nodded, giving quick instructions before the

officers escorted the prisoners out. He stayed behind to take Han's statement.

They moved to the dining room. Han recounted the events, her voice calm and precise. Alex listened, his admiration growing.

'What happened at your place?' she asked when she finished.

Alex glanced at Lewis. 'Tim should explain.'

Lewis sighed. 'Truth is, Han, we screwed up.'

He outlined the sequence of events, admitting they had overlooked the possibility of a rear entry and the ease of entry via the bay windows. He repeatedly apologised to Alex.

Then he turned to Han. 'And I owe you an apology too. We didn't realise they were watching the school. We assumed they'd focus on the bank and Alex's house. You ended up carrying the burden, and you did it with full honours. Thank you.'

Han waved it off. 'I don't think they knew, initially, that I had Sarah, Tim. If they did, they'd have ambushed me on the way here.'

Lewis considered this. 'Maybe. When they saw Alex enter the bank without her, they probably decided to focus on the money first. Then, when they didn't get the call they were expecting from their man at Alex's house, they realised Sarah was their only leverage.'

'But how did they know she was with me?' Han pressed.

Lewis rubbed his chin. 'They've been monitoring the trial. They've seen you there with Alex and Sharon. When they realised Alex handed Sarah off to someone at the school, they guessed it was you. Finding your address wouldn't have been difficult for people like them.'

'So is this over?' Han asked.

Lewis exhaled slowly. 'I think so. We can never be a hundred per cent sure, but with your help, we've taken out their enforcers, their muscle. The real players are the loan sharks—probably a syndicate. As we speak, Hancock is getting grilled in prison. We're closing in on his moneylender. If we're lucky, these two muscle men might even testify against their bosses. One way or another, we'll make sure they leave Alex alone.'

Alex sighed, relief washing over him.

A loud thud upstairs broke the moment. Then the pounding of feet on the staircase. Anya and Sarah came rushing down.

'We're hungry! Is dinner—' They froze mid-step.

Sarah's eyes widened in shock as she took in the scene before her. 'Alex! What are you doing here? You said you had some work this afternoon, and that's why I had to come here for a sleepover. Why aren't you telling me the truth? It's about Mr Hancock, right? He escaped from jail, right?' She came down and stood next to him, looking at him accusingly, hands on hips.

Feeling sheepish, Alex said, 'Sorry, Sarah. No dear. Hancock is safely in jail. I had some other work, and it got done quicker than I expected. If you want to come back home with me, I'll take you.'

'No, thank you. I want to stay over with Anya.' Sarah pouted.

'Okay. No problem.'

'And who's this big man here?' she asked, looking at Lewis.

'He's a friend of mine and Han's. He was helping me with my work this afternoon.'

She turned to Han, Lewis now forgotten. 'We're hungry, Han. Right, Anya?'

'Yes. Very,' Anya chipped in.

Han smiled. 'Sorry, dears. Dinner is done. Why don't you help me lay out the table? Our visitors can also join us if they like.'

Lewis and Alex sat with them at the table and nibbled some food.

'What kind of work were you helping my grandpa with this afternoon, Tim?' Sarah asked.

Lewis looked at Alex, nonplussed for a moment, then he recovered. 'Your grandpa was teaching me about economics. About how to save money.'

Alex grinned.

'My grandpa's an expert on economics and money,' Sarah announced proudly. Then she turned to Alex and said with concern, 'Will you be okay sleeping alone at our house?'

Both Han and Tim smiled.

'Absolutely, dear. I'll miss you, but then I'll see you soon again. Tomorrow, right? At school pick-up.' He gave her a hug, then hugged Han and Anya as well.

He left with Lewis, who drove him to his house.

'Will you be okay, Alex?'

'Yes, yes, Tim. Many thanks for all you've done. Big relief for me.'

'Well, just to reassure you, I have two men, incognito, sticking around the neighbourhood, including on the parallel road behind you. We don't want a repeat to happen. We'll have to tie this all up with more formal interviews and statements, perhaps in the next day or so. But for now, I wish you a good night's rest.' Lewis waved goodbye and drove off.

Alex entered his house. It felt strangely quiet and peaceful. A couple of hours ago, there'd been mayhem.

He made his way to the bay windows and ensured they

were indeed locked. He was going to have to take measures to ensure better security.

Then he sat on his sofa again, an ice pack on his side, and reflected on his latest adventure. One too many, perhaps.

TWENTY-FIVE

'I'm so excited, Alex! Mum will be here next Friday!'

Sarah practically bounced on her toes as she spoke, her excitement lighting up the room. They were at Kay's house, getting everything ready for her return from PNG.

Sarah was agog with excitement. She'd told everyone she knew—her friends at school, her teachers, parents of her friends, Alex's next-door neighbour, Ella Webster—that her mum would soon be back. She and Alex had prepared a welcome-back card for Kay, with Sarah doing the drawings, and Alex writing the message.

Then they'd gone to the supermarket and now the house smelled of fresh bread, fruit and groceries. The fridge and pantry were well-stocked—muesli without fruit, soy milk instead of dairy, olive oil for cooking, no butter, no cheese, and definitely no snacks.

Sarah had made sure everything was just as her mother liked. Alex was struck at how well the little girl knew her mother's preferences. At seven years old, she was already a careful observer of the world around her.

'Can you buy some of those chips and cookies, Alex, and keep them at your house?' she asked, tilting her head in that exaggeratedly innocent way that always made him chuckle. 'For a weekend, you know.'

He grinned. 'Sneaky. But sure.'

Alex enjoyed her excitement. He'd miss his little granddaughter once she returned to her mum's home. He struggled to fathom how he'd become so attached to this seven-year-old over a relatively short period.

He recalled the phone call from his daughter three-and-a-half months ago. He'd been aghast that she was leaving the kid in his charge to live with him. He hadn't had a clue about child minding. But he'd been given no choice. Yet it had all gone by so quickly that he now regretted Kay hadn't delayed her return.

Sarah and he had become mates. They knew each other's habits, likes, dislikes, quirks, and idiosyncrasies. She was very adult in that way.

'Did you enjoy your stay with me?' he asked as he tucked in the sheets on Kay's bed.

Sarah was perched on the edge of the mattress, swinging her legs. 'I'm going to miss you, Alex. Mum's way stricter. Not as much fun. But, you know … she's my mum. I love her. So I have to stay with her.'

'Yup,' he said softly.

'But I'll come every weekend. We can still play, right?'

'Absolutely.'

They took a break, Alex with his coffee and Sarah with a glass of milk. He watched her sip absentmindedly, her little brow furrowed.

'How's Cassie Hancock? Doing okay after her dad left?'

'Oh yes,' Sarah said, brightening. 'She's happy. No fighting at home anymore. And her mum has more money to buy her goodies. I hope Mr Hancock stays in prison forever. Will he, Alex?'

Alex sighed. 'I don't think that'll happen, but her mum will probably get a divorce. He won't be coming back to the house to stay with her, that's for sure.'

'Good. I'm never getting married.'

Alex raised an eyebrow. 'What was that?'

'I said I'm never getting married. Boys and men are always fighting.'

'Not always,' he said. 'And only some of them.'

'I hate the boys at school. And I won't marry,' she repeated stubbornly.

Alex let it go. She was seven. Time had a way of reshaping even the most resolute convictions.

'So what do you want to be when you grow up?'

'A karate expert.'

'I thought you wanted to be a magistrate. That's what you said the last time we discussed this.'

Sarah thought about it. 'Can't I be both?'

'I've never come across a magistrate who was also a karate expert. But, perhaps, you can be the first.'

'I want to be just like Han. I'll beat all the boys in my class. And all the bad men. Alice and Cassie are going to train too.'

A small, determined army in the making.

'Look, Sarah, you're a clever girl,' he said, smiling. 'You've got your mum's brains. She's an economist, you know—makes a lot of money. Wouldn't you like to do that too?'

She tilted her head. 'Can I be an economist and a magistrate and a karate expert?'

Alex shrugged. 'Maybe. Though that's going to take a lot of study and work.'

He hadn't realised how deeply Han's self-defence takedown of Hancock had impressed the children. It was as if they'd witnessed a superhero in action and decided to follow in her footsteps.

'Okay,' he said, standing. 'Let's finish up here and get home for dinner. We've done your room, your mum's room, and the kitchen. What's left?'

'You haven't cleaned the bathroom.'

'Right. Let's get on with it.'

~

A week after the hectic encounters with the musclemen of the mob, Alex decided it was time to get back to his gym routine. The bruises had faded; the soreness was gone, and surprisingly, he missed his workout routine. It'd become a part of him, like an old song he hadn't realised he loved until he stopped hearing it.

'Hey, Han,' he said in greeting when he walked in. She stood behind the reception desk but quickly came around to give him a warm hug. The Hancock case had brought them closer, and he admired her deeply—not just for her strength, but for her kindness. A businesswoman, a dedicated mother, a martial arts expert, and effortlessly fit.

'You feeling okay after everything?' she asked, concerned.

'All good. Ready to go again.'

'Great! I'm holding a body pump class in half an hour. You should join.'

Alex hesitated. His usual workout with Arun was enough for him. Body pump? It sounded suspiciously intense. 'I'll think about it.'

He spotted Arun, waved, and got started on the rowing machine. While moving into a rhythm, he reflected on how much he'd changed. If someone had told him a year ago that he would be a regular at the gym, he'd have laughed.

'Alex!'

He looked up to see Laura dressed in gym gear. His appreciative eye noted how well she wore it.

'Good to see you back,' she said, smiling. 'You've been off the radar for a while. I thought of calling you to check if everything was okay.'

He stopped rowing. 'A lot has happened,' he said. 'We need to catch up. I haven't forgotten about the podcast.'

'How about lunch at Betsy's on Saturday?'

'Sounds good.'

'I'm off to Han's body pump class now,' she added. 'You should try it.'

That was the second invitation. He hesitated.

'Come on,' she urged, sensing his hesitation and his interest. 'You can take a back row, so you needn't be self-conscious. See if you like it. I'll help you along.'

Alex sighed. Maybe it wouldn't be so bad. And working out next to Laura had its appeal. 'All right, I'll give it a go.'

She beamed. 'Good choice.'

Alex wiped down the rowing machine, picked up his stuff and followed her into the body pump room. The dummies were there in one corner. Several attendees were picking up various pieces of equipment from the other corner and setting up their mats and bench tops in rows across the room.

'Come. I'll show you.'

Laura took him to the equipment corner and helped him get a mat and bench top for himself. Then she showed him the other equipment.

'You need a barbell. Here, take one. Click on weight plates on each end. I'd suggest you begin with light ones, perhaps the two and a half kilos at each end.'

She helped him lay out his mat and bench top. The barbell on the side.

'The exercises work most muscles of the body. That's the great thing about body pump. And they're all done to a music beat. Once you get the hang of it, you'll lose yourself in the music and enjoy the exercise.'

He nodded, though dubious. The equipment before him already looked overwhelming. What made it worse was that most of the attendees were women, all with well-toned muscles, slim and fit. Anyway, he was here now, hopefully unnoticed in a corner. Laura set up beside him, giving him encouraging looks.

Han entered the room and welcomed everyone chirpily. She noticed Alex in the corner, waved and gave him a smile and a thumbs-up.

The music began, and Han led the exercise with continuing instructions. The high-energy music played while Han guided them, encouraging them to keep to the beat.

Alex struggled to get the cadence of the movements. The exercises were demanding, some complex. He had to get them right while keeping to the beat. A seemingly impossible task. But the others and Laura appeared quite skilled at it.

'You'll get it in time. No worries,' she assured him.

He was grateful for the regular, though short, breaks between exercises. Some exercises were beyond his capability, such as the lunges. Han came to his rescue, suggesting he do squats instead if those were easier.

At the end of the forty-five minutes, he felt exhausted but

exhilarated. The endorphin rush left him feeling euphoric. He was on a double high. One from the exercise, the other from working out next to Laura. Her regular encouragement added to his high.

Han came up to him after the session. 'I'm really impressed, Alex.'

He grinned sheepishly. 'You're having a go at me, Han. I hope I didn't make a fool of myself. I'll need time to get the hang of this.'

'Relax, Alex. We all had to start once, and we too went through the phase of getting the rhythm and exercise right.'

Other attendees now gathered around, patting him on the back, encouraging him and saying they hoped to see him back at the next session.

Feeling good, he walked with Laura to the gym exit and waved a goodbye to Han and Arun.

'Thanks, Laura. I'd have never started if not for you.'

'You'll soon find it addictive, Alex. I'm glad you've joined. I'll now see you more regularly, right?' She grinned.

He grinned back. 'We'll catch up in any case on Saturday at Betsy's, twelve noon, for lunch and to finalise our podcast.'

They went their separate ways, she to her car, he walking home.

TWENTY-SIX

Though it was a Friday and a school day, Alex let Sarah stay home. Today was a day for goodbyes and new beginnings. Besides, they had work to do.

The morning unfolded in a flurry of packing. One by one, Sarah's belongings found their way into the car—her favourite teddy bear, stacks of books, a jumble of toys, her iPad, clothes, toiletries, and an assortment of little treasures only she knew the significance of. Alex was amazed at how much one small child could own, how many objects carried pieces of her world. Her excitement bubbled over while they worked, a stark contrast to the quiet heaviness settling in his chest. His home would soon feel emptier, the air quieter, the rhythm of his days forever altered.

No more school drop-offs or supermarket runs for her favourite groceries. No more tiny uniforms to launder and press. Soon, he'd be dining alone again, perhaps reacquainting himself with the news programs he'd abandoned in favour of bedtime stories and giggles. But he would adjust. More than anything, he was grateful—grateful for these weeks, for the bond they'd built, for the way she'd filled his life with warmth and noise and love.

When the last of her things were packed, they drove to her mother's house and carefully unloaded them.

'We have to keep everything neat, Alex, or Mum'll be upset,' Sarah reminded him, her voice carrying both authority and resignation. He watched as she smoothed out her blankets, lined up her toys, and arranged her books with methodical precision. She was already bracing herself for the shift, adapting as only children could.

By noon, the move was done.

'Okay, Sarah, I have one more treat for you before we head to the airport.'

Her eyes lit up. 'What's it?'

'How about McDonald's for lunch?'

'Yeah!' she squealed, then clamped a hand over her mouth. 'But we can't tell Mum.'

'Agreed. One more secret.' They exchanged mischievous grins.

While Sarah devoured her fries and burger, Alex watched her with amused affection. McDonald's had perfected the art of capturing young hearts, their menu a siren song for kids everywhere. He had to admit, even he found comfort in the ritual—the simple joy of indulging in something forbidden, just the two of them.

At the airport, they arrived well ahead of Kay's flight. On their way towards the gate, they passed a small flower shop.

'Would you like to get some flowers for Mum?' Alex asked.

Sarah nodded eagerly. 'Yes, please! She loves flowers.'

Kay's flight from Port Moresby, connecting through Brisbane, was a domestic arrival, so they waited right at the gate. Sarah pressed her nose against the glass, watching as planes taxied across the tarmac. When her mum's plane landed, she grew still, eyes wide with fascination as a ground crew member guided the massive aircraft into its designated spot. The passenger bridge extended towards the plane like an outstretched arm, locking into place with a quiet finality.

As soon as the first passengers emerged, Sarah rushed to the front, clutching the bouquet in one hand and Alex's hand in the other, bouncing on her toes.

Then there she was—Kay.

'Mum! Mum!' Sarah dashed forward, flinging herself into her mother's arms, peppering her face with kisses. Around them strangers paused, smiling at the heart-warming reunion.

Alex swallowed against the lump in his throat. There was something profoundly pure about the love between a mother and her child—something that words could never quite capture.

Kay finally looked up, her gaze landing on Alex. A smile broke across her face, and then, unexpectedly, she stepped forward and hugged him.

He stiffened for a moment, caught off guard. Physical affection had never been part of their relationship. But there was nothing forced about her embrace; it was warm, genuine.

When she stepped back, she studied him with curiosity. 'Dad, you've changed.'

He chuckled. 'I doubt it.'

'No, you have. You look … different. Happier. And you've lost weight.' She tilted her head, as if trying to pinpoint the difference.

He smirked. 'Sarah's orders, right, Sarah?'

'Yep,' Sarah confirmed proudly. 'Alex's become a good boy. He eats healthy now. And does exercise.'

Hand in hand, the three of them made their way to the car. Sarah refused to let go of either of them.

When they arrived at Kay's house, Alex turned to her. 'I made pasta and salad for you and Sarah's dinner.'

Kay's eyes softened. 'That's really thoughtful. Thank you, Dad. Stay and eat with us?'

He hesitated. Their relationship had always been distant, cool at best. But something was different. Warmer. 'All right,' he said finally.

Kay went to freshen up, and Alex and Sarah curled up with her iPad for a round of Angry Birds. At dinner, Sarah dominated the conversation by recounting every detail of her latest adventures—including how Han had taken down Hancock.

Kay, already familiar with the tale, shot Alex an incredulous look. 'And you couldn't stop him?'

He shrugged. 'More details another time. For now, just listen to Sarah.'

He hardly got a word in, but he didn't mind. He had a hundred things he wanted to ask Kay about—PNG, her work, the economy—but they could wait. Tonight belonged to mother and daughter.

Before he left, he and Kay made plans for lunch while Sarah was at school.

'No way!' Sarah protested. 'You're not allowed to have lunch without me.'

Both adults laughed.

Driving home, Alex felt a quiet sense of contentment settle over him. He was happy for Sarah. Happy for Kay. And, for the first time in a long while, happy for himself. Maybe, just maybe, he and his daughter had found their way back to each other. Mabel would be pleased.

It was Saturday, and Alex sat alone at the breakfast table. Bacon and eggs sizzled on his plate, a meal he usually relished, but today it tasted oddly bland. The house was too quiet. No chatter, no little footsteps, no Sarah. He'd grown used to her presence filling every corner of his home, and now, with her gone, the emptiness pressed in on him like an unwelcome guest.

But he looked forward to a lunch with Laura. At noon, he stepped out, thinking about how he and Laura would finalise their plans for the podcast. He barely made it past the front door before Ella Webster's voice rang out.

'So Alex, feeling lonely with Sarah gone?'

He turned to face her, forcing a smile. Over time, he'd developed a certain patience for her relentless curiosity.

Before he answered, she added, 'I hope you're not up to any more mischief now that she's not around. That incident the other day still has me shaken. I double-check all my locks now before stepping out. You'd best do the same.'

'Sure, Ella. You have a nice day,' he said, excusing himself swiftly. He had no intention of letting her nosiness dull his anticipation for lunch.

The moment he walked into Betsy's, his eyes found Laura's. She'd secured her usual quiet corner table—a mystery, considering how often it was in demand. She stood and greeted him with a warm hug and a light kiss on the cheek. Heat rose to his face.

'I've missed our chats, Alex,' she said, studying him. 'You vanished after our city trip, apart from that quick encounter at the gym. I'm glad you're sticking with body pump. It'll do you a world of good. But what kept you away all week?'

He exhaled. 'Let's order first. It's a long story.'

Over lunch, he recounted everything—the courtroom drama, his and Han's testimonies, Hancock's defence, and his eventual conviction.

Laura let out a breath. 'That's a relief. I only know Sharon Hancock in passing, but I'd heard whispers about what she endured. Domestic violence infuriates me. And yet, I haven't seen a word about the court case in the papers.'

'The law prevents the media from reporting on domestic violence cases to protect victims' privacy.'

'Maybe, but I still think these stories should be told. The more we expose this plague, the better chance we have of fighting it.' She paused. 'At least Sharon can move forward now.'

'Cassie says her mum is much happier—and so is she.' He took a sip of water. 'But things didn't end with the trial. I found myself in a bit of trouble afterward.' He detailed the extortion attempt and how Han, with the police's help, had put an end to it.

Laura shook her head. 'That's terrifying. And Han—she sounds like a force of nature.'

'She is,' Alex admitted. 'I owe her more than I can say.'

Laura gave him a knowing smile. 'You do seem to be living quite the adventure these days, Alex.'

He grinned. 'I could do without the dangerous ones.'

'Who would've thought? A retired professor, an esteemed economist, a pillar of the community, caught up in all this intrigue. You should write a book about it.'

He chuckled. 'Maybe I will. *The Remaking of Professor Bobbins.* What do you think?'

She laughed. 'Perfect.' Laura leaned forward. 'And Sarah? She's back with her mum?'

'Yes. A couple of days ago. The house is eerily quiet. But on the bright side, I have more time for our podcast.'

'Which brings me to our last discussion. If you recall, I wanted us to talk about domestic violence and its impact on the economy. The cost is estimated to be over fifteen billion dollars annually. Did you check the sources I gave you?'

'I did.'

She tilted her head. 'You were adamant this was a social issue, not an economic one. Are we starting our debate there?'

Alex hesitated, a faint smile playing on his lips.

'What's wrong, Professor? You're not usually speechless on economic matters.'

He sighed. 'Laura, I've had a change of heart. No academic study or statistic could have opened my eyes like living through the Hancock case. Domestic violence isn't just a social issue—it's an economic one, and a serious one at that. Government intervention isn't just warranted, it's essential.'

Her eyebrows shot up. 'Am I hearing this right? The champion of neoliberalism, the man who insists the government should stay out of people's lives, is calling for intervention?'

'Yes,' he admitted. 'I still believe in free markets, but I now see that some crises demand action.'

Laura's face broke into a delighted smile. 'I'm thrilled to hear that, Alex. But now I must insist on a title change for your book.'

He raised an amused brow. 'Oh?'

'*Bursting Bobbins' Balloon.*'

He threw his head back, roaring with laughter, tears forming in his eyes. She remained mock-serious.

'Or better yet—*Popping Bobbins' Cocoon.* Though that would ruin the alliteration.'

'You're brilliant, Laura.' He gazed at her, momentarily captivated by the woman before him.

She raised her glass. 'Sarah pried open that cocoon of yours, Alex. Out emerged a lighter, more open-hearted, and—dare I say it—charming man.'

He clinked his glass against hers. 'To new beginnings and getting closer to the loveliest woman I have met in a long time.'

A NOTE FROM THE AUTHOR

If you enjoyed this book, I would be very grateful if you could write a review and publish it at your point of purchase. Your review, even a brief one, will help other readers to decide whether they'll enjoy my work.

If you want to be notified of new releases from myself and other Alkira Publishing authors, please sign up to the Alkira Publishing email list. In return you'll get a free ebook by an Alkira Publishing author. You'll find the sign-up button on the right-hand side under the photo at www.alkirapublishing. com. Of course, your information will never be shared, and the publisher won't inundate you with emails, just let you know of new releases.

ACKNOWLEDGMENTS

I am deeply grateful to my wife, Matilda, whose steadfast encouragement and belief in this project kept me moving forward, and to my children, Shefali and Gerson, along with their spouses, Evan and Julie, who offered their unwavering support, thoughtful feedback, and many moments of inspiration throughout the writing journey.

Special thanks go to Conrad Saldanha, whose encouragement helped shape this novel, and to my dear friends, Joseph Grossman and Divya Yadav, who generously read through early drafts, offering invaluable feedback that made the story stronger.

I extend my sincere appreciation to Tahlia Newland of Alkira Publishing, and her team, for their professional guidance, expert editing, and unwavering encouragement in bringing this book to publication.